CREATURES
of the
NIGHT

CHAPTER ONE

Every day is the same mind-numbing routine. I wake up, venture from the tunnels, serve breakfast for the hunters, weed the gardens, make lunch, clean the tunnels, and then cook dinner. And finally, the most important step—go back into the tunnels and don't leave until sunrise. I thought that by the time I turned nineteen I would've been able to hunt like everybody else. That I'd already have ventured farther than the tree line that guards our village. I was wrong.

"Did you slice the carrots, Milena? Remember, Charles likes them extra thin."

The carrots on the chopping board lie in crooked chunks beside the blunt knife. "Yes, Cynthia."

Her gray hair pops up from behind the wooden countertop, her thick eyebrows pulled together as she eyes the hacked-up carrots in front of me. Darius, her thirteen-year-old son, lingers behind, pulling a face behind her back. In charge of food preparation, Cynthia has been bossing me around for half my life now, so her disapproving tone barely affects me.

"That's *not* thin." Her nose wrinkles. "You're turning twenty this week, child, yet you still don't know a slicer from a knife."

My best friend, Flo, who stands beside me, warns me to keep my mouth shut with a shake of her head, and I bite my tongue. The only time I ever talked back to Cynthia, I was put on cleaning duties for a month. Alone. I couldn't go more than a few hours without having to pick dirt from my fingernails.

"I'm sorry. I'll try again."

"Good." She brushes her hands on her apron. "All the vegetables need to be sliced and in the pot. You have an hour before the hunters return, two before the sun sets. Make sure dinner is prepared and ready in the tunnels."

"Yes, Cynthia," Flo and I chime. The matron turns on her heels, grabs Darius's hand, and drags him outside, the door swinging shut behind them.

Flo's shoulders slump, red hair spilling over them. "She's *such* a nightmare. I know the hunters are important, but I'm pretty sure how thin the carrots in the stew are is the last thing on their minds when they get back."

"Yeah." Still, I'm slicing the carrots as thinly as I can manage. "Who would've thought that I'm days away from turning twenty and still stuck on cooking and gardening?"

"You get to clean sometimes too."

"Oh, joy."

"Come on, Millie." Flo picks the bucket of potatoes up off the floor and dumps it on the wooden countertop. "It's not *that* bad."

CREATURES
of the
NIGHT

GRACE COLLINS

wattpad books

wattpad books

Content Warning: Assault, Murder, Violence

Published in Canada by Wattpad Books, a division of Wattpad Corp.

36 Wellington Street E., Toronto, ON M5E 1C7

www.wattpad.com

First Wattpad Books edition: July 2021

ISBN 978-1-98936-549-6 (Trade Paper original)

ISBN 978-1-98936-550-2 (eBook edition)

Library and Archives Canada Cataloguing in Publication information is available upon request.

Printed and bound in Canada

1 3 5 7 9 10 8 6 4 2

Cover design by Laura Mensinga
Images © CHUTTERSNAP via Unsplash and
© Andrew N. via Adobe Stock
Typesetting by Sarah Salomon

"Easy for you to say. Charles let you hunt the moment you came of age."

"You turn twenty soon," she says without looking at me. "And then you'll get your wish."

"Everyone else only had to wait until they turned sixteen." Flo peels the potatoes, as there's nothing she can say to make me feel better. She knows it's true. My entire life, I've been prohibited from venturing into the forest. While everyone else had some freedom starting at sixteen, Charles kept me here, wanted me safe. "Come on," I say. "Let's weed the garden while we wait for the stew to boil."

Chucking the carrots and the rest of the potatoes into the simmering pot, Flo follows me out of the wooden shack we use as a kitchen. The sun glares down at us as we wander toward the vegetable patch behind it. The village we live in doesn't look like much. With one, sole building aboveground, the rest of the clearing consists of gardens and a thin stream before a large, clear area that separates us from the reaches of the forest. To a passerby, the building would be as inconspicuous as a run-down shack.

As Flo tugs at some weeds, I lean back on my heels and gaze across the clearing at the tree line. The sun bathes the tips of trees in gold as it begins its descent, dipping between the distant mountains. Figures of hunters form in the gaps between the trees. Charles is first to come into the open, a dead boar thrown over his shoulder and four hunters following behind. Like every other day, a crowd gathers around the entrance to the tunnels beside the kitchen shack, mostly children, welcoming the hunters back. Life seems normal, like a regular day of hunting. But it isn't. The hunters never return early.

I nudge Flo. "What?" she asks, still pulling weeds from the ground.

"The hunters. They're back early. They're *never* back early."

She shrugs. "I'm sure it's nothing."

Charles weaves through the villagers, eyes scanning the crowd.

"Charles." Cynthia greets him first. "You're back early."

He nods. His movements are stiff and intentional. Different. "I'd like everybody in the tunnels. Curfew starts early tonight."

Cynthia scurries away, ceaselessly obedient. Charles surveys the crowd, the limbs of the animal on his shoulder flopping left, and then right as he turns. A gentle breeze blows my dark hair across my face. "We should get the food." I tug on Flo's arm to pull her up. "Cynthia will be angry if we're not ready."

She drops her tools and together we hurry back to the kitchen. I peer over my shoulder as we fly through the center of the village. Charles is looking at me from across the clearing, green eyes sharp. A silent message passes between us—I know what he's trying to tell me. Night is coming, and so are they.

~

Dead—my mom, my dad, my whole family. Charles says there was a raid the day I was born. That the creatures broke into the tunnels and killed my parents. He raised me, and though he provided me with the necessities, there was never any warmth in his embrace.

"The stew is good," Charles says once we're secure in the tunnels. He sits at the head of the tunnel with a group of hunters. "Thank you, ladies."

"You're welcome, Charles." Flo smiles brightly.

Even though she's one of my only friends, the way she sucks up to Charles annoys me like nothing else. I move my piece across the checkerboard and kick Flo to let her know it's her turn. She nearly knocks her bowl off the table as she turns back.

"Milena," Charles calls. "Come here. I want to speak with you."

Pushing myself to my feet, I move toward him. "Yes?"

He nods to one of the hunters sitting beside him, who gets up and moves away. "Please sit." As I do, the other hunters at the table stare at me, but I ignore it. I do their cooking and cleaning, but I'm not allowed to hunt, and that makes me an outcast. "What'd you do today?" Charles asks.

"What?"

"I'm asking what you did today." He lifts his spoon to his mouth, stew catching in his gray beard. "I'm trying to have a conversation."

Charles never tries to converse with me. My childhood consisted of instructions and scolding; I can count the number of casual conversations we've had on one hand.

"Cooking and gardening with Flo, like every other day."

"You didn't do anything . . . unusual?"

"No. Why?"

"No reason." He stirs the spoon in the bowl. "You can go now."

"Charles, what brought the hunters back early?"

"We finished early."

"You never finish early." He ignores me, turning to say something to the woman next to him. "I'm turning twenty in two days, Charles. I finally get to hunt. Isn't it time you let me in on things? Isn't it time I get to learn a thing or two about the hunts?"

I've never been afraid of Charles, and although he's never been kind, he's never hurt me either. But as he stands and stares down at me, I feel so very small. "We finished early. The reasoning is none of your concern."

"Right. Sorry."

"Go. I'm sure Cynthia could do with some help cleaning up."

I step away as he ventures around the corner to the cleaning station. We're in the room designated for dining and recreation, separated from the stone walls blocking the entrance by a mere three steps. And despite the fact that there are fewer than two hundred of us living in the tunnels, the rooms always feel crowded.

"You okay?" Flo appears at my side and puts her hand on my arm. "I know he's harsh, but he cares about you. He doesn't want you to get hurt."

Memories of my childhood blur my mind: begging Charles to carry me through the tunnels, crying when he refused; scraping my knees against the ground and hanging my head in shame when he told me to grow up. If Charles won't allow me to hunt because he cares too much for me, he has a funny way of showing it.

"I'm going to have an early night," I say. "See you tomorrow."

Before she can respond, I take the two steps that lead to the narrow halls. Unlike the main rooms in the tunnels, the hallways aren't well maintained. Carved from compacted dirt, they're thin, winding passageways littered with dips in the ground and badly attached pipes that drip water. Their only purpose is to connect the various rooms. I take the familiar corner, ducking my head to avoid a low-hanging pipe protruding from the entranceway of my room.

When I was younger, I stayed with Charles in his quarters—the largest and most extravagant of the rooms. But when I turned ten, he left me in a box-sized room right at the end of the passageway, separate from the rest. He said it was time for me to mature, to grow up and start being more independent. I cried out for him every night for the first two weeks. But tonight, lying in my stone room void of anything save for a lumpy bed and set of drawers, I enjoy the loneliness. The blanket scratches against my skin as I pull it to my chin. I trace the crooked letters Flo and I scratched into the wooden bed frame when we were kids—an *F* and an *M*—with my finger. The distant howls coming from above provide a familiar comfort. They allow me time to sort through my racing thoughts.

My entire life I've waited for my twentieth birthday. I thought people would be more inclusive, would accept me as one of them—a hunter. But the closer the day gets, the more secretive Charles becomes, and the more ostracized I feel. And today was no exception.

Bang. I jolt up in bed. *Bang.* The screeching starts. It rebounds off the stone walls, rattling my brain. I put my hands over my ears and listen: deep, familiar growls echo through the tunnels—sounds that make my chest burn. But these growls aren't coming from above. Shouting fills the halls. Footsteps barrel past my quarters. I slide out from beneath my covers, throw a coat from the floor on, and pull the sheet covering the doorway open—then leap back in fright.

Charles stands in the doorway. "You're still here," he says, relieved.

"What's going on?"

"Don't leave this room."

"Charles—"

"Listen to me: do not leave this room until I come back for you!" His voice shakes me to the bone. I can do nothing but nod as he slips from the room, the sheet billowing as he exits. His footsteps get farther and farther away. Panic blazes through my body like wildfire. I stand frozen, staring at the door. Night has broken into the tunnels, and so have the creatures who own it.

~

The screaming ends before the night does and a piercing silence takes its place. I don't leave my room. I don't venture into the halls. I don't disobey Charles. I stay in my quarters, hugging my knees and waiting for the screaming and growling to start again. It never does.

When Charles finally appears in my doorway, I know, from the absence of howling, that the sun has risen. "You did as you were told, good." His shirt is torn across the chest, his head of gray hair mussed.

"Yes."

He clears his throat, the dark circles under his eyes more prominent than usual. "Cynthia called for you. They're preparing breakfast in the kitchen shack."

I grab his wrist before he can leave. Why is he acting like everything is normal? Nothing like last night has ever happened before. "Charles, what happened last night?"

"Everyone is safe and accounted for." He pries his hand from my grip. "The rest is none of your concern."

He spins and exits without another word, not addressing my curiosity. Whatever happened last night, however abnormal, I'll have to ask somebody else about it. I throw on a light-blue shirt and braid my black hair to the middle of my back before venturing into the cocoon of the morning sun. The village is quiet, the songs of birds wafting through the trees surrounding us. On a warm day like today, children are usually playing in the small stream that runs through the clearing, but everyone is still in the tunnels.

"Millie!" I turn as I reach the kitchen to see Flo rushing toward me, Darius's hand clasped in hers. She wraps her arms around me and squeezes. "You're okay! I couldn't find you anywhere last night."

"What *happened*?" I ask.

"Don't tell me you slept through it," Darius says, blue eyes wide.

"I heard screaming and growls. Charles made me stay in my room."

Darius opens his mouth. "They caught—"

"You're okay, that's all that matters," Flo says, shooting Darius a look.

"It was *terrifying*," he says. "The entrance wasn't sealed properly. Someone—something—broke in. It had red eyes and matted fur, and it was in the tunnels."

"A creature of the night . . . you saw one?"

"No. But Flo did," Darius says. I stare at Flo but her eyes are focused on the ground. "She said it almost killed her but the hunters got there just in time."

"They killed it?"

"No." He leans closer. "They *caught* it. It's down in the tunnels, chained up."

A creature of the night alive and in the tunnels. It broke in and we're still alive. *What's it like? Why didn't they kill it? Why didn't anybody tell me?*

"Hey!" Cynthia appears behind Flo, hands on her hips and a scowl on her face. "What do you think you're doing?"

"Mom!" Darius yells. "They have one in the tunnels. Flo said the hunters caught it and—"

"Stop spreading nonsense and complete your chores, Darius," Cynthia snaps, looking at Flo and me. "Get inside and get to work. The hunters need a meal before they leave."

We follow her timidly into the kitchen and stand to attention. A gust of wind rattles the pots hanging on the wall. There are three other girls present—Allison, and the twins, Katie and Alexis. The twins started in the kitchen with me and Flo less than a year ago, but this will be their final year before they're promoted to hunting. "Allison and Flo, Charles wants you on the hunt today," Cynthia says. "The rest of you: gardening, cleaning, and cooking."

"I'll clean the tunnels," I say.

"You're on breakfast."

"After breakfast, then. Instead of gardening. I need a change of scenery."

"Fine," she says, and the tension in my shoulders releases when she looks away. "Get to it."

Flo gives me a sheepish look before exiting with Allison to prepare for the hunt. Alexa hands me a pot full of water collected from the stream. I kneel down to the basket of supplies Cynthia brought from the tunnels, for once glad I'm not getting my chance to hunt today even though I'd like to go with Flo. Today, I have other plans. None of what Darius said makes sense. They should have killed the creature. Stopped it before it got to the entrance. But as the hunters leave soon, the tunnels will be unguarded, and I'm going to see a creature of the night.

CHAPTER TWO

Aside from mealtimes, nobody likes being in the tunnels during the day, so when I appear belowground with a bucket and cloth, Darius and I are surprised to see each other. With a smile, I hold up my bucket to answer his question about what I'm doing down there today. "Cleaning duty. Shouldn't you be at school?"

There are only around thirty kids in the village, but until the day they turn sixteen, they're stuck here like me. They spend most of the morning at school, where they're taught writing and reading in the tunnels, or if it's a nice day, in the patch of grass before the kitchen. I was never given that luxury. When I was a kid, Charles made me learn to cook while other kids were taught to write. He said I was good at it, and it'd be a waste not to take advantage of that.

"Mom's mad at me again." He sighs. "You know what that means—cleaning duty."

"What'd you do this time?"

He shrugs. "Aren't you usually on gardening?"

"I wanted a change of scenery."

He shrugs and wipes down the table. I've always liked Darius. He's only thirteen, so he hasn't hunted yet, and doesn't look down on me because I haven't either. Hunting is a rite of passage in the village—everyone, even Cynthia, participates every now and again. And it always happens the same way: When they're young, they're kind to me; and then they go on their first hunt. The next day, I'm a distant memory and lucky to receive a smile, as if being a hunter makes them so much better than me. The only one who's stuck around is Flo.

Darius smiles at me. "So, the creature. . . . Is that why you wanted to clean?"

"No." I look at the wall again and focus on the distant dripping of water.

"Don't worry, I won't tell anyone."

I keep my head down. Seeing the creature won't be worth it if Charles finds out.

"You wanna see it?" Darius asks.

"Really?"

"Yeah. They came down a while ago to attach the new chains."

"The new chains?"

"It broke through the old ones. These ones are silver, though. They seem to have an effect on it. Charles said I have to give it this medicine every hour to keep it alive, otherwise the silver will kill it." He shows me a syringe filled with a dark-red liquid. I eye it warily. This is why I came down here, but now that the offer is

GRACE COLLINS

right in front of me I'm struck with hesitation. "Come on, Millie." Darius leans closer and the edges of his mouth tilt up. "Live a little."

"Okay."

"Let's go," he says, dropping the syringe in the bucket and turning down the hall. Taking a deep breath, I follow him. With the absence of people, the tunnels feel colder, darker. The glow from Darius's lantern crawls along the damp, narrow halls as we move. Sweat beads at the back of my neck; the farther we get from the entrance, the thicker the moisture in the air gets.

"It doesn't talk," Darius warns. "I don't even know if it can."

Each step feels like I'm breaking an invisible string that Charles has tied me to. The deeper we venture into the tunnels, the more my shoulders tense, and the more I want to turn around. Nobody goes this deep unless there's something wrong with the pipes, and there's only two people in the whole village who work on the pipes. I'll be punished if I'm found down here, but I can't ignore my nagging curiosity. These are the creatures that murdered my parents. They're horrendous, bloodthirsty beasts hell-bent on killing innocent humans, but I've never seen one. And though the idea terrifies me, I can't stop myself from following Darius around the corner.

"You'll see," Darius says, his voice a mere whisper. "It's nothing like I expected."

I grip his sleeve as if he can protect me from the dark shape forming in the corner of the room. My fists clench as I take a step forward. When we're young, we're told stories of the creatures— contorted bodies, pointed teeth, claws for hands, matted hair, and spiraled horns that point toward the moon. The creature faces us, hunched in the corner and crouched on its haunches. Dark, thick fur covers its frame—a large wolf-like creature with red eyes glowing like fireflies in the darkness. The air is thick with the taste of iron; scarlet blood coats the thick metal chains attached to the creature's neck.

"It's huge." When I speak, the creature looks at me.

"Ugly, isn't it?"

It looks stealthy and graceful and strong. The only savage thing about it are the bald patches of skin rubbed raw around its limbs. "It's nothing like I expected." Darius moves toward it but I grab his wrist. "What're you doing? Don't get too close."

"I have to give it the injection." He pries my hand from his wrist and creeps forward. The creature follows Darius with his eyes, terrifyingly still. I shiver.

"Are you sure this is safe?"

"I've done it before. It won't hurt me. It knows it will die without this." He reaches the creature and presses the needle into the mangled skin of its shoulder. "See?"

Before I can respond, a low growl echoes off the walls and suddenly the creature flies at Darius. I yank his arm and fall back, scrambling across the floor until my back is pressed against the wall. The creature strains against the chains as it reaches for us, its breathing ragged and heavy. It stands taller than either of us, with broad shoulders and an intimidating stature. It looks unworldly.

"Don't worry." Darius brushes his hands on his pants and helps me up. "It does that every so often. It's trying to scare us."

"I shouldn't have come down here."

"We can go," Darius says.

The creature makes a low, guttural sound. It unsettles me, and it has nothing to do with how it makes me want to run away. "I think that would be best."

I leave first, desperate to be aboveground, away from the frigid air and the stench of blood. Darius's hand slips into mine and he squeezes.

He'll come for me.

A chill creeps up my spine. The words come from behind us, low and gravelly. I don't stop myself from looking back. The creature still stands, an animal with a glowing glare. "Darius, did you hear that?"

"Hear what?"

My entire body goes rigid.

"Milena! *Milena!*"

Charles. The hunters were supposed to leave an hour ago, and Charles never stays behind. "We need to get out of here." I tug on Darius's arm. "*Now.*"

But it's too late. Charles stands at the end of the tunnel wearing a murderous expression. He marches toward me and rips my hand from Darius's.

"What do you think you're doing?"

For the first time in my entire life, I'm afraid of Charles. He has scolded me plenty but never with such venom.

"Charles!" Darius's voice is excited. "She said it spoke but I heard nothing—"

My wrists sting where Charles's nails dig in. "What did you hear?"

"It said 'He'll come for me.'"

Charles shoves me aside and strides over to the creature. He picks up a long, metal pole with a sharp point and stands in front of it, a snarl on his face. "Who's coming?"

The growl emanating from the creature makes my hair stand on end, and I press myself farther into the wall. Charles jerks forward and shoves the metal pole into the creature's abdomen. It convulses around the pole and the room erupts with a body-shaking roar.

"Answer me!" Charles retracts the pole and the creature's lips lift to reveal sharp teeth.

"The one who rules the night." It looks at me, abdomen dripping with blood and voice filling my head. "And when he comes, you'll wish you were never born."

~

The inside of Charles's quarters reminds me of my bedroom—barren and void of personality. While bigger than my own, they consist of a small bed, a wooden desk, and a dresser with a missing knob. Standing in front of him with Darius, I wish there was something to look at to distract myself from Charles's wrath. "Do you understand how stupid you were today?" he scolds.

"Yes," Darius says, hanging his head. "I betrayed your trust. I shouldn't have taken Milena down there."

"No, you shouldn't have." Charles frowns. "Leave us, Darius. I'll deal with you later. You're going on your first hunt."

"*What?*" I demand. Nobody goes on a hunt before they turn sixteen. Nobody gets to know anything about it when they're as young as Darius.

"But, Charles, I'm only—I'm only thirteen."

"I've made up my mind. Now I'd like to speak to Milena." His voice is stern and cold. Darius doesn't move. "Alone."

"Of course." Darius nods and stumbles through the doorway.

We stand in tense silence. I can't stop thinking of the creature. Save for its bloodstained fur, it didn't look like a beast at all. But

GRACE COLLINS

its eyes glowed. That *thing* was no wolf. "I'll instruct Cynthia to reassign you to gardening duty until your birthday," he says eventually. "And you must do it alone. No more cooking or cleaning with Flo, gardening duty only."

"You can't be serious."

"I'm deadly serious."

Defiance surges through me but I bite my tongue. Arguing with Charles will only grant me a greater punishment. "And Darius? You *rewarded* him with a hunt when he's barely thirteen."

"What if it had broken through the chains again?" He ignores my comment. "You could've been killed."

"And Darius couldn't have?" None of this makes sense. "Why'd you hide this from me? You should've known I'd find out you caught one of them."

"I did know," he says lowly. "I, however, didn't believe you were stupid enough to go and visit it."

"He was—*it* was chained up. I was curious."

"You were *stupid*. You're lucky to be alive."

The icy air nips at my arms. Darius's lantern sits on Charles's desk, creating a looming shadow on the wall. When I was younger, I used to make drawings for Charles. He would pin them up on the wall of his quarters so that it didn't look so barren, but when I drew a picture of him and me as a family, he tore down all the drawings and told me that they were childish. He lets out a long, low sigh. "All these years and you still don't listen. Have I taught you nothing about obedience?"

"I said I was sorry." Something about being scolded this way makes me feel like that child again. "I won't disobey you again."

"I hope not. Or you won't be alive for your first hunt. A very important day. One you simply can't miss."

I could melt into the floor. I'm ashamed, upset, confused. Charles moves to stand in front of me, his shadow on the wall like an ominous figure threatening me from behind. For a second, I think he's going to touch my cheek, but his hands stay by his sides, and I feel foolish for thinking otherwise, for assuming there would ever be tenderness between us.

"Charles?" He hums in response. "The creature . . . it spoke to me. About somebody else—somebody more dangerous. Is he really going to come?"

"I've heard of it before." He pauses. "A creature who rules the night and those who run under the moon. We've been hunting it for years, we've never found it to be anything more than a myth."

"Do you think it'll come?"

"If it is out there, it'll track the creature right to us. We can't be seen as weak. They thrive off weakness."

"You're going to kill it?"

"The execution will be tonight, in front of the whole village, just before the sun sets. We need to send a message."

I shudder. "What do you think it's like? The one who rules the night?"

"That, Milena, is something I pray you'll never find out."

~

Make your way home at five, nobody out past six. Be in the tunnels as the sun begins to fall, seal the entrance as the sky turns ember. Be locked away *before* you need to be, leave enough room for malfunction. These are the rules I grew up with, the ones I never dared to break. But tonight is different. The sun is falling but the entire village stands in the clearing as we stare at the

GRACE COLLINS

creature chained to the kitchen. With all paws on the ground, it looks exactly like a wolf, but the red behind its eyes reminds me of the truth. It looks just as terrifying as it did in the tunnel. The chain around its neck has penetrated the skin, the area red and swollen. But it doesn't look afraid.

The adults murmur among themselves; they've been on the hunts, this isn't their first time seeing a creature. But the children cower between the legs of their guardians. I spot Darius across the crowd next to Cynthia, standing bravely with his chin in the air. Beside me, Flo grips my hand and looks at the sky. I know what she's thinking; the sun will set in less than an hour, and the creatures will come out to play. We've never been aboveground this late before.

"Justice will be served tonight!" Charles walks in circles so that everybody can get a good look at what's behind him. "We have our revenge. We will have its blood. And the lives of all those before us will be honored!" He scans the clearing, stopping on me. "Soon, we won't be weak."

The creature holds its head high—those red eyes narrowed as Charles paces, and I'm transfixed but also terrified. It doesn't look afraid of Charles's words. A cool wind rustles the trees and travels through the clearing, stirring up the fallen leaves and loose dirt scattered across the ground.

"Why are we doing this so close to dark?" Wilhelm, one of the hunters, steps forward. A few others murmur in agreement. "We need to get into the tunnels."

"Don't worry, we'll be in the tunnels before nightfall," Charles says. "We needed to do this as close to the moon as we could so that its beast will truly die. Look at it!" Charles raises the pole in victory. "A creature of the night!"

He thrusts the pole into the creature's chest but this time he doesn't take it out; he twists it. The creature roars, teeth morphing into pointed daggers. I clutch Flo and we stumble backward as we watch the creature morph into its . . . bloodied, long-fingered, hairless, skinned, and arched body. It almost looks *human.* The creature's bones crack as it convulses, causing the chains to cut deeper. I don't understand what I'm seeing.

When Charles pulls the pole from its chest, its body morphs before our eyes and slumps against the ground, all beast, thick blood seeping into the ground. But the hole closes right in front of our eyes. The clearing is silent as we watch this dark and dangerous creature writhe in pain. My whole life I've heard them at night, howling, growing, destroying—it's surreal to see one right in front of me.

"Any last words, beast?" Charles snarls, getting in the creature's face.

It lifts its head, eyes human but body completely animal. And then I hear it: the voice inside my head again. "You foolish thing. You have no idea what you've done."

Charles doesn't falter. "I know exactly what I'm doing."

He plunges the pole in again. The creature's howl is ear piercing, sending the birds nesting high within the treetops scattering above our heads. It looks out over Charles's shoulder and scans the crowd as we cower back. And though the sun still peeks above the ice-capped mountains and the sky has not yet shifted red, something howls back.

"But . . ." Charles looks stumped. For the first time in my life, his eyes hold fear. "But the sun . . ."

Darius screams as the howls turn to growls. People begin to push and shove, trying to make it to the tunnel entrance on the other side of the clearing. But I can't move. Charles stands in front of the beast, shaking and filled with uncertainty. And then, amid the chaos, red eyes focus on me, and a wry smile thaws my frozen body.

"He's here," it says. "And you're all about to die."

That's the last thing I hear before a bloodcurdling scream, and Wilhelm's head lands at my feet and rolls across the ground.

"Go! Everybody go! Get to the tunnels!"

Flo pulls me so hard my arm feels like it'll tear from its socket, but in the chaos, I don't resist. I can't see them but I know they're here—shadowed blurs cutting down anyone who gets in their way. Somewhere in the havoc, Flo and I become separated, my arm wrenched from her grip. I reach the tunnel entrance in a few seconds and stare desperately out at the clearing. The creatures move too fast to be seen in the low light—fast-moving shadows taking down villagers dashing for the tunnels.

"Milena!" Charles is in my face, blood splattered across his chest, limping on one leg.

"I can't find Flo!" I cry, gripping his arm. "She was with me one second and the next she—"

"Forget about Flo. Go to your quarters and don't turn around."

Cold terror claws at my throat. "Charles—"

"*Go.*" He turns and starts to slide the door across at the same moment there's a scream. *Flo.* I can see her beyond his shoulder, limping toward the entrance, tears streaming as she calls out to Charles not to shut the doors. The ends of her dress drag across the ground, torn and dirty.

"*Flo!*"

"Help!" she cries. "Wait!"

The entrance is sliding shut. "Charles, do something!"

He turns around, furious. "I told you to get out of here."

Flo's knees buckle and she falls to the ground.

"Flo's still out there!"

He doesn't care. The gap between Flo and me shrinks. She pulls herself up and tries to drag herself to the door, her hair dark with blood and face contorted in pain. A split second later, I dart through the gap. The doors graze my skin, the whisper of death brushing my arm.

I'm on the other side, the sky darkening around me. Racing to Flo, I can see her arm is slashed and her leg points at an unnatural angle. The kitchen shack lays between us and the tunnels. "Millie, look out!" A shadow hurtles toward us. Screaming, I jump on top of her and roll us across the ground—the creature goes sailing past.

"We're going to die," she cries. "*You're* going to die and it's my fault! Charles is going to kill me—"

"Flo, stop!" I say, pressing her into the wall of the shack. "We're in this together, okay?"

Her eyes flutter. I grab her arm and put it to her chest, trying to stop the bleeding.

"Leave me. Go, get safe. You—you have to."

"Flo, stay with me. *Flo!*"

"Go. You don't . . . understand, you—you can't die, you're almost . . . twenty, you can't—"

"What're you talking about? Neither of us is going to die, okay?" Her eyes flutter shut. "Flo?"

But she's unconscious. I shake her, willing her to wake, but to no avail. A growl comes from behind, and I turn my head. The faces of an army of wolf-like creatures with snarling mouths and glowing eyes are simply *there*. They move in, jaws snapping, teeth bared, ragged breaths clouding in the night air. But one howl stops them all. The wolves halt and lower their heads to the ground.

With my back against the side of the kitchen there's nowhere for me to go, nowhere for me to run. I'm surrounded but they aren't attacking. Something emerges from the tree line. No, *someone* emerges from the tree line. The broad-shouldered figure walks toward us, the earth shaking beneath its feet.

As it gets closer, I squeeze my eyes shut when it stops in front of me. If I'm going to die, I don't want to see. The growls stop but the screams continue, ricocheting off the trees that surround us.

A low demanding voice says, "Open your eyes."

Power fills the air, fizzing and bubbling—the same power that made each and every one of the wolves lower their eyes. "*Open your eyes.*"

The command calls to my body in more ways than one, and I obey, eyes opening like they have a mind of their own. There it stands in front of me—the creature who rules the night. And it—*he*—looks just as human as me. He towers far above me, chiseled chest bare and covered in scratches. He has regal, refined features, dark hair, and a strong jawline. A faded scar runs from his jaw to his collarbone. But it's his eyes that make me hold my breath—they contain the golden glow of sunlight yet completely lack the warmth.

"A human. Interesting." There's something so frightening about this creature, and it has nothing to do with the wolves that prowl behind him, waiting to attack. "What's your name?"

"Milena."

He waves a hand and the wolves around me stand and bolt into the forest, howling into the darkness. My pulse jumps at his unwavering stare, but then his head snaps up, toward the tunnel, like he's heard something.

"I'll see you soon, Milena," he says, as if talking to a child. "Sleep well."

And like a moth succumbing to the fatal heat of a flame, I fall into the night.

CHAPTER THREE

Cold pierces my skin, infiltrates my bones. I try to open my eyes but pain flourishes across my forehead. A familiar voice, sweet and gentle, reaches into the void, calling my name. A twisted groan escapes my throat.

"Milena, wake up." This voice is more demanding, rough.

Figures form above me, illuminated by the warm glow of the lantern. But I feel so cold, ice inside my veins, robbed of life. I'm lying in my quarters, the familiar aroma of dirt filling the air. The voice I recognize as Flo's; her face coming into focus is streaked by tears and her arm is in a makeshift sling. Beside her stands Charles.

"What happened?" My voice is sandpaper against my throat. "What time is it?"

"You don't remember?" Flo asks.

"You left her." I sit up and glare at Charles, my head pounding. "You *left* her."

Flo looks at the ground. "Millie—"

"Don't defend him. He was going to leave you to die. He was going to shut the doors before you could get back."

"It's all right."

I push myself backward, ignoring the ache in the back of my head. "Are you kidding?"

"It was for the greater good," she mumbles.

"The *greater* good?" I say, glaring at Charles. "Are you even *sorry*?"

"Fifteen people lost their lives last night. Of course I'm sorry. Don't question my integrity, Milena. If I hadn't shut those doors when I did, we'd be talking about a much higher number."

My stomach tightens with grief—grief for children missing their parents and parents missing their children. It feels like there's a weight pressing on my chest.

"What happened to you last night?" Flo asks. Images appear against my eyelids: Flo passing out, the wolves with their glowing eyes.

"Flo has told me all she remembers before she passed out. The two of you were found unconscious by the kitchen," Charles says. "With all the creatures aboveground, I don't understand how you're still alive."

Wolves crowding in, teeth bared, creeping closer and closer until . . . golden eyes.

"I—" Charles's eyes pierce me as if reaching inside my brain. "The creatures, they abandoned us there and I—I think I fainted."

My room is so quiet I can hear the blood pounding in my

GRACE COLLINS

ears. The blanket scratches against my skin as I twist in the bed, leaning up against the cold stone wall. Charles clears his throat.

"They *left*? Just like that?"

"Yes."

"You didn't see anything else?"

Golden eyes; a creature so normal he couldn't possibly be a beast.

"I fainted. I don't remember."

"I see." He examines me. "Preparations for the memorials will commence this morning. We'll hold the ceremony at three, and then we'll hunt later."

Tell him about the man. Tell him about the one who rules the night.

"Does Cynthia need help preparing the food?" I ask.

He glares for a few tense moments. "How does your arm feel?"

Instinctively, I shift my arm. A white bandage has been wrapped around my bicep, red prickling through. It stings slightly but I barely even noticed it. "Fine."

"You're still being punished, then, till your birthday," he says. "The garden needs to be weeded."

"Right."

"Florence will help Cynthia and the others prepare." He gestures to Flo, who nods and hobbles from the room on a makeshift crutch. "As for you—"

"Gardening, got it."

If there's anything I hate more than cleaning, it's gardening, and Charles knows that. The weeds among the crops are relentless— you pluck them one day and they've already choked their way around the plants the next. The conversation seems finished but Charles doesn't leave. He stands halfway through my door, the white sheet swaying softly when he moves.

"You could've died, you know? The night before your hunt. You're so stupid," he says. "You're lucky to be alive."

I could've died; I *should* have died, but Flo should've, too, and Charles doesn't care about her, memorial for the dead or not. He threw her to the creatures without a second thought. Charles is my guardian, but that's all. He's never cared about me before, about my first hunt, so why now? "I'll be better." I blink back tears. "I promise."

He sighs and, holding the sheet back, turns to look at me. "If you remember anything about last night, you know where to find me."

I nod, body rigid at the warning in his tone. He leaves the room and I sink back into the bed, shoulders slack as the previous night's events rip through my mind. The dim light of the lantern highlights the aged scars etched into the ceiling, and I try to think of those who lost their lives, but only the golden-eyed creature fills my mind.

~

I'm hot, filthy, and frustrated by the time I arrive at the memorial. Behind the kitchen shack, beneath the blazing sun, the village stands. It's only in seeing the horror-struck faces that I feel guilt deep in my bones. My head aches, my feet sting, and the ends of my sleeves are black with dirt. Still, I'd rather be gardening than attending this memorial. Because the crowd is missing familiar faces.

Wilhelm, a devoted hunter and excellent cook. Abby, the woman who taught me before Charles pulled me out of school. Freya, Alex, Nieve. These are the people I grew up with, and

GRACE COLLINS

despite their indifference toward me, their taunts, and how they mocked me, the crushing weight I feel by their passing doesn't ease.

I had spent the remainder of the morning before the memorial plucking weeds from the vegetable garden by the stream, gazing out at the journey it takes through the forest that surrounds us. My mind played tricks on me, making me believe there were eyes watching me from deep within the trees. When I turned, there was nothing there, but the eerie feeling followed me to the memorial.

The event passes painfully slow; everyone has a memory to share, a final good-bye. The sun beats down on us, the day mocking those in mourning. I find Flo among the cluster of bodies after the ceremony. She links her arm through mine and wipes her eyes.

"You okay?"

"Yeah." She sniffs. "I just hate the creatures. I hate them so much."

"Yeah," I say, ignoring the twisting of my stomach. "Me too."

"Do you want to play checkers? We can bring them up and sit by the stream in the sun. I was supposed to hunt but Charles gave me the afternoon off. I need to take my mind off everything."

"Can't. I'm still on gardening duty, remember?"

Her shoulders slump. "Right."

"Hey, it's not all bad." I nudge her and force a smile. "You should ask Charles if you can hunt tomorrow instead. He's taking me on my first one."

"What?" She stops in her tracks.

"It's my birthday tomorrow, finally. What's wrong? You know I've been waiting for this day since forever."

She looks like she's seen a ghost. "I'd forgotten it was tomorrow, with everything that's happened."

"Flo." I put my hand on her shoulder but she sidesteps it. "Aren't you happy for me?"

She avoids my eye and backs away. "I have to go."

"Flo, wait, I—"

But it's too late—she's already gone, fleeing through the center of the village like I'm some sort of disease she can't get away from fast enough.

~

It's late afternoon by the time I reach the vines. The wooden wall built to support the tomatoes was partially snapped last night, and fragments are scattered in the garden surrounding it. A layer of sweat covers my forehead and my hair is a tangled pile atop my head as I move around in the heat, tidying up.

There's a reason gardening is the worst job to do alone—because it's the one task that never truly ends. As soon as I mount the square wall back upright, I notice the weeds clawing through the dips in the wood. I drag my tools along the ground and hack at the browning vines gripping the wood for dear life. The whisper of the breeze brushes my skin, a ripple of leaves in its wake, and I hear it, then.

Turning, I expect to see Cynthia about to scold me for the crooked wooden support. But it isn't her. It isn't anyone. "Hello?"

The edge of the forest, usually inviting and fruitful during the day, looks ominous—branches reaching out to me, crying for me to get lost in their depths. It swallows the other end of the stream, shadowing the clear water. Turning back around, I snip the root of a weed and tug it from the wall, trample it. And then I pause; there are the burning, golden eyes staring right back at me.

He stands only a few feet away, barefoot, clothed in black. I stumble back until I hit the wall; it falls behind me, the wood snapping as I brandish my cutter in my hands like it can somehow protect me. The tomato patch is the only section of the clearing not visible from the tunnel entrance, blocked by the back of the kitchen shack.

"Don't come any closer." He tilts his head, glancing at the cutter in my hands. "I'm serious. I'll, I'll—"

"You wouldn't be able to hurt me even if you wanted to."

Though he looks and speaks human, there's an otherworldly beauty to him that I can't describe, but one look at his biceps makes me gulp—he could snap my neck before I could call for help.

"I could scream."

He starts to walk closer. "But you won't."

I hate that he's right. I hate that I don't understand *why* he's right. Our afternoon was spent mourning fifteen of the people I grew up with—why am I not disgusted by the mere presence of this creature? *Because he didn't kill you when he had the chance.*

He's nearly in front of me, hand reaching out, and there's nowhere for me to go—if I step back, I'll tumble over the unsnapped section of the wall mounted crookedly in the ground. His fingers close around the cutter pointed at him, and he pulls it from my grasp.

Scream. Call for help.

"Why did you come here?" I ask.

"I said I'd see you soon."

"Why didn't you kill me?"

"You're no monster."

"And the others you killed are?" The ghost of a smile appears but he doesn't answer. "Who are you? Why does your kind kill so many innocent people?"

His expression falters ever so slightly. "You shouldn't believe everything they tell you."

"I know you kill. I *saw* it last night. Fifteen people died. They were *murdered*."

"The killing isn't the part you shouldn't believe."

In the distance, laughter filters through the clearing. A group of hunters heads toward us from the tree line. Charles is at the front of the path, with Darius right by his side. When I look back the man is gone—so fast it's as if the breeze carried him away. Charles spies me standing by the wall.

"Milena?" He approaches me. "What happened to the wall?"

"I—uh—it must've been broken last night. I was trying to fix it."

He looks past me, to the forest, where the man had emerged. "The sun will set soon. Best get to the tunnels."

The sun lingers in the crevice of the mountains; it'll be hours before the sky is dark. But after yesterday, nobody will take any chances. I pick up my tools and fall into step with Darius. With a glance over my shoulder, I hold my breath, half expecting the creature to be watching me leave. The tree line is empty, like he was never even there.

My entire life I've been told of the beasts, bloodthirsty creatures with no humanity. They're the ones who killed my parents, the ones who ruined my life, the ones I should hate. But the golden-eyed man was no beast; he was beautiful the way the icicles lining the gutters in winter are—enticing yet untouchable.

"Hey, Darius," I say. "How was your first hunt?"

"Fine." His voice is tight and firm, nothing like the light, joking tone he used in the tunnels the day prior.

"Everything okay?"

"Yes."

I grab his arm, halting him. "What's up with you? Are you really going to ignore me now too?"

The look in his eyes, his scowl . . . it's familiar. It's the one they all return with after their first hunt; it's the way his mother, Cynthia, looks at me. I let go of his arm. "Good night, Milena." His face is so young, but his voice is so cold and knowing. "I'll see you tomorrow for your first hunt."

He strides away. Tomorrow, I turn twenty. Tomorrow is the day I've been waiting for my entire life—the day I get to experience my first hunt; the day I get to join the ranks of so many people before me. I should be excited. But I only feel heaviness thrumming through my veins.

~

The mood in the tunnels feels different, and it has nothing to do with the fact that families are mourning the loss of their loved ones. People stare at me when I walk past, averting their eyes when I catch them, as if somehow last night was my fault. I hold my head high as I search for Flo in the main room, her quarters, and the hall, but she's nowhere to be seen. There's so much on my mind.

Darius's attitude change makes my head spin, and Flo's absence is peculiar. And the hunt tomorrow—what does it involve? The hunters usually return with dead animals for meals, although sometimes with nothing. But there's always an air of mystery that surrounds them, a huge secret I feel left out of. And yet it's the creatures who plague my mind, intrigue and fear warring against one another.

I retire to my quarters early, giving up on finding Flo. At exactly a quarter past seven, Charles arrives at my door with a stoic expression. "How are you feeling?" he asks.

I shrug halfheartedly. "I'm all right."

"Good. You'll need your energy for tomorrow. Make sure to sleep well tonight. I need you at your very best."

I nod eagerly, thoughts of finally uncovering the mystery of the hunt shooting a surge of energy through me. "Charles." I catch his arm before he can leave. "Did the hunt go well today? With Darius?"

"Of course."

"He seemed different."

Gently, he wraps his hand over mine and untangles my fingers from his arm. "That's the hunt, Milena," he says. "It changes everything. You'll see." And then he turns and exits, leaving me alone with a messy arrangement of thoughts to sort through.

CHAPTER FOUR

Charles arrives at my room early the next morning with a pair of brown trousers and a white shirt that he instructs me to put on. I'm twenty. It's the most important day of my life. Today, I'll become like everyone else—a hunter. And I can feel like I belong here for the first time, maybe ever.

I'm aboveground within five minutes. Despite the early morning sun, the air has a bite to it. This isn't unusual heading into winter—what *is* unusual, however, is the absence of life both in the tunnels and around the village.

"Where is everyone?" I ask Charles, tugging my trousers by their waistband.

"Busy." He waves my question off with a flick of his wrist and heads toward the forest. The wind whistles through the empty clearing, an eerie emptiness following us from the underground. "Keep up, Milena."

We pick up the pace and take the forbidden step into the forest. I'm awestruck, briefly forgetting where I am—that I've left the village and am in the territory of the creatures. I forget that I've waited twenty years for this moment. I forget that I should be nervous.

The trees tower overhead, touching the sky as rain runs down in rivulets, dampening my arms. From inside the village, the forest always looks ominous, but the trees widen their branches in welcome and the chirping of insects bounces through. Leaves crunch beneath my feet; a melancholic song echoes off the tree-tops as birds flutter from one side of the forest to another.

Charles bashes through the plants, whacking them aside haphazardly, widening the flattened path before us. He isn't careful; he shoves through it, unnecessarily disrupting the peace of the inhabitants who call this place home.

"Where are all the other hunters?" I ask. Charles uses his machete to chop a low-hanging branch to the left of us. His knife glints in the sun and reflects in my eyes.

"They're waiting for us."

"Where?" I frown. "Where are we going? When do we start? Don't I get a weapon?"

"Patience, Milena." The irritation in his voice only grows so I shut my mouth. I'm not about to blow it because a few things seem out of the ordinary. We walk deeper into the forest. The farther we get from the village, the further I feel I'm being stretched. It feels strange to aimlessly wander through a place I've been forbidden from entering my entire life—ludicrous, even.

Snap.

Charles pauses in front of me. The sun filters through the branches, creating a patchwork of light on the forest floor. "What was that?" I ask.

Charles turns. "This is an important day."

"I know." I step over a fallen log. It's picturesque but a sinister feeling tickles my spine as the distant hum of chatter wafts toward us. "People are talking. Can you hear that?"

"Close your eyes."

"What? Why?" We're the only two there among the trees. "Is this how everyone's first hunt goes?"

He steps toward me. "My people have been waiting a long time for this day. Close your eyes."

He stares at me, fingers fidgeting restlessly at his sides, and I ignore the nagging voice in my head. This is Charles. The man who took me in when my parents died, who has always kept me safe. So I shut my eyes, my other senses tuned, suddenly, to what's around me. Charles wraps a hand around my wrist and guides me forward, trees brushing against my skin as I clamber through the bush, struggling not to stumble over loose rocks and roots that get in my way.

Despite the frigid air, a bead of sweat travels the line of my spine. Charles instructs me to lift my feet to avoid fallen branches, hand tightening around my wrist as a reminder to keep my eyes closed. And then we stop. "Can I open my eyes?"

Silence. A chill caresses the bare skin of my arms. Charles's grip loosens until he isn't touching me anymore and, for a brief moment, I think he's left me alone as some sort of test. I open my eyes. The trees have thinned around a pond-like body of water, shrubs and dirt surrounding the edge. People linger at the edge of the trees. We are not alone.

"Charles?" My foot catches on a root and I fall backward, elbow stinging as it grazes the ground. Charles stands over me, the large machete in his hand raised to his shoulders. "What are you doing?"

"I'm sorry, Milena."

Peering past him, I see Cynthia standing at the front of the pack with a blank expression, a scowling Darius by her side. My stomach plummets as I scan the rest of my village standing by and watching. Something isn't right. "What's going on?"

"I'm sorry," he says again, stepping forward. "But this must be done."

"*What* must be done?"

He moves closer still. I try to push up but my foot gets caught and my head smacks against the dirt. I look at Darius, the memory of his cruel words and cold eyes jolting me. The ostracism, the judgmental looks, the isolation—it all clicks.

"Is this what you do to everyone on their first hunt?" I get up, ignoring the pounding in my head. "Is this why they come back so different? So stuck up? Do you *torture* them?"

"Our first hunt is when we learn the truth about you," Darius says, spitting at the ground.

"Quiet, Darius," Cynthia hisses.

"The truth?" I repeat. "What truth?"

"Enough talk." Charles takes another threatening step toward me. "We've waited twenty years for this—I don't want to waste another second."

He lifts his arm and the machete shimmers like glass. I leap back. Nobody moves; everybody just stands and watches. "What've you been waiting for? I don't understand!"

"This moment."

"*What* moment?"

His breath is ragged as he lifts his chin and rolls his shoulders back. Terror grips an iron fist around my heart and wrenches it out of my chest. I've known him all my life, but this side of Charles—uncontrolled and wild—I do not recognize.

"The moment you die."

The trees spin. My legs are frozen, hands paralyzed at my sides as I wait for him to laugh, for the look on his face to turn less twisted, to hear the punch line to his joke. But it never comes. He takes another step toward me, machete raised, and I leap sideways. Death strokes my arm as the blade breezes past. A scream escapes—strangled and hollow. There's no time to think, no time to feel betrayed. I turn on my heel to get away but the villagers surround me on one side, and the pond circles me on the other, blocking my escape.

"Let me out!" I cry and shove against them. "Please! Let me out! He's trying to kill me!"

Thump. Thump. Thump. Footsteps. One after the other. I turn just in time, the machete coming down a whisper from my left leg. Charles scowls in annoyance when I dart away. Over his shoulder, a ribbon of red—curls billowing in the wind, wide green eyes. Relief floods through me.

"Flo!" My voice is hoarse. Cynthia pushes me back when I try to reach her. "*Flo!* Help me!"

She averts her gaze to the ground and I almost drop and succumb to the threat of the machete. My very best friend, the only one who ever showed me kindness. The only person in this entire world who truly loved me. Or so I thought. I race in the other direction but Cynthia grips my arm and twists it back, her iron grip holding me tight, forcing me to stare at Charles who stands inches away with his machete. My cheeks are damp, a mixture of dirt and tears. There's nowhere for me to go, nowhere to run, nowhere to hide. I'm trapped.

"*Please.* Why? I—I don't—please, I—don't let me—"

"You're making this harder on yourself, girl," Cynthia hisses.

Charles stands in front of me now, mossy eyes narrowed as he raises the machete. A sob rolls through my body in waves, rendering me incapable of forming coherent words. Cynthia lets me fall to my knees, drained. The sun bathes Charles in a bar of shimmering gold, like some sort of angel—a cruel contrast to reality. And despite my disorientation, my fear, my ultimate desire to simply lie back and stare at the sky, I don't break from him, as if I can somehow change his mind, as if we can go back to the village and act like nothing has happened.

"I'm sorry, Milena."

"Why are you doing this?"

His jaw tenses and he closes his eyes, lifts the machete.

Bang.

The weapon flies from Charles's hands and clatters to the ground a few feet away. Flo screams. Charles reaches for the machete but the blade is yanked from his grasp. A figure stands in front of him, clothed in black, a hood pulled over their head so only their smile and a bit of white hair spilling out are revealed. They raise the machete at Charles. In the shadow created by the hood, the figure's eyes shimmer silver.

A creature of the night.

"Beast," Charles hisses.

"Beast?" The voice is sweet and high-pitched, an enchanting laugh following. "Well, that's ironic."

Cynthia moves forward, toward the girl, but she's too fast—in the blink of an eye, I'm yanked from the ground and across to the other side of the clearing, by the pond. She stands over me, swinging around and slashing the hunter coming for her with the machete before facing me.

"Run," she says. "And don't turn back."

I don't need to be told twice. Spinning directionless through the trees, my elbows scrape against bark and low branches tear strands of hair from my head. Adrenaline propels me, faster and faster, until the sounds of screaming and shouting are nothing but a distant echo between treetops. And when I can't run anymore, I walk, stumble, crawl. But I don't stop. Time passes in a blur. Seconds, minutes, hours. I can't think clearly; I can barely see.

Charles tried to kill me. Flo didn't stop him. I have nowhere to go.

Warmth seeps from the forest as the sun dips lower. My legs should ache and the grazes on my knees and elbows should sting, but the excruciating pain of betrayal is overpowering. Noises ring out—the howls. The wind carries them toward me until they come to a halt. I'm no longer alone.

The only announcement of their arrival is the slight drop in temperature. My fingers quiver as I half turn. The forest alights blue, brown, green, red, and silver. Shadows surround me, closing in. I sink to my knees in defeat. Someone steps through the group of wolves, a human. His black hair is shaved close to his head, muscles flexing beneath his skin—skin marked with burns. But it's his eyes that are familiar—glowing a bright red. This is the creature Charles tried to torture, and he stands before me unrestrained. "Stand up," he orders. He watches me wobble to my feet, mouth in a straight line. "Now walk."

"What?"

"*Move.*"

I open my mouth to scream but he slaps a hand over my mouth, the other going around my neck. I am choking; his hand cuts off my airway. We're the same height but I feel so small.

"You can do as I say and walk silently, or I can force you to listen to me." His mouth presses to my ear. "Your choice."

I do exactly as he says, my knees knocking together and my throat aching as I join the group of wolves traveling through the dead-quiet forest. I ran from my village right into the hands of monsters, but I'm alive.

CHAPTER FIVE

We walk for what feels like an eternity, each hour longer than the last. A thick blanket of cloud conceals any light from the moon, but my eyes adjusted to the darkness long ago. It's the glacial air that stuns me, leaving me quivering in nothing but my thin clothes.

Nobody speaks. Nobody touches me. Nobody looks at me. Three wolves lead the way, setting an almost impossible pace, and the creature we tortured lingers behind. I can't see him but I know he's there, a terrifying energy warning me not to turn around. The terrain is no longer flat, leaving me gasping for air as we climb hills and stumble down the other sides. My body threatens to shut down but fear keeps me moving toward the looming landscape ahead. I've stared at these mountains from my village every single day of my life. They were far away, distant shadows that rose like jagged teeth from the ground. But we head toward them and they grow in size until I can't see anything beyond them anymore.

The wolves ahead come to a stop, turning their heads to look behind me. I tense in the silence as the man steps forward, eyes locked with one of the wolves. They stare for a while longer before he turns to me. "We're here." He takes my arm, grip a lot gentler than before, and ushers me forward. "Don't make a sound."

We step past the wolves and through the trees. It's only when they begin to thin that I understand what he's talking about. Warm light stretches through the trees, the hum of life—laughter and music—vibrates toward us.

"Where have you taken me?"

"I told you to be quiet."

We don't move toward the light—the man directs me around it until we reach a vast stone wall that cuts us off from it. Thick vines crawl upward, towering far above the treetops where the stone reaches. It's some sort of castle—like the ones in the picture books Flo and I would try to read when we were children. The man pulls me to a wooden door. He releases my arm to shoulder the door but it only budges. I'm so entranced by the castle I forget my terror, trying to twist my head to catch the sights at a better angle. The man captures my attention by cracking the wooden door when he shoves it open, turning back to look at me.

He takes my arm again and pulls me behind him. It isn't dark like I thought; lanterns are strung up along the plain stone walls, illuminating the towering arched ceilings and narrow halls leading off the sides. If it wasn't such a large space with high ceilings,

I could almost believe I was back home in the tunnels.

"Took you guys long enough, I've been here for hours."

The man, unalarmed, strolls toward a staircase and leans against the banister. "We didn't all have the luxury of running, Cassia."

She—Cassia—sits sideways on the banister of the stair, picking at her nails. She notices me looking and swings her legs to hop to the ground to walk closer. Her face is angular, sharp cheekbones and jawline framed by her sleek, collarbone-length hair. Her hooded, wide eyes flash silver. "You were there," I say. "You were there and you . . . they . . ."

"I saved your life."

I want to disagree with her, to deny that my own people tried to kill me, but I can't. "You're one of—you're—you're—"

"A beast? A monster?" she suggests. "What else did they tell you about us, huh?"

Though she looks and talks like me, the way her eyes flashed when she stood over me with the machete reminds me that she isn't human.

"What am I doing here?" I ask. "Are you going to hurt me, punish me for what we've done to you?"

"You're safe, Milena."

"How do you know my name?" No answer. The idea that I'm even sitting here in front of one of them is terrifying—the only thing that keeps me from running is the knowledge of what they might do to me if I tried to escape. "I—let me go. I don't understand what's happened but I . . . please let me go."

"I *saved* your life."

"You've killed so many of my people. You've murdered in cold blood."

"You mean the very people who just tried to murder you?" the man says, pushing off the banister. "I'm the one your people *tortured* in cold blood, the one your leader impaled multiple times, who was tortured while *you* stood there and watched like it was all some sick game."

"Eric," Cassia hisses.

Eric lifts his lip in a snarl. "Doesn't matter if she's not one of them, she was raised with them."

"She didn't—*doesn't*—know."

"That's no excuse," he says, starting toward me. "She should be treated like we treat the rest of those hollowers."

"*Eric!*" Cassia grips his arm and yanks him back.

"Let me go!"

"Listen to me, dammit. Don't touch her. You're not thinking straight."

He stares at me, hatred in his eyes. "You don't belong here. You'll *never* belong here." And then he turns around and disappears down the hall, accelerating my pounding heart.

"Sorry about him." Cassia offers a sheepish smile. "He hasn't exactly forgiven your people for . . . well, you know. I don't blame him."

Nothing makes sense. I don't know where I am, why I'm here, why I'm not dead. "I don't trust you."

"I wouldn't expect you to."

"I don't understand what's going on."

"I know you don't." She sighs. "Look, I'm not going to hurt you, okay? Do you believe that?"

I want to trust her, and something tells me that I should. But I feel so disoriented—my reality is so distorted I can't pick what's real and what isn't anymore. "All I know is that I've been taught my entire life that your kind are hell-bent on murdering anything that gets in their path, and now you stand in front of me looking just as human as me and I don't understand."

Cassia steps closer, holding her hands in front of her in surrender. "Will you follow me? I want to show you something."

"Do I have a choice?"

"Of course." She nods up the stairs. "Come on, I won't touch you, I swear."

With nowhere else to go, I tentatively follow her up the staircase, legs aching in protest. At this point, I've been awake for over twenty-four hours, and the only thing keeping me conscious is the fear. The staircase is narrow, the stone walls maintaining their height the entire way up. We reach the next floor, and Cassia simply steps through the first wooden door.

This room is brighter, lit by lanterns, but also by the light filtering through the large window on the far wall. A large bed divides the room, taking up much more room than a bed should. High arches tumble to the floor. Cassia moves to touch my arm.

"Stay back," I warn, as if I could hurt her. "Don't come any closer."

"Turn around, look out the window."

Cautiously, I angle myself to peer out the window, squinting to adjust to the brightness. The view is breathtaking. I've never seen anything like it. We're one floor above the ground, but it's enough to see the village stretched out below. Unlike the place where I come from, this is entirely aboveground, the clearing home to vast open spaces. Wooden shacks, like our kitchen, litter the landscape, lined up to create narrow streets with people bustling through them, wearing colorful clothes, and ducking in and out of their homes. And the trees at the edge of town stretch on for miles, only thinning once they reach the base of the mountain.

Putting my hand on the window ledge and leaning out, I momentarily forget my current situation. I want to store everything in my memory. "Many of those people, they're like you," Cassia says.

"Imprisoned?"

"No, and you're not either. They're *human*. They're safe here, we coexist.

"But you kill humans."

"No, we don't."

"I've seen it. Fifteen of my people were murdered."

"I'm not denying that. I'm saying we don't kill humans."

I turn and face her. "That can't be true."

"It is." I turn at the sound of a familiar intruder. He stands in the doorway, an inch ahead of Eric, arms by his side. I tremble in his presence—the one who rules the night. This man makes Eric seem amicable. I have so many questions to ask—why he didn't kill me, why they don't look like beasts, if it's by his order that I'm kept here. But only one question comes out.

"What're you saying?"

"I'm saying"—he enters the room, eyes flashing amber—"the people you grew up with are not human."

My chest aches like I've been struck. "What?"

"They're hollowers," he says. "Your entire life you've been led to believe that *we* kill humans, but it's them. *They're* the ones killing. We're trying to protect humans."

"No. You're crazy."

"I'm telling the truth."

"You can't be. I would've known because they would've said—"

"They lied to you," Eric says. "Get over it."

"Why should I believe anything you say?" I ask.

"It wouldn't be the first thing they lied to you about, would it?" he says in reply.

I know he's right, and deep down, I believe him. My entire life, I've been led to believe that the creatures of the night were nothing but animals, but here three of them stand, looking as human as me. But I don't *want* to believe him. Because if I do, that means accepting that my entire life has been a lie, that I've been groomed and raised only to be killed by the very person I trusted more than anyone else.

"What are *hollowers*?" I ask.

"Hollowers are . . ." He searches for the words. "They hollow humans to survive."

"*Hollow humans?*"

"Eat them," Cassia clarifies, waving a hand. "Feed off their humanity, relish in their memories, steal their energy—yada, yada."

I look at the golden-eyed man to provide me with confirmation but his expression gives nothing away. "That sounds crazy."

"You don't believe us?"

"I don't know what to believe."

"Believe this: Your friends, these people you believe are like family, the ones who raised you and tried to murder you? They lied to you, betrayed you, and they probably would've hollowed you if I hadn't sent Cassia to watch over you." His words are lethal—they cut right through me. "Your entire life has been a lie, Milena. You've been lied to, misled, *betrayed*—"

"Elias, stop," Cassia demands. "Can't you see she's had enough?"

He pauses, jaw clenching. The fire in his eyes disappears so fast I almost wonder if it was ever there at all. "Excuse me," he says softly, turning around and exiting the room without another word. The air sizzles with his departure.

"Tell the girl about hollowers," Eric says. "I'll be in the office if you need me." And then, as quickly as Elias, he exits the room.

"Sorry about that," Cassia says with a grimace. "Elias isn't usually so rude."

I feel shaken—like somebody has wrapped their hand around my heart and is trying to wrench it from my chest. Not to mention my fingertips have gone completely numb. "You said I'm not imprisoned here."

"You're not."

"Will you let me go?"

She frowns. "No."

"Then I'm imprisoned."

"We're keeping you safe, Milena. Where do you want to go? Back to your village?"

She's right, I don't have anywhere to go. But just because they say I'm safe doesn't mean I believe them. It isn't possible to throw everything I thought I knew about their species out the window in five minutes.

"Tell me more about the hollowers," I say. "Why do they have to eat humans?"

"They don't *have* to eat humans, they do it to live longer. They could live off human food perfectly fine, but eating other species gives them abilities."

"Abilities?"

"The average lifespan of a hollower is around twenty. When a hollower reaches sixteen years of age, they begin to age very quickly and then die. Eating different species gives them more time."

"Like immortality?"

"Not quite," she says. "They hate other creatures because they're jealous of us. Eating a human makes them age like one, but eating a shifter ages them like shifters and gives them the strength of one. And wispers, well, they're not around anymore to try it out."

Her words make my head spin. "Shifters?"

"I believe you call us creatures of the night. Or, you know, beasts. Though I'd have to argue with that."

"And wispers?"

"Let's just stick with shifters and hollowers for now."

I look out the window. The sky is still dark, and with no sign of the moon, it's impossible to tell how far away sunrise is. "I think I want to be alone."

"I'm not so sure—"

"You say I'm not a prisoner here, so leave me alone. I need to be by myself. I haven't slept in over a day, I'm exhausted."

"Okay. I'll be by to get you in the morning." She walks to the door, shooting me one last glance. "There's a bathroom to your left. Get some rest, okay?" She closes the door behind her. I watch it, waiting for somebody else to barge in, but it remains shut.

I don't recognize myself in the mirror on the wall. My brown eyes have dark circles beneath them and my skin is dull and dry. Black, thick hair knots at the nape of my neck, littered with twigs and leaves. I look dull and lifeless, so unlike me.

I have to get out.

The door handle doesn't budge when I yank on it—it's locked

from the outside. So I tear a piece off the nearby curtain and throw my fist into the mirror until it shatters onto the floor. Using the sharp shards of glass, I slice the curtains and sheets into thick strips and tie them together in a mismatched patchwork. I dangle my makeshift rope from the windowsill to a spot inches above the ground. Clambering down the material, I use the holes in the cobblestone wall to rest my weight. After a few moments, I'm on the ground.

The trees welcome me as I walk through them, heart running and mind speeding. I don't know what I'm doing or where I'm going; all I know is that I was almost killed by my family and now I'm being held captive by the very creatures I've been hiding from my entire life. I need time to sort through this information, but each step I take through the trees, I feel less confident about the decision.

The air moves around, branches groaning in the wind. I stop moving and stare ahead as nature screams, aware of a more powerful being lurking in its presence. I'm not alone.

"Where are you going?"

I don't turn around. I can feel Elias's terrifying presence, like a pulse of lightning. "How'd you find me?"

"I'll always find you." There's a mocking tone to his voice, but beneath it, a threat. "Why did you run?"

"I wanted to be alone. I couldn't think locked in that room."

He's in front of me in mere seconds, leaning lazily against the tree. "Where are you running to?"

"Nowhere," I say. "Why me? Why did this happen to me?"

"I'm still trying to figure that out. It doesn't surprise me that they tried to kill you, it surprises me that they waited so long," he says. "Why raise you for nineteen years, keeping you in the shadows and hiding who they are when they kill every other human on sight?"

I stare at the ground. His gaze makes me feel like every move is being noted and dissected. "This is crazy. It's all crazy. *You're* all crazy."

"Denial isn't going to get you anywhere."

I scoff, wiping under my eye. "You don't get it. I don't know where I belong anymore."

He pushes off the tree and steps toward me, his expression softer. "You don't believe us."

"I don't know what to believe. Don't you understand? My entire life has been ripped apart. I can't go home, the only people I'd remotely consider family tried to *kill* me, and here you are telling me they had planned to all along—that all this time I've been hiding *with* the murderers when I thought I was hiding *from* them. What would you believe?"

"I'd want to stay where I've been shown I'm safe."

"I was safe for the last nineteen years of my life," I say. "I thought I could trust *them*. Wouldn't it make me foolish to trust *you*?"

"Using that logic, I suppose so."

Elias is rational and controlled, and I stand in front of him one strand away from falling to pieces. It isn't like there's anywhere I *could* go, but learning that every aspect of my life has been manipulated and controlled to fit someone else's plans makes me want the freedom of choosing for myself.

"Then let me go."

"We can't let you go," he says. "We won't."

"*Why?*"

"They'll kill you when they find you."

"Why do any of you care? Why do you care? Why me?"

"I don't."

They shouldn't, but his words sting. "Then let me go."

"They *will* find you, Milena."

And in my hysteria, in the state where all I want are answers, I can only think one thing: *Let them have me.* But I stare at him then, and while the world seems to spin, he remains clear and still, eyes brighter than the sky above. He looks ethereal, like an angelic figure that visits you in your dreams. I've never allowed myself to fall victim to the harsh trap of beauty—not that any of the men in my village ever paid me any interest—but there's something about Elias that makes my breath hitch.

"We should get back," he says. "You must be tired."

"I don't want to go anywhere with you."

"Milena, look at me." I don't. "*Milena.*" He stands in front of me and lifts my chin. His touch is gentle, fingertips warm against my skin as he forces me to look at him. It occurs to me that he could snap my neck in seconds, and I would be completely defenseless. I don't care.

"You're tired." His voice is a low hum that vibrates in my chest. "You should sleep."

And as I stare at him, eyes burning like they did in the bedroom, weakness washes over me. And then, as if my body obeys his every command, my eyelids grow heavy, my limbs go numb, and everything is black.

CHAPTER SIX

The setting sun wakes me up the next day, bathing the bed in a pink hue. I stretch my achy limbs above my head, looking around the room. The last thing I remember is running into Elias in the forest; it had been the middle of the night then, and now, the sun is already setting. I must've slept all day.

The new, gray sheets are silky against my skin, a stark contrast to the scratchy blankets I'm used to, and I feel slightly disgusting as I crawl out of bed and stare down at myself. I pull the twigs out of my hair and try to brush the blackened dirt off my clothes. I cringe, moving to the bathroom connected to the room and fill the tub with water.

My head pounds as I sink into the water, rubbing my legs and shuddering at the way the water turns brown. Last night doesn't feel real. And if it wasn't for the extravagant room I woke up in,

I could almost have believed everything was a long nightmare. But the memory of Charles standing over me with that machete is etched so clearly in my memory it's hard to shake.

There's a knock on the door. "Hello?" I call.

"Milena?" It's Cassia, her high voice carrying through the door. "How are you feeling?"

Memories of my encounter with Elias come to mind, of everything I've learned since I've been here. "Fine."

"I was wondering if you wanted to go for a walk. I could show you around the village."

"It's dark outside."

"We don't have to worry about that here," she says. "I can explain all that if you come with me."

I don't *really* want to spend all my time locked in this room, and even though the prospect of being outside after dark still scares me, I have to take advantage of whatever opportunity I have to find out more information.

"Okay, I'll be out in a minute."

"Great! I brought you some clothes. I don't know if they'll fit so I added a belt, just in case." The door creaks open, and a neatly folded pile of clothes slides across the floor. "I'll wait out here."

I take a deep breath and peel my clothes off, then slide into the warm water with a sigh. Bathing back home was nowhere near as pleasant as this—the bathroom was all open plan. With a washcloth and a bucket of cold water, nobody looked forward to it. And yet, as I lie in the water and rub soap through my tangled hair, part of me wishes that I'd open my eyes and find myself with a bucket of cold water and a washcloth.

I take my time washing myself, and then dressing, pulling the brown sweater and black pants on. Cassia's slim, taller than me, and has a lot more muscle, but we're not all that different in size. Part of me hopes that by the time I emerge from the bathroom, Cassia will have given up. I don't know if I want to see anyone right now, do anything. But she's sitting on the bed, legs folded beneath her, and a bright smile on her face. When she sees me, she pushes herself to her feet.

"Ready?" I nod, my wet hair dripping on the floor. "Great." She turns on her heel and starts down the hall, gesturing for me to follow. "If people stare, just ignore them, we're not so used to strangers."

I swallow my nerves. The castle is entirely made of stone, furnished with mismatching bits that don't quite fit. The narrow halls are empty as we wander through to the bottom floor; it opens into a wide foyer, the floor covered with a lavish, red rug that leads right up to the wooden exit. Cassia pushes the doors open, and I want to run back. The vast night sky looms over us.

"It's okay," Cassia says, urging me forward.

The village lays at the foot of the castle, and is teeming with life. The streets are carved from the dirt, flattened and hardened with gray stone, and long wires lined with lanterns light the pathways. A man plays with a ball in the middle of the street, groups of people bustle together, laughter fills the air, and somewhere in the distance, music dances through the fog of the night.

Cassia watches me, but she's not the only one. People sneak curious glances while smiling at Cassia, who greets each of them by name. Shyly, I shift behind her. "No one will hurt you," she says. "We can go back inside if you like."

"I'm fine." Past her shoulder, the wooden cabins spread farther than I can see. "How many people live here?"

"In this colony, there are only around five hundred of us," she says.

"*Only?*" That's more people than I've seen in my entire life. "And it's a settlement of both humans and . . ." *Beasts. Creatures of the night.*

"Shifters," she fills in for me.

"But everybody here looks human."

Cassia smiles over her shoulder at me. "Most of the shifters are off running."

"Running?"

"We can only shift forms in the dark when the moon is out. And it's the only time our teens can roam the forests without fear of the hollowers attacking them."

At the mention of my people, I cringe. "Because we—*they* hide?"

"Yes." She nods as we come to a stop in front of the source of music. "This is where you can come to get a drink. It's the only bar in the village, but it's great."

The building is all wooden but it's painted a bright red and decorated with lanterns that glow a variety of bright colors. Laughter pulses from inside, mixing with the music to create a beautiful melody. It fills me with a sense of longing.

"Anyway," she says, "hollowers hunt during the day and hide at night because they know they can't take down shifters when we're not in human form. We hide during the day and roam during the night."

"You guys hide?"

"Sort of." She twists her lips in thought. "We don't actively go into hiding, not like you're used to. The hollowers would never risk coming here during the day, they'd be outnumbered, but our young are prohibited from leaving the village in daytime. Only a select few of us are allowed out."

"And when you do go out, do you kill my people?"

"They're not your people, Milena."

I know she's right—I know I'm not one of them, but even knowing they tried to kill me doesn't make it easier. It doesn't erase the past nineteen years—the laughter I shared with Flo, our conversations while gardening. It doesn't erase chasing Darius through the clearing and trying not to laugh when he got scolded by his mom. That stuff doesn't go away, not even when your so-called family tries to kill you. It's just another thing that twists around my throat and chokes me whenever I think about home.

"That's not an answer," I say.

"I think you know the answer." I look at the forest, my stomach in a knot. Yes, just as my people hunt them, they hunt my people. "They tried to kill you, Milena. They've been killing us for decades."

"They *raised* me."

I stare at the sky above. It's clear, littered with stars, and I momentarily forget where I am. We saw them so rarely growing up—one or two would dot the sky as the sun went down, but it was nothing compared to this. There are thousands of them, stretching across the darkness so far that all my problems feel insignificant.

"You said your kind could only shift during the night, so why was Eric an animal during the day when he was at my village?"

"They used silver on him. It weakens us and it prevented him from shifting back." She grimaces. "That was complete torture, you know, not allowing his body to naturally shift in the daylight."

Guilt hammers at me. Despite the fact that his temper terrifies me, I understand it. "And Elias?"

"What about him?"

"The night when I first saw him—" I stop myself, the memory of that night leaving a bitter taste in my mouth—of losing something that was never really mine. "The others listened to him."

"Yeah, he runs things around here, has for a while. Like a chief of sorts."

"Was he born into power?"

"No, we don't do things by birth here. It's because he's strong. He's different from the rest of us, and we trust him to take care of us."

"Different how?"

"He doesn't shift," she explains. "He doesn't need to, he's strong enough in his human form."

"Did he tell you to watch me? Back at my village?"

"After we got Eric back, he sent me to watch over you. He found it suspicious that the hollowers had a human living among them. Usually, he would've just taken you then, but he was intrigued and wanted to see what they would do, so I watched over you for the next little while, to make sure they didn't harm you."

"Why did any of you care if I was harmed?"

"We protect humans, it's what we do."

"But I'm sure there were more important things you could've been doing, and yet you were stuck watching me."

She studies me. "Elias is complicated, but he's a good man. I trust him and don't question his actions, and you shouldn't either. He asked me to watch you, so I did."

Elias is an anomaly, and Cassia is offering no explanation. "Can we go back now?"

Walking back the way we came doesn't seem so magical. It's a reminder of where I've come from, what has happened to me. The only thing that holds me together is the uneasiness I feel. The minute I let myself fall apart, I fear the creatures will pursue their attack.

The stone castle is lit by an extravagant lamp in the foyer. Light dances on the walls, stretching high up to the ceiling. My feet patter against the stone floor as I follow Cassia, a reminder that I'm being watched, that though they try to deny it, I'm trapped here. Not that I have anywhere else to go.

When we reach my bedroom on the second floor, Cassia turns and smiles brightly at me. "I'm really sorry about everything that's happened," she says. "I know this must be hard. But we really do only want to help you."

"Thanks."

I'm exhausted when I flop onto the bed, nearly missing the bolt on the window and brand-new mirror. The curtains have also been replaced. Drifting to sleep, I see remnants of the past. The rare moments Charles tucked me into bed; splashing through puddles with Darius when it rained; gossiping with Flo while we prepared food, muffling our laughter with our sleeves. I think of my parents. If what the shifters have told me is true, they couldn't have been killed by the creatures in a raid. But the idea that they could still be out there seems impossible, terrifying, even. If they are out there, how did I end up with the hollowers?

~

The following days pass in a blur of isolation and hysteria. The sun rises and sets, Cassia comes and goes with trays of food and various methods to spark conversation. Her attempts are futile. The village bustles below my window and at night, I dream of machetes and of parents I've never known breaking into the castle and saving me. But nobody comes except Cassia. No one— not Flo, not Darius, not Cynthia, not Charles—is going to save me. I don't even know if I need to be saved.

On the third night I sit by the window, watching the moon shift beneath the clouds, listening to the laughter wafting up from the village below. No matter how many nights pass, I never get used to the darkness—to being exposed to the moon and the potential threat that comes with it.

The thoughts that race around in my head become less like a distant dream. My village's betrayal sinks in deeper. I grew up believing I'd be accepted when I joined the hunts, but their plans for me were much more sinister, and in hindsight, I feel stupid, like I should've read into their hostile stares and snickers in the shadows. I was never one of them. But then there was Flo—the only one who made me feel as though I belonged.

My dearest memory is a distant one. Flo and I had thrown a birthday party for Darius when he turned eight. He'd never made many friends with the younger kids, lingering around the two of us whenever he had free time. And though we invited kids his age, none of them came. I think that's why I always had a soft spot for him—we were both outcasts.

Darius was upset. He cried for an hour until Flo and I snuck him outside of the village to play. We played a game of creature and villager, chasing one another for hours around the perimeter that surrounded the village. We ran until we were out of breath, and Charles caught us and shouted at us for leaving the safety of the ramparts.

I was put on gardening duty for a week as punishment, but it was one of my happiest memories. Running until we were pink faced, stomachs hurting from laughter, tickling Darius who squealed with joy when we caught him—it was euphoric.

Was Flo thinking of my death when it was her turn to chase me around? Was she thirsting for my blood our entire friendship? Did she always know who I was? I'm torn between the heartache of losing my best friend and the realization that, maybe, she was never truly my friend at all.

Every moment shared between us plays like a song in my head until it twists into a scream. What *was* her motivation for being friends with me? My village tried to kill me, my guardian tried to kill me, Darius wanted me dead, but at least none of them had pretended to love me. But Flo? Her betrayal hurts the most. It buries itself deepest and leaves invisible scars inside my chest.

There are three knocks at the door. I don't respond but the door is pushed open anyway. "Hey." Cassia appears with another plate of food. "I brought you dinner."

The tray has a few sandwiches, an apple, and a large glass of water. My stomach rumbles, but every time I try to eat, the food comes right back up within a matter of hours. "Thanks."

She lingers by the bed. "You need to eat."

Despite me ignoring her, she moves and settles on the window seat opposite me, strands of hair escaping the knot at the nape of her neck. She puts her hand on my knee. "I'm not going to hurt you."

I draw my knees to my body. "I just want to be alone."

"You've been alone for three days. We're all worried about you."

I turn away and stare back out the window. Cassia exits

without saying anything, quietly shutting the door behind her. I know she's right; I can't carry on like this, and starving myself isn't going to help. But I don't know what to do. Gingerly picking up a slice of apple, I unfold my legs and wander toward the door. It looms over me, daring me to open it. When I do, it creaks the same way the doors to the tunnels used to creak at nighttime.

Being in such a large structure with nobody else is still something I haven't gotten used to. While the halls are narrow, the high ceilings make the space feel so empty, with arches and the occasional artwork lining the walls amid a labyrinth of rooms. I've barely left my room since being here, but from Cassia's ramblings, I know she, Eric, and Elias are the only ones who live within the castle, with the exception of occasional visitors.

I try to memorize my path through the halls, nibbling on my apple slice as I come to a stop in front of a half-open door. Orange emanates from the door and the crackling of a fire entices me inside. I peer in before shoving the door open, then exhale in awe.

Back in my village, there were very few books. When I was young, we were read stories of the creatures, warning us of the danger that came when the moon replaced the sun. In school they were all we read. Charles always had a few books in his room that he'd never let me touch, and Cynthia kept a few in which she scribbled instructions for all her favorite recipes. But this room . . . the walls are lined with rows of books that tower right to the ceiling, lit orange by the warm glow of the crackling fire. I chew the last of my apple and run my finger along some of the spines as I enter an aisle. One book catches my eye, the spine a vibrant red. I pull it out and hold it in my arms before continuing, gathering books of vibrant colors and with interesting

GRACE COLLINS

looking titles—some fiction, and some appearing to be history-type books with titles I struggle to read.

I was never an avid reader—I didn't have the chance—and I doubt I'll understand much of what's written here due to my lack of experience beyond children's books. But the prospect of getting lost in different worlds while mine is falling apart is much too appealing. I stand on the tips of my toes to reach a book on a higher shelf.

"Starving yourself isn't going to solve your problems, you know."

I jump, dropping the book in my hand as I see Elias standing at the end of the row. In his hands is the book I just dropped.

"I'm not starving myself," I say, finding my voice.

"Your trays of food are always left full."

I hold the other books tight against my chest. It's been a few days since I've seen him; I'd forgotten how on edge his presence makes me. "This room is amazing," I say. "I've never seen so many books."

"I like to read. It's a good way to pass time."

"Hunting hollowers and running a village isn't interesting enough for you?"

He smiles. "Do you like to read?

"I'm not so good at reading. I only needed to know one thing: creatures of the night are bad, and I should be afraid of them." I don't know why, but it embarrasses me to admit that I can barely read. "Have you figured anything else out? About why they waited to kill me?"

He's silent for a few moments. "No."

"And you expect me to just sit around here doing nothing while you figure it out?"

"I expect you to do what you like. You're the one choosing to sit around and do nothing."

"And what if I want to leave?" I insist.

"You're free to leave the castle any time you like."

"You know that's not what I meant."

"Well, I'd say no," he says, stepping closer to hand me the book he caught.

"Why?"

"I told you, they'll kill you when they find you."

He's close, a mere whisper away. There's energy between us, pulling me toward him. "And I asked why you cared."

"You're important to the hollowers for some reason, we have to figure out why."

I know Charles waited until the moment I turned twenty to kill me even though they apparently kill every other human on sight. And it must mean something, so I understand why Elias and Cassia don't want to let me go until they've figured out what.

When I turn back around, Elias hasn't moved. He still looms over me. "You need to stop starving yourself."

"I'm not."

"If you promise to start eating properly and stop hiding away, I'll let you help me figure this out."

"Really?"

But before he can respond, there's a shout. Elias wraps his hand around my wrist, warm and tight. "Stay here," he demands. "Don't leave this library."

"Elias—"

But he's already gone, as if he was never there at all. The only evidence of his presence is the tingling of my wrist and the way the curtains wave in the breeze. I discard the books on the shelf before heading into the hall, my heart pounding in anticipation. The voices grow louder as I come to the foyer. Cries, shouts, low murmurs. I reach the top of the staircase and my breath catches.

Crimson red. Bodies drenched, skin void of any color. Three dead bodies lie at the foot of the staircase, a man crying hysterically over them as a woman tries to pull him off the corpses. Cassia hovers, Eric to her side, consoling a man with his head in his hands. Elias stands among the bodies, head held high as his eyes pass over the victims.

The door bursts open and a man stumbles in, the collar of his shirt stained red. He falls to his knees at Elias's feet, tugging the bottom of his shirt so viciously Elias stumbles forward. "They were everywhere! They took him—they took our son," he breaks off, choking. "They won't stop, they won't stop, and they'll come back."

"Harrison, slow down," Elias says. But Harrison has already succumbed to the hysteria, releasing a squeal so piercing I have to cover my ears. His body slumps over and he lets out a heart-wrenching sob.

"They said they won't stop coming until they get what they want."

The room falls silent, the soft weeping of the man in Eric's arms the only sound. Cassia turns and looks at me.

"What *do* they want?" one of the women asks. Harrison frantically scans the room until he stops and lifts his finger, pointing. Everyone looks at me. The room is cold but the stares are ice. My hand slips from the railing as their eyes drill into me—looks of curiosity, anger, fury.

"They want *her*," Harrison says, venom dripping from his words.

Elias steps in front of him. "Stand down, Harrison."

"They killed these people because of her," he snarls over Elias's shoulders. A few in the crowd nod. "We should give her to them. Give them what they want!"

Eric starts up the stairs toward me and wraps a hand around my wrist. "Come on."

I let him pull me up the staircase and back through the hall. He flings open a door and pushes me inside. I stumble backward, rubbing where his nails pierced my skin. The room looks like some sort of office, a deep-brown desk in the center and a small bookshelf lining the wall behind. The floor is covered in a worn, dark carpet. I hug my body. Images of the dead are printed on my eyelids—their lifeless faces, limp bodies, blood-stained clothes.

Eric steps to the side the exact second Elias stalks in, Cassia and Harrison a beat behind. "Tell me what happened," Elias says calmly.

Harrison, standing next to Eric, pushes his hair from his face. There's dried blood speckling his cheeks. "It was an ambush. They were waiting for us, like they *knew* we'd be passing the western route. It was *barbaric*. I tried to get as many bodies as I could but they took the rest."

"And did they say anything else?" Elias asks.

"They said we have someone they want, and they won't stop until they get her." Harrison glares at me. "We rarely have visitors. It didn't take much for me to figure out *who* they were talking about, and it won't take others long either."

"Don't talk about this with anybody else." Elias straightens so he towers over Harrison, who cowers in his shadow. "Understood?"

"I understand." He nods reluctantly. It's my turn to cower as Elias's eyes drift to me. Harrison continues, "What do they want with her? Who are we harboring?"

"I don't know," Elias muses, more to himself than anyone else.

"What *is* so special about you?" Cassia chimes in. "You seem like any other human—no offense."

"None taken."

"They kept talking about *immortalia sacrificium*," Harrison says. "How they're running out of time."

"The sacrifice for immortality?" Cassia looks to Elias. "You don't think . . ."

Eric huffs, but doesn't look at me. "No, you must've heard wrong, that doesn't make any sense."

"None of this makes sense," Elias says. "Harrison, did you see who was leading the attack?"

"The same one as always. Green eyes, gray hair—"

"Charles," I breathe. But he wouldn't do that to innocent children, he couldn't—not the Charles I knew. *The Charles you knew was a lie.*

"I told you," Harrison says coldly, "she's one of *them*."

Cassia stands in front of me. "She's human."

"She lived with them her whole life. We can't trust her," Harrison replies.

I glare at him but feel a wave of grief. The people I thought I belonged with tried to kill me and the people who don't want me dead don't trust me.

"I'll make that call, Harrison," Elias says, looking at me curiously. "You knew their leader? Is he the one who tried to kill you?"

"Charles is—he took me in when my parents died."

"You see!" Harrison says. "He was her caregiver! She was *close* to him!"

"How did your parents die?" Elias asks, ignoring him.

"I don't know. Charles always told me the creatures killed them soon after I was born." I don't need to say the rest, that that must've simply been one lie in a web of lies Charles raised me on. To think they might still be alive just adds to the growing disorientation.

"I see."

"You think they might be alive?" Eric wonders.

"No," Elias says bluntly, his words like a punch to the gut. "If they got her when she was a baby, her parents were already dead or they killed them. The hollowers don't leave humans alive."

"Except for me?"

His eyes meet mine. "Except for you."

"That's it then?" Harrison concludes, glowering. "We're not giving her to them?"

"No, we're not."

His face burns red and he clenches his fist. "She means nothing to us and they're killing us because of her."

"We'll tighten security and enforce a curfew," Elias says. "I've made up my mind, Harrison. We protect humans, always."

Though Harrison looks like he wants to argue, he keeps his mouth shut and turns to glare at me. "Please excuse me. I have seven funerals to plan." He slams the door behind him, his last words echoing in my head. Seven people. Dead because Charles wants me.

"Don't listen to him, Milena," Cassia says. "This isn't your fault."

Eric scoffs. I remember his body tied to that pole, Charles

impaling him as Eric roared in agony. I stood by and I watched—I didn't even try to stop him. "Don't lie to the girl. Harrison's right, they wouldn't be dead if it wasn't for her."

She frowns. "You can be really awful, you know that?"

"That hurts, Cassia, really, my heart is broken—"

"That's enough," Elias says, silencing them both. Cassia looks down, cheeks dark, but Eric just folds his arms. "Eric, come with me. Cassia, go through the books in the library and see if you can find anything about the sacrifice."

"What about me?" I ask.

"You can help me," Cassia chirps. "There are way too many books to go through myself."

Elias watches me, waiting for me to object, to admit that I can't read. But Eric's belittling gaze is enough to deal with. I keep my mouth shut and he nods. "It's sorted then, let me know if you find anything."

And he and Eric disappear through the door.

CHAPTER SEVEN

"They hate me." I peer around the room, conscious of all the eyes that flit to me when I look away. Cassia dragged me out and we're sitting at the bar in the village she showed me that first night, claiming the library made her tired. A wooden table is set against the wall and several people sit on stools there, talking in hushed tones.

Cassia flicks through a book on the table. "They don't *hate* you."

"When we walked in, everybody stopped talking to stare." I shift uncomfortably in my seat. "I don't blame them."

"They're just not used to strangers. There's no way they know about what happened this morning, or not why, anyway. Come on." She clicks her fingers so my attention is back on the book on the table between us. "We need to focus."

For the past hour, Cassia has been trying to teach me about their world, despite the fact that we're supposed to be going through the books she gathered from the library. The truth is, I was too embarrassed to admit that I couldn't read and hammered her with questions instead.

"You guys can communicate without talking?" I ask.

"Sort of. It's kind of like telepathy, I guess. But only when we're in our wolf forms."

"When I first saw Eric, he spoke to me, but I was the only one who could hear him—the first time, anyway."

Cassia nods. "We can channel different frequencies. Each one accesses a different species. When Eric saw you, he was confused because you didn't smell like a hollower. He spoke in different frequencies to see which one you'd respond to."

"And I heard the human one?"

"Yeah. I think he tried the shifter one first, but it didn't work."

Somebody wanders through the wooden doorway, shoots me a scowl, and takes a seat on one of the bar stools. I avert my gaze.

"Do you think they want me because of the sacrifice?" I ask.

"It's the only thing we have to go off right now. Which reminds me, we should really keep focused. I've only gotten through three books within the past few hours, and I've got a whole stack in my bag." She empties her backpack onto the table, books spilling out. "Here, take this one."

"Yeah . . . uh, I sort of can't really read," I mumble, cheeks warming. "Charles didn't want me to learn."

Cassia's mouth opens, eyebrows raised in surprise. "Those hollowers are real idiots."

She pulls out a piece of paper and a pencil, scribbling words on it before sliding it over to me. "Here. Flip through the pages, and if you see any words that look similar to these let me know. Rituals, sacrifice, or immortality."

I smile gratefully, grabbing the book, opening it, and running my finger along its musty pages. These books look delicate and old. In my mind, I see Elias running his fingers along the spine, flipping through the pages in the chair by the fire.

Flipping page after page, I try to find similar-looking words until I reach the end, then I pick up the next book, for once feeling like I'm doing something constructive and useful. That's something I like about Cassia—she doesn't make me feel like some useless burden the way Eric does; she makes me feel like I have something to offer, as if they need me as much as I need them, even though I know that isn't true.

We sit there for what feels like forever, moving through endless pages of endless books, when finally I spot something. I nearly read past it, my fingers instinctively turning the page. But an alarm goes off in my head and I quickly flip back, scanning the word to be certain.

"Cassia," I breathe, running my fingers along the letters. *Sacrifice*. "I think I found something."

Cassia leans over, head turning to read upside down. She glowers in concentration, then looks up at me. "I think you did."

"What does it say?"

Her eyes go back to the book. I watch as they go from left to right, tracing the words, mumbling incoherently to herself.

"What is it?"

"We should find Elias."

"Is something wrong? Is it . . . *bad*?"

"It's . . . interesting." Cassia starts packing up the books again.

GRACE COLLINS

"Come on, I'll explain when we meet Elias. He needs to know about this."

Cassia doesn't even bother to wait for me, spinning on her heel and flashing out of the bar before I can even blink. I scramble, trying to keep up with her as she weaves through the village for the tree line, pausing when I reach the edge, eyes to the sun still sinking in the sky, and then head in after her. I don't stop to think about why going into the forest could be a bad idea, or about running into a hollower, because the curiosity pushes me forward. Thankfully, we reach our destination before any hollowers can reach us.

Elias and Eric stand in the center of a clearing. Their eyes turn to Cassia and me, faces filled with surprise. Elias's chest is broad and muscular, scars and scratches across his stomach, his skin shimmering with perspiration. Eric is in a similar state, but it's Elias I can't stop staring at.

"What *happened* here?" Cassia asks incredulously.

I survey the clearing, the smell of smoke rising to the sky. The trees around us are charred black, leaves burned, mixing with the brown of the dirt below.

"Some kids started a forest fire," Elias says.

"*Again?*"

"Again." Elias nods, looking at Eric, who shrugs his shirt over his head. "Is something wrong?"

"Milena found something in the books." Cassia speaks so fast she nearly stumbles over her words. "About the sacrifice."

Elias goes rigid. He picks his shirt up off the ground and pulls it over his head. "What is it?"

"I think we should wait until we're somewhere a little more private."

Elias nods. "We'll meet in my office."

~

Elias's office feels a lot bigger without Harrison's looming presence. I sit on the opposite side of the desk to the others, nervously twiddling my thumbs and wishing more than anything that I could read more of the words etching deep frowns on their faces.

"Impossible," Eric mutters under his breath.

"But what if—"

"There are no ifs," Eric says. "You know I'm right. We're missing something important."

"Eric's right," Elias says, "it's impossible."

"What's impossible?" I demand. "Can someone explain to me what's written on those pages?"

Elias sighs deeply, looking back down at the book. "You remember when you first got here, and Cassia told you about shifters and hollowers?" I nod. "She mentioned wispers too. Do you remember?"

"She said there weren't any left."

"There aren't. Wispers went extinct long ago."

"What *are* wispers, anyway?"

"Wispers were . . . special," Cassia says. "They age like shifters and look like humans, but they have gifts."

"Gifts?"

She nods. "Wispers were born with a gift the same way a shifter is born with another form. Some gifts were completely useless while others were extremely powerful. It was luck of the draw, really."

"Like what sort of gifts?"

"We don't know much about them," Eric says.

"They went extinct a while ago." Elias runs a hand down the side of his face, looking back at the book. "There isn't much information around anymore."

"I think I read something in the book about a list of abilities they had." Cassia looks down at the book, flipping through a couple of pages. She puts her finger on a page and begins reading aloud. "Here. Telepathy, mind reading, mind control, breathing underwater."

I shiver. "Those all sound pretty powerful."

"It also says one had the ability to sing people to sleep. You see, they come in all shapes—some *are* completely useless."

"It doesn't matter what they could do," Eric says. "They're not around anymore. None of that matters."

"What does that have to do with the sacrifice then?" I ask.

"That's where things get weird." Cassia looks back at the book. "It says that in order to gain immortality, the blood of all three species must be combined and consumed. One shifter, one human, and one wisper."

Their eyes rest on me, gauging for any reaction. "I don't see how this helps."

"It doesn't," Eric says. "Not really, it just makes things more confusing."

"They had Eric, a shifter," Elias says. "And it wouldn't have been hard to find a human. All they needed was a wisper."

"You're saying—you think I'm . . . a wisper?"

"You're definitely not a wisper." Elias shakes his head.

"Then why did they wait so long to kill me?"

"That's why this is so confusing," Cassia says. "Wispers don't get their gifts until they turn twenty. Before then, they're about as useful as humans. For some reason, the hollowers were going to use you as a wisper."

"This doesn't make any sense." Charles waited for my birthday to attempt to murder me even though he could have done it the day I was born. "What if I'm . . . what if I'm not human?"

"You are," Elias says, leaning forward. "We *know* you're human."

"But *how*?"

"If you were a wisper, you wouldn't have heard me speaking inside of your head that night in the tunnels," Eric says. "And if you had a gift, you'd know."

"What if it was a useless one, though? One I wouldn't even notice?" I ask.

Eric shakes his head. "You'd still know. When wispers get their gifts, it's an incredibly painful experience—excruciating. It's a similar sort of pain us shifters feel when we shift for the first time. It's not something you'd easily forget."

I let out a breath of relief. I don't know why, but the reassurance that I'm completely human steadies me. If I'd found out another thing that uprooted who I thought I was . . .

"What now?" I ask. "The hollowers are wrong, then. Can't we somehow prove it to them, so they'll stop coming after me?"

Eric's eyes brighten. "That might not be a bad idea—"

"No," Elias says. "The hollowers are barbaric but they're not stupid. They must know Milena is human, which means we're missing something. Nobody is going to the hollowers until we find out what that is."

Eric scowls. "Don't be foolish, Elias."

"I've made my decision."

Tension lines Eric's shoulders but Elias stares back, unbothered. "Fine." Eric glares. "Don't say I didn't warn you, Elias."

"Cassia, come with me. Eric, take Milena to get appropriate

wear for the weather up north." They both stare at him, confused. "We're going to see Ana."

"You want me to babysit her and take her shopping?" Eric deadpans.

"I want you to protect her and get her appropriate wear for the mountains," Elias says, as if he couldn't possibly understand why that'd be a problem.

"*Great.*"

Elias ignores him, stepping through the door and motioning at Cassia to follow. She nudges Eric on her way past. "Be nice."

"No promises."

And then they're gone and I'm left alone with the one person I'm convinced actually wants me dead.

~

"Can you keep up?" Eric complains. "Quit dragging your feet."

"I'm sorry I don't have superhuman abilities," I say, leaning against the wall of a wooden cabin to catch my breath. Thankfully, the village is mostly empty; the only people loitering around have normal eyes, which means they're human. So far, shopping has consisted of me standing by as Eric rakes through piles of clothing and throws the occasional item haphazardly into an oversized backpack. Something tells me this job would have been quicker if Eric had done it alone.

"Why do I need all of this stuff, anyway?" I ask, eyeing the thick wool coats atop the pile. "It isn't that cold here."

I've never seen so many different types of clothing before. Back home, we rarely got new garments. We didn't have the resources. Wilhelm was the one in charge of distributing them to people in the village. He also did repairs, but we always had limited supplies. Here, there's a wider variety of clothing. But from what I've picked up from conversations, it seems as though shifters trade their acts of service to the village for goods.

"It snows in the mountains," Eric says, taking another turn. We're on our way back to the castle and I couldn't be more grateful.

"We're not in the mountains."

"Wow. Pretty and smart, who knew?"

I frown. "Are we going to the mountains?"

"No, Elias made me take you shopping for nothing."

"Is Ana in the mountains? And who is she?"

"You ask too many questions." He looks at me over his shoulder. It's taken a while, but the unnatural color of his eyes doesn't frighten me so much anymore. Though he doesn't like me, something about him makes me feel comfortable. Where Cassia is all smiles and Elias is all mystery, Eric is an open book. He doesn't wear a mask, and after discovering everyone I grew up with wasn't who I thought they were, I appreciate it. He doesn't like me, and he doesn't care if I know it.

Suddenly, I'm yanked backward. "You! It's *your* fault my son is dead!" a man screeches, grasping me by the collar of my shirt and lifting me off my feet. My shirt tightens around my neck. I flail, feet in the air, choking and grasping at my neck. And then I'm released and fall to the ground. The man who grabbed me lies on the ground, too, his lip split. Eric stands over him, back to me.

"Give her to me!" the man cries. "She killed my son!"

"Get out of here, James," Eric snarls.

James doesn't run. He clambers forward and tries to break

past Eric, but he's too slow. Eric pulls him up by the shirt and holds him near his face. "Go *now*," he hisses. "And never try anything like that again or you'll answer to Elias. And I assure you, he'll be much less forgiving."

He drops the man back to the ground. The man's expression is torn as he glares at me before scampering off into the trees, body morphing in the air until he lands on four paws. My breath shakes as Eric comes toward me. He leans down to pick me up and dumps me on my feet, turns to pick up the backpack again, and continues toward the castle entrance ahead of us.

"Thank you, Eric. If you hadn't been there I—"

He spins so fast I jump in fright. Mere inches away, he glares down at me with vicious, red eyes, teeth bared. "Don't mistake me following orders for kindness. If it was up to me, I would've let him have you. If it was up to me, I would've given you back to the hollowers." He stabs a finger at my chest. "I'll protect you for as long as Elias asks me to, but the day he decides you're not worth it anymore, I'll be the first to let the hollowers know you're theirs."

He drops the backpack and tears off into the forest, leaving me alone at the castle doors.

~

When I was eight, Charles punished me for crying over a pet snail I'd kept in the tunnels for three days. I'd found it while gardening, all alone among the tomato plants, and promised to take care of it. When Charles found it in my room three days later, he squashed it and scolded me for crying. He used to shake his head and scowl at me when I mourned the rabbits they brought back from the hunts. I used to think that my tendency to get upset by violence and death was the reason he wouldn't allow me to hunt, but now I know the true reason was much more sinister.

Eric's words, while harsh, bring me back to reality. I'm petrified of going back. The thought of seeing Charles again fills me with a terror so violent it makes me shake. And yet, by being here, I'm hurting people. Seven people were ambushed and killed because of me—they felt the same terror I did when Charles stood over me with that machete. Somebody brave would run away. They'd give themselves up to the hollowers and accept their fate, for the good of others. Fear paralyzes me, and, like a coward, I lug the backpack up the staircase and into my room. It isn't empty. Elias stands by the window, his back to me, blocking my view of the night sky. Bathed in the moonlight, he looks angelic.

He turns around when he hears me, eyeing the backpack in my hands. "Where's Eric?"

"He left."

If Elias is surprised, he doesn't show it. "You have scratches on your neck."

"I, um, tripped in the forest."

"You're a terrible liar, you know."

"Eric didn't hurt me."

"I know he didn't. He wouldn't dare."

Thankfully, he doesn't ask who did. "Yeah, well, he sure doesn't like me much."

"He doesn't have to like you to protect you." Elias moves toward me, gliding across the floor with the grace of an assassin. "You weren't thinking of leaving, were you?"

"It's not like I have anywhere else to go."

"That doesn't mean you're not thinking about it."

"Of course I think about it." I drop the backpack with a sigh. "I don't exactly belong here."

"Is that how you feel, or what Eric told you?"

"Does it matter?"

"Yes."

I pause, then look up. "I don't know where I belong anymore."

There's something about his expression that's comforting somehow, like he understands. But he can't. Elias is valued here, anyone can see that. "You should have something to eat and get some sleep," he says eventually. "We'll leave for the mountains tomorrow night."

He's so close that if I was to reach out, I could touch him. "What's in the mountains?"

"Ana."

"What information are we looking for, exactly?" I press.

"Anything helpful, really."

Irritation flares in my stomach and my mouth runs before I can stop it. "People keep dying because of me, Elias. The people I grew up with are out for my blood, and I'm fighting them with our mortal enemies. It isn't fair of you to keep me in the dark and hope I'll be quiet. You said you'd involve me in figuring this out, so *involve* me."

An icy breeze wafts through the window, billowing the curtains. "I don't want to scare you, Milena."

"I'm already scared."

The room is dead silent. Elias looks at the window, where light from the village filters in and creates jagged shapes on the floor. "Ana is an elder shifter," he says. "She's very old, and she knows a lot more about the hollowers and sacrifices than I do. I'm hoping she'll be able to shed some light on *immortalia sacrificium*. We have to be missing something."

"How long can hollowers last without the sacrifice and just feeding on others?"

"On humans, they could live a human lifespan, depending on how frequently they feed. On shifters, around one hundred to one hundred and fifty years. But it's much more difficult for them to capture shifters."

"How old are *you*?"

"*I* am only twenty-six," he says. "Cassia will explain more tomorrow, but for now, you should rest." He steps to the door.

My mind reels. Before a week ago, I'd never traveled past the tree line around my village, and now we're trekking all the way into the mountains.

"Milena," Elias calls from the door. I turn and stare at him. "Some of us aren't meant to belong."

He closes the door behind him and leaves me alone, all the warmth in the room escaping with him.

CHAPTER EIGHT

The following day passes in a blur of funerals and strangers bringing food to my room. From my window, the courtyard is visible. Crowds gather wearing dark clothes, taking turns paying their respects to the weeping families who huddle together at the foot of the well, which is surrounded by flowers.

Watching firsthand the destruction my presence has caused makes me sick to my stomach. And though it's like a form of torture, I can't look away. Each new family that passes by the well serves as another hit, another family I've hurt by being here. It makes me think of my own. Of Charles and Flo, of Darius, and of the parents I never got to know. Grief for a life that was never mine suffocates me.

Cassia comes by my room sometime in the afternoon, after the last funeral finishes. She wasn't visible in the mass of people, but it's clear from her expression where she's been.

"Good afternoon," she says. "Good to see you've eaten."

The sun is descending. By this time, we'd already be locking ourselves in the tunnels, ready to sleep. But I've never felt more awake. Behind me, Cassia rifles through the backpack of clothes discarded at the end of the bed.

"Ugh," she grumbles. "Eric could've at least *tried* to pick something a little less drab." She holds up a long-sleeved navy shirt. "I guess I shouldn't have expected more from someone who exclusively wears one type of shirt. He owns, like, fifteen versions of the same thing."

"It's just a shirt."

"Hollowers didn't teach you much about clothes, did they?"

I gesture to the plain shirt I'm wearing. "I guess not."

"You know, of all the things I've heard about your childhood, that is definitely the saddest."

I laugh. "How come you didn't get the clothes instead?"

"I'm second in command. It only makes sense that Eric gets the crappy jobs."

"*You're* ranked above Eric?"

"We don't really call it that, but yeah. Surprised?"

"No. I just—"

"Don't forget, I saved you from at least thirty hollowers."

"It isn't that, I was just surprised because Eric seems so . . ."

"Domineering? Bossy? Arrogant?" Cassia jokes.

"I was going to say disrespectful toward you, but those fit too."

"The whole ranking thing doesn't mean he has to obey me or anything, it just means that if something happened to Elias, I'd be in charge." She continues to pull clothes from the bag, making snide remarks about a couple of items before gathering her chosen pieces in her arms. "Here, go put these on."

I head to the bathroom. "We're leaving soon? Because it's safer to travel at night?"

"Exactly," she grins. "Now go, get changed and I'll fill you in on the details before we meet Elias downstairs."

In the bathroom, I change into the clothes: tight, black pants; a fitted long-sleeved shirt; and a gigantic coat with a fur hood. They're different from the clothes I've been borrowing from Cassia. These items hug every inch of my body from my neck to my ankles. Without the coat, I feel completely exposed.

Cassia knocks on the door. "Coming in!" She leans against the frame, assessing me. "Eric did well. The shirt could be a little tighter, though."

If it was any tighter, it'd be like a second skin. I tug at the neckline and stare at myself in the mirror. My skin doesn't look as dull as it did the other day but the dark circles beneath my eyes haven't disappeared. "It's very . . . fitted."

"Good. You can't keep running around in my clothes, or those baggy rags you brought with you—you'll be tripping all over the place." I never minded the clothes I grew up in. They weren't formfitting, and not at all flattering, but they were comfortable. But she has a point; it'd be a lie to say I hadn't tripped over the ends countless times. "Sit down," Cassia says, picking up a pair of scissors from the drawer. "Let me do your hair."

"What's wrong with my hair?" It's the longest it's been since I can remember, thick tresses reaching my midback.

"Nothing is *wrong* with it, it's just so long. Doesn't it annoy you?"

Memories surge through my mind—Charles hacking my hair with a pair of blunt cutters. He didn't like it getting past my shoulders. The first time he did it, I cried as the black locks fell to the ground, but it became a mindless routine after that. "No."

"Okay, no cutting. At least tie it back." I take the band she offers me. "It'd be a lot easier if you let me just cut it off, you know."

I stare at my reflection in the mirror, remembering the loss of control I felt each time my hair got cut back. It's stupid, I know, to think so highly of something so superficial. But I'm keeping my hair because I want to. And having that control feels better than I could've imagined.

~

When I imagined how my life would be after I turned twenty, I saw freedom and acceptance. I imagined returning from a hunt and joining Charles at the main table, laughing with the other hunters, finally *belonging* somewhere. Twenty was the age that everything was supposed to change, and to pass that milestone feeling more alone than I did before is crushing. If it wasn't for the shifters waiting for me downstairs, giving in to the despair would be all too tempting.

Cassia and I meet Eric and Elias in the foyer; they are talking in hushed voices, both with large bags on their backs. Their conversation cuts off when we emerge, and they both look up at us.

"You're running late," Eric says.

Cassia flips her hair back. "It takes time to look this good, I wouldn't expect you to understand."

"It takes time to get to the mountains too."

"How are you only twenty-five? You act like *such* an old man."

Eric huffs and opens his mouth to retort. "So," I blurt, looking at Elias, "when are we leaving?" He's clothed in all black, dark hair a disheveled mess. The pinched skin of the scar on his jaw stands out against the black coat.

"Now," he says. "Cassia and Eric, you go on ahead. We'll be right behind you."

Cassia casts a curious glance my way before shrugging and starting through the door, smirking at Eric on her way past. He begrudgingly follows, leaving me with Elias. "I wanted to talk to you, without snide remarks from the others." He gestures to the doorway. "After you."

I head through, stars glimmering above us as we ditch the village and aim straight for the forest. Cassia and Eric are swallowed by the night. The wind whistles through the trees; I hug my coat around me as Elias falls into step with me.

"Did the villagers ever speak of the sacrifice? Even in passing?"

I shake my head, hiking the backpack higher onto my back. "I don't think so."

The trees crowd around us, creating a canopy that blocks out all light from the moon. "And with Charles. Nothing was ever suspicious to you?"

His line of questioning makes me feel stupid—like I'm foolish for not having noticed that they were out to kill me the entire time. "Everybody else was allowed to hunt when they turned sixteen but Charles wouldn't let me go until I turned twenty— not that his intention was for me to hunt, anyway. I always thought he was trying to protect me."

"Hollowers start to rapidly age around sixteen. It makes sense that's the age they start hunting and training."

"But why twenty? If we're sure I'm not a wisper."

"That's what we're going to figure out."

My breath clouds in front of my face. Walking through the forest when it's dark isn't as menacing with Elias beside me. There are no fears of strange monsters emerging in the night and grabbing at my ankles, not when the one who rules it walks a beat ahead of me.

"How far away are we?" I ask.

"We should arrive in the mountains by tomorrow night."

I pause. "Are we going to walk during the day?"

"Yes."

"Isn't that dangerous? With the hollowers?"

"You don't need to be afraid, Milena."

He travels with the grace of a wolf stalking its prey, and I'm a stumbling toddler in comparison. "You don't say a lot."

He looks at me, surprised as he lifts a low-hanging branch to let me past. "What do you want me to say?"

"I don't know. I know nothing about you."

Leaves crunch beneath my feet, filling the beat of silence between us. "You don't need to know anything about me."

"But it wouldn't hurt, would it?"

He turns to look at me. "It might."

"But if you—"

He spins so fast it startles me. The scar on his jawline catches my eye, skin jagged and pinched in contrast to the smoothness of his neck. "You don't need to know about me any more than I need to know about you, Milena. All you need to know is that the hollowers are after you, and all I need to know is why. Anything else is just useless filler."

Useless filler.

His words sting. Despite his hardened exterior, there always seemed to be something gentler about him, an energy that drew me closer. But that desire shrinks back in fear. He's like fire—enticing to the eye but dangerous if you get too close.

"I'm sorry, I shouldn't have asked."

His expression softens. "Don't apologize."

"Sorry—"

He closes his eyes for the briefest moment. He turns then, running a hand through his hair, before disappearing from sight. I blink, disorientated; the only sign of his presence is the buzz in the air. Cassia's words linger in my mind: *He doesn't need to shift. He's different.* I'm not afraid of him but everything inside of me tells me that I should be.

In moments, Cassia and Eric show up, replacing Elias without a word. And we continue on, my feet aching and mind racing. The moon rises higher as we wander deeper into the forest, and as I think of Elias's words, fragments of my world slip beneath my feet. *Some of us aren't meant to belong.*

Charles never said the words, but his actions spoke volumes—I didn't belong with them either. I can't keep fooling myself. Despite Cassia's warm smile and Elias's enchanting presence, I'm treading on thin ice. The only thing keeping me safe here is the mystery surrounding my attempted murder. Perhaps uncovering this mystery won't be such a good thing for me after all.

~

The morning is as dark as it is cold. Though the sky transitions from black to navy with the arrival of day, the air is thick with a glacial fog. My breath clouds around me with each exhale. I sit on a log next to a pile of sticks as Eric constructs a fire, grumbling under his breath when it doesn't light. Cassia hasn't even put her coat on, and Elias, who joined us again, wears his coat unbuttoned and with the hood down.

"You all right, Milena?" Cassia asks. I pull my knees to my

chest and nod, teeth chattering. Cassia looks at Elias. "She's not going to survive the mountains if she's shivering that much down here."

Elias doesn't look at me. He hasn't looked at me since he returned, and it only makes me colder, like I've done something to warrant his indifference. He says something to Cassia and she reaches into the backpack discarded on the ground to pull out another sweater.

"Here, take your coat off and put this on."

"I'm okay," I say, mostly because the thought of taking the coat off is worse than sitting here shivering.

"Your lips are blue. Put it on," she says. Reluctantly, I take the sweater from her hand and brave the cold. "How's the fire coming along, Eric?"

"Would be coming along a lot faster if you actually helped."

"Charming as always." Moments later, the fire flickers to life, burning through the thick fog. It's small, but the change in temperature is drastic. "Are you hungry?" Cassia asks, offering a sandwich.

"Thanks."

"Dammit!" Eric kicks the tree beside him when the fire dies out in a sudden gust of wind. "The wood is too wet, it won't catch."

"A grown man having a hissy fit," Cassia says under her breath. "Amusing."

"You try to light it then, I give up! I don't need this damn fire anyway."

"Cassia, there's a stream half a mile west of here," Elias says, moving to the fire. "Can you get some water? Milena, you too."

"Milena's seconds away from becoming a human ice block. I doubt going to the stream will make that any better."

"Cassia."

"Fine. Fine." She reaches over to scoop up one of the back-packs. "Come on, Milena, let's leave Elias to deal with this grown child."

Eric glowers in her direction. "Cassia, I swear to—"

"Just go, Cassia," Elias says.

She hooks her arm through mine and pulls me up with a sat-isfied smile. "Men. So easily agitated." The trees are clearer in the morning light so I don't have to focus so intently on where I place my feet. I shove my hands into my pockets and wrap the coat tighter, knees knocking together.

"How far are we from the mountains?" I ask.

"We've nearly reached the base. It's only going to get colder from here, and we need to be more careful since it's daytime."

I glance over my shoulder. "You think the hollowers could be there?"

"They don't know about anyone residing up in the mountains. But that doesn't mean they won't be lurking around down at the tree line."

"But it's so far away."

"From your village, maybe." The trees thin out and some-where close by, water gushes. "But they're not the only village of hollowers, just like we aren't the only village of shifters."

"There are more of them?"

"Scattered all over the place. We've only ever had problems with your colony because they're closest to us. Here"—she tosses me a bottle—"fill this up, will you?"

She disappears ahead. The wind picks up, whispering warn-ings through the trees. I shudder. As Elias said, the stream is there, a steady flow of water weaving in and out of the trees.

Cassia bends over, dips her bottle in the water. The last thing I feel like doing is getting near the icy water but I follow her lead. It takes us a few minutes to get back to the others, but the fire has been lit—ruby embers crackling beneath the blackened wood.

"Impressive," Cassia says.

Moving closer to the fire, I pull my hands from my pockets and hold them in front of the flames, staring at Elias. The flames dance around him, turning the tips of his hair copper. I shuffle closer, but this time, it isn't the fire that lures me. It takes only a second for his entire demeanor to change.

"Did you hear that?" Cassia says. Elias holds a hand up to hush her. We stand in tense silence, Cassia's hand wrapping tightly around my wrist. Eric stamps the fire out then squeezes a water bottle over the embers.

"What's going on?" I ask.

They exchange glances, then Elias looks at me. "We're not alone."

Sweat beads at the back of my neck and my heart thumps. Cassia gathers the bottles in her backpack and Elias and Eric speak in hushed whispers. They all look at me.

"Climb the tree," Elias says. "We don't have enough time to run, they could be tracking us. Here, I'll give you a lift."

He places his hands on my waist and hoists me up like I weigh nothing more than a feather. I wrap my arms around one of the branches, lifting myself up and perching in the crevice where it meets the trunk. The branches obscure my vision but Cassia clambers up the trunk behind me to perch next to me. Squeezing my eyes shut, I force myself to sit still, disorientated by the height.

The sun makes an appearance, piercing through the canopy of

leaves and warming the back of my neck. "Why are we hiding?" I whisper. "Can't you take them on yourselves?"

"We could, but contrary to what you've been told, we don't *like* to kill others." I open my mouth to respond but she raises a finger to her lips. There's shuffling below. Voices.

"You sure it was over this way, Henry? I could've sworn it came from the north." They appear between the gaps in the leaves. There are two of them, clothed in thick coats and carrying matching machetes. My chest tightens. I don't recognize either of them, but their weapons are all too familiar.

"Reports from the west say they left the creatures' grounds," Henry says. He bends to the ground, placing his machete beside him and rubbing his fingers in the dirt. He looks at his companion and smiles. "The remains of a fire."

"Can't be the creatures then, they wouldn't be so stupid. They don't need it to stay warm."

But Henry's smile doesn't waver. He picks up his machete. "The creatures don't. She's with them. She must be, and if we want to get that deal, we've got to be the first to find her."

Cassia and I exchange alarmed looks. She shifts her weight, the backpack brushing against the trunk of the tree. And then, before either of us can stop it, her foot slips on the branch. I grab her arm to steady her, and we both breathe sighs of relief. But it isn't over. Her backpack topples over and a bottle slides out, spiraling to the ground and landing with a thud between the hollowers. They freeze. And look up.

The earth stands still as our eyes meet. Henry's eyes grow and he steps forward. My knees knock together. Cassia grips my arms, holding me against the trunk, but I'm the only one they can see. "Come down, sweetheart," Henry says. "I promise we'll be nice."

"Over my dead body," Cassia hisses, maneuvering on the branch so she's blocking me. At the sight of her, Henry falters, gripping his machete in front of him.

"Give us the girl and we'll spare your life."

"Tell me why you want her and maybe I'll spare yours," Cassia retorts. She grabs the collar of my shirt and puts her mouth to my ear. "Climb higher, try to get to the next tree if you can."

I dig my nails into the bark, sliding slowly across the branch and eyeing the one above. I rise to my feet, slightly off balance in order to reach it. One of the hollowers catapults their machete into the trunk of the tree, causing it to shake. Cassia, balancing on her feet, nearly topples over but catches herself at the last minute. I slip. The air escapes my lungs as I fall through the air.

I land with a thud on my back, my lungs constricting. Two faces blur above, reaching toward me. In my dazed state, I drag myself backward. My attempts at escape are futile, I can barely take a breath after my fall. Henry grips my ankle, but I jut out my leg and kick his stomach. He doubles over, clutching his gut.

"You little *brat*," he wheezes. I push to my feet, swaying as the other hollower grapples at my arms.

"Let me go!" I smash his nose with my elbow. His grip loosens and he spins me around before throwing a fist at my face. I duck, but his fist hits the side of my cheek and I tumble to the ground again. Dirt fills my mouth as I drag myself across the earth, desperate to escape the man with a machete standing over me. I don't know how to fight or defend myself. I'm trapped.

Tears spring to my eyes as the adrenaline burns away and fear sets in. Where are the others? Why aren't they helping me?

"You're coming with us," the man says. Henry stands beside him, still holding his gut. "Whether you're conscious or not depends on whether you put up a fight." He cuts my struggling short by pressing the machete against my throat. The cool blade brings rancid memories of Charles standing over me.

"What do you *want* from me?"

"You're worth a lot to some very important people," he says, getting right in my face. "I'll be honest, I don't think you're worth it."

One second, Henry stands in front of me, the next, his head is swept from his body, decapitated, spurting blood onto the ground as it rolls across my feet. I suck in a breath as Elias appears behind the man—he looks like an avenging angel in the light of the morning sun. "Wrong answer, hollower."

Before I can blink, the other hollower flies through the air and lands with a thud on the ground, a hole in his chest. Elias stands above them, his arm a sleeve of blood. I choke and scramble backward, eyes wide, stuck on the two fallen bodies that lie before me, the fauna around them stained red.

"Milena." Elias kneels in front of me, reaching a hand toward my cheek. I flinch backward when his hand caresses my skin, the bone aching at his touch. "I'm sorry I didn't intervene sooner. I'd hoped they would reveal important information. I didn't think they'd harm you before taking you back."

Cassia appears behind him, rubbing her arms, but I pay her no mind. All I can focus on, besides Elias's red arm, is Henry's head to my left—and the pungent smell of blood.

"You killed them."

Elias shows no remorse. He says nothing at first, eyes growing dull. "They would've taken you if I hadn't."

I know he's right, but still, bile rises up in the back of my throat. He rises to his feet, wrapping his clean hand around my forearm to pull me up. I collide with his chest and almost forget the red on his arms, the look in his eyes as he ripped a head from its body. But Elias is quick to create space between us, letting go and stepping back. I can't look at the bodies on the ground. When they look human and act human, it's hard to believe they're not.

What could Elias do to me?

Cassia steps forward. "I'm sorry, Elias, I didn't mean—"

"Come on," Elias says. "We're wasting time."

He turns away and continues forward, the heat of his gaze leaving my body burning. But I can't look at him. As I step over the fallen bodies on the ground, I quiver in fear. Because for the first time since meeting him, I want to run in the other direction.

CHAPTER NINE

The closest we ever got to snow growing up was the ice that froze along the roof of the kitchen shack deep in the winter, and the sleet that hammered the windows during the colder season. I always imagined snow to be gentle, but the reality is a lot harsher. The wind howls, stirring the snow up and making it nearly impossible to see more than a few feet ahead. It cuts into the bare skin of my face and reaches past the tops of my boots, numbing my toes.

The sun is long gone. We've been walking for hours and I haven't breathed a word, mind still spinning at what happened in the forest. Elias tore the man's head off like it was a weed in the ground. It's a harsh reminder of the world I've walked into. I've spent the last few days coming to terms with the fact that the creatures aren't who or what I was told, but that doesn't mean there isn't any truth to the stories. The creatures of the night might not be trying to kill me, but that doesn't mean they don't kill.

Cassia walks behind me, Eric in front, and Elias a few feet ahead of us all. Questions swim around in my mind, but I don't dare speak unless spoken to. I don't want to shatter the fragile ice I walk upon. The trees thin out as we climb into the crevice between the two mountains, a rocky terrain covered in a mixture of dirt and snow. I step over a branch protruding from the snow but the end of my boot catches and I slam face first into Eric's back. He moves unnaturally fast and catches me before I can hit the ground.

"Watch your step," he snaps.

"Sorry."

He grumbles under his breath and turns around. Ahead, Elias narrows his eyes at me. "Are you warm enough?" I nod. He weaves seamlessly through the snow to stand in front of me. "Show me your hands."

"What?" Instead of answering, he reaches into the pockets of my coat and pulls my hands out, holding them in front of my face. The bottoms of my fingers are white, the tips red. They're so numb I barely feel the heat from Elias's fingers.

Cassia rifles through the back. "Let me look for the gloves."

"You should've said you were cold," Elias says.

"I—" I stop myself from apologizing again. "I didn't want to slow us down."

"You'll definitely slow us down if you get frostbite." Warmth exudes from his hands as they wrap around mine, his calloused palms rough against my skin.

"Here." Cassia holds out a pair of black, woolen gloves. "Put these on."

Elias takes them from her and opens the gloves so I can slip my fingers in. A gust of wind blows the hood from my head, exposing me to the bitter cold. Elias reaches out, hand stopping a few inches away from my face. "Pull your hood up," he says. "You'll lose a lot of heat from your head." He turns back to Eric and continues moving.

"Come on, Milena." Cassia hooks an arm through mine. "We're almost there."

I let her tug me. She stealthily guides us over hidden branches buried in the snow. "Is Elias always like that?" I ask.

"Like what?"

I search for the right word. Elias is cold, but there are moments when warmth peeks through his gaze—a warmth that stirs something inside me—but it disappears before I can even acknowledge it. "Distant."

"Yes," she says. "Always." Her expression grows cold and she walks ahead of me so I can't see her face anymore.

The mountaintops arch around us. Elias slows as we reach the highest point. The chill lingers but the gloves thaw my frozen fingers. The journey up the mountains was steep and winding, littered with trees, but the earth below plateaus into a craterlike dip surrounded by rock walls. Snow covers dead grass, straw-like shrubs peeking through. But it's mostly barren, and, aside from the whistling wind, dead still.

"Why have we stopped?" I whisper. This can't be it, there's nothing here.

Elias turns to Eric. "Did you hear that?"

"Hear what?"

"I thought I heard—" He shakes his head. "Nothing. I must've imagined it. Let's keep going."

He starts down the steep edge. The snow slides beneath his feet but he manages to remain steady. I take the same steps Cassia leaves imprinted in the snow to avoid hidden roots, only much slower. "Are we here? I thought there was a village."

She offers me a hand from where the ground flattens, steadying me over a significant drop. I land in the snow with a thud. "Ana lives alone up here." She nods over her shoulder. On the other side of the crater, two rocks arch together to create the mouth of a cave that swallows Eric and Elias.

Trudging through the snow after them, we reach the entrance. The darkness is impenetrable; my shadow melts into the walls. "Someone lives *here*?"

Up ahead, a fire sparks, creating a backlight for two dark shapes. We move toward them. The wood in Elias's hand burns, hot ribbons casting shadows along the jagged rock walls. The pathway is wide but low so Elias has to crouch slightly so as to not hit his head on the ceiling. Small, loose stones scatter the floor, echoing against the dense walls when disturbed, but it's a welcome change from the snow.

The darkness eases as we round the corner, a bright glow emanating from the end of the cavern. I duck my head around Elias's, trying to make out what lies before him. The path comes to an opening, but it barely resembles a cave. The end is a bulbous shape, widening to stretch around the corners. A worn rug covers the expanse of the floor, dirtied footprints marking a path to the narrow passageway opposite us. There's a bed in the corner beside an old rocking chair, and crumbling bookshelves stretching all the way to the ceiling line the two walls. The only light comes from a single lantern string running along the ceiling on a thick wire.

"This is it?" I ask, shuddering. It's freezing inside. "Where is she?"

Elias walks forward to run his finger along the bookshelf, disrupting the dust gathered along the wood. He seems relaxed, unconcerned. "She must've gone out for something."

I sneak my head around the corner, wishing I could borrow some of his courage. Despite the fact that I spent over half my life in underground tunnels, the cave suffocates me, like the walls will buckle inward and trap us.

"Wait here in case she comes through the back," Elias instructs. "Eric and I will have a look around outside."

A small stream travels through the cavern, no exit visible. I turn to the bookshelves as Eric and Elias wander away, leaving us in a dull light. The bookshelves are covered in a thick layer of undisturbed dust, like nobody has been here for a while. The passageway on the other side is much narrower than the one we came through, and dark. "Where does this lead?"

"Probably deeper into the mountain," Cassia says. "There are lots of springs around here, and Ana would need a water source close by."

"Have you met her before?"

"No." Cassia is settled in the rocking chair, boredly inspecting her hands. "I've only met the elders on the coast. But I've heard a lot about her."

"The coast? How far away is that?"

"A four-day run for me. For you, much longer." Charles never said anything about a coast. I always just imagined the trees stretching on forever, and beyond the mountains, I wasn't sure. But I never planned on having to find out; I never thought I'd venture much farther than the tunnels underground.

Eyeing the books on the shelf, I walk the expanse of the room. It's even smaller than the room I grew up in, and much more cluttered. But despite the freezing temperature, there's something cozy about the decor. I lean against the wall, back to the passageway. My finger grazes the book closest to me but before I can put my hands around it, a sharp point presses into the center of my back. I freeze. A mouth presses to my ear. "Who are you and what are you doing here?"

Cassia leaps up from the rocking chair, body in a low stance as she swings around to face us. The dagger at my back pierces the skin. "Ana?"

"Who's asking?"

"My name's Cassia and that's Milena." Ana's grip on me doesn't loosen. "We're here with Elias. We came for your help."

"Elias is here?" She pauses, still holding me close but the pressure of the dagger eases. At that exact moment, Elias and Eric come around the corner, freezing when they catch sight of us. Cassia grabs me; I turn to face Ana. Her appearance is deceiving and speaks nothing of her strength. Her body is hunched over and frail, long, gray hair braided down her back to reach her waist. She hobbles forward, and Elias moves to meet her. She reaches up to embrace him, her body dwarfed by his. And when she pulls away, she swipes a hand tenderly across his face. "I didn't know you were visiting."

"I didn't have time to send word," Elias says, pulling away. "Where have you been? It's freezing down here. You haven't been using the fire I set up for you."

She waves a hand. "Sit down, you must be tired from the journey." Against his will, she forces Elias to sit on the edge of the bed, before moving over to Eric and wrapping her arms around him too. Then, she turns to me. "My apologies for our encounter, I don't usually have unannounced visitors." I force a shaky smile, still on edge. "You're human?"

"I am," I say.

Ana smiles warmly as she examines me, curious. "You must be freezing, dear. Sit down so I can make you a warm drink."

I settle in the rocking chair. Ana turns her back to us and kneels down to the hole dug into the stone, igniting the fire and then placing a pot full of water over it. "We came because we need your help," Elias says. "We've had issues with the hollower colony."

"What do you mean?"

"We think they're trying to complete the *immortalia sacrificium.*

She pauses, two mugs in her hands, and turns to look at him over her shoulder. "That's impossible. They'd need a shifter, a human—"

"And a wisper, we know," Elias finishes. "And for some reason, they think Milena here is a wisper."

She looks at me, intrigued, and begins to pour water into the first mug. "What makes you think that?"

"They raised me and tried to kill me on my twentieth birthday, a few days ago."

She stands up suddenly, her cup dropping and shattering on the ground, shards of glass spreading out around her feet and steaming liquid seeping into the rug laid across the floor. Elias leaps to his feet and grabs her arms to keep her from stepping on any of the fallen shards. "You okay?"

She looks frazzled, her wrinkled hands shaking. "Yes, I just lost my balance for a moment there."

"Are you sure?"

She nods firmly. "I'm fine. Leave it, Elias, I'll clean it up later."

After she's settled back on her chair, he gently brushes the shards into his hand and discards them in a pile by the wall. I shift uncomfortably, because Ana won't look away from me.

"You lived with the hollowers?" she asks me.

"They caught me a couple of nights ago," Eric says. "I noticed they had a human living with them and thought it was strange."

"We decided to leave it to see what they would do with her," Elias continues. "Cassia kept an eye on her to make sure she was all right, but they tried to kill her a few days ago. And hollowers have mentioned the *immortalia sacrificium.*"

Ana doesn't say anything, pulling her gaze from me and looking at the floor. "Elias said you might know something," I say. "About the sacrifice, or why they might want me."

"Elias is mistaken." Her voice is low and quiet. "I'm afraid I can't help you."

I look at Elias, whose frown deepens. "But—"

"Did you cover your tracks on the way here?" she asks, standing up from the chair and looking at me. "Hollowers have been getting closer."

"Not this high up, no," Cassia says.

"I'd best go do that," she says, standing up and patting down her dress. "Elias, would you help me? Would you three mind cleaning up here? Feel free to go through my books but I doubt you'll find anything helpful."

Cassia frowns and Eric narrows his eyes, but neither of them protests. Elias stops me with a hand on my arm. He reaches beneath his coat and into the waistband of his pants, and holds something out to me: a silver, sheathed dagger.

"You should have some way of defending yourself," he says, wrapping my fingers around the hilt. "Just in case."

And then they walk away. I slip the dagger into the thick pocket of the coat, and turn to Eric. He's watching me. "I don't know how to use this."

"The hollowers didn't teach you how to fight?"

"They taught me how to cut vegetables, I wasn't allowed to hunt."

"If you can, always go for the jugular," he says, gesturing to his throat. "If you must stab, use as much force as you can and aim for the stomach, direct the dagger upward to the heart."

"The throat or the stomach," I repeat. "Right." This is my life now. I have to know these things.

I slump into the chair, deflated. I'd placed all my hope in getting the answer from Ana, but she was so cold, so adamant she didn't know anything more than we did. I don't know where we're supposed to go from here. "Should we help them cover the tracks?" I suggest.

"It's snowing, they're already covered." Cassia looks at Eric. "Was she always so strange?"

Eric's still staring after them. "Yes, always."

"How do you know her?" I ask Eric. He ignores me.

"There used to be a small village of elders here," Cassia says. "Years ago, all the elders picked up and moved to the coast. But Ana stayed."

"Why?"

She shrugs. "I don't know what happened, some conflict. Anyway, Ana raised Elias."

It makes sense in the tender way he treated her. There's a thud in the distance, and both Eric and Cassia tense. "What was that?" I scan the passageway Elias and Ana went through. "What if they're here?"

"Hollowers don't know about this place," Eric says.

"But what if—"

"Stop asking questions. You're giving me a headache."

I shut my mouth and listen, trying to shove my anxieties to the back of my head. If they say there's nothing to worry about, I have to learn to trust them.

~

The hour ticks by painfully slow. Elias and Ana don't return. Eric leans against the wall, flipping through pages of books while Cassia stands with me in the center, giving me lessons on how to kill somebody with a dagger. For practice purposes, she made me use a blunt one.

"You have to hold it tighter than that," Cassia says, adjusting my grip on the dagger. "Otherwise it'll slip as soon as somebody knocks you."

To demonstrate her point, she strikes forward and hits my arm. The blunt dagger clatters to the floor.

"See?" She picks it up and hands it back to me.

I sigh, gripping the leather hilt and tightening my fingers around it. "Like this?"

She knocks my hand before I can even blink but I keep hold of the knife. "Better. Now try what I told you."

I flick my wrist forward, going for her throat. She catches my wrist before I can reach her and twists it behind my back. I let out a sigh of defeat. "I'm terrible at this."

"You'll get better," she assures me, releasing my wrist. "Trust me, you'll be surprised how much damage you can do when you're fighting for your life."

The thought of plunging the dagger deep into somebody's stomach to save myself makes bile rise to the back of my throat. "My life being at risk didn't help me much that day you saved me," I say, remembering how I'd dragged myself helplessly along the ground. I'd stared Charles right in the eye and accepted that he was going to kill me.

"That's different. You were severely disoriented and that wasn't a fair fight. Even if you'd had a weapon, you were outnumbered."

"That didn't stop you."

Cassia smiles, pulling her short hair into a ponytail at the back of her head. "I'm flattered. But that's not a fair comparison, I've been training my whole life. It's a shame they never taught you how to fight."

"That really wouldn't have helped their Kill Milena agenda."

"Good point," she says, and pulls one of the books from the shelf. She opens it on her lap. "When we get back to the village, Elias will show you how to fight better."

My stomach twists at the thought. I don't doubt Elias already sees me as weak, and teaching me how to fight definitely won't help my case. I watch her as she flips through the pages just as Elias wanders back in. His eyes are cold, expression dead. "We should leave now."

Cassia frowns. "We just got here."

"Ana can't help us and we should be getting back."

Nobody says anything for a few moments. Eric, silent in the corner, studies Elias with narrowed eyes. "Elias, what'd she tell you?"

"Nothing, Eric. We need to—"

A short, sharp scream echoes through the tunnel. My body goes rigid and Cassia darts a hand out to grab my wrist. "What was that?"

Elias moves so quickly I barely see it. "Come on." Cassia drags me behind her as we run from the cave. The icy air rushes through my hair as we sprint through the dark after Elias, the light at the end of the cave getting closer. Elias stands stationary at the end of the cave, his back facing us. Eric's a few steps ahead of him, kneeling down in the snow. There's a steely stench to the air. I cover my nose with the sleeve of my shirt and step forward. "Elias?"

At the sound of my voice, his head turns, golden eyes gazing at me. But they don't seem the same—they seem far away, lost somewhere distant. "I didn't sense them," he says. "The tracks were covered. How could they—how did they . . ."

"Get back in the cave," Eric demands, rising to his feet. "Gather your things, pack up as many of Ana's books as you can hold. We have to leave. *Now*."

Cassia disappears back into the cave. I stay still, stepping forward to where he was so intently focused only moments before. Suddenly, I wish I'd never looked at all. The color is the first thing I notice—stark red against white. It smells pungent and steely, making my eyes water. Lying delicately in the snow is a lone hand, torn from its arm. But Ana's gone.

"Elias, we have to go," Eric says.

Elias's eyes are on Eric's face, but he isn't looking at him—it's like he's not even there. "It doesn't make any sense."

"*Elias*. We have to go. Now."

A tense silence stretches between them. Elias snaps into action, turning away from the bloodstained snow, and marches back into the cave. Eric grabs my arm on the way past and pulls me with him. When we get back to Ana's corner, Cassia's frantically shoving books into backpacks. I try to help her but she swats me away.

"How can we get down?" I ask. "If they're out there?"

"They took Ana but didn't attack. They want us to know they're there, waiting for us," Eric says, looking around. "So they can ambush us when we come down the mountain."

"But it's almost night," I say. "They won't wait much longer, they won't risk it."

"We should wait it out, then," Cassia says. "Until nightfall."

Elias shakes his head. "They have Ana, we're not waiting."

"Elias is right," Eric agrees, looking at me. "If they know she's with us, I don't think they'll waste much more time waiting around."

The hollowers are here. *Charles* could be here. "Switch coats with Cassia," Elias says. "They must've seen you already, they wouldn't risk attacking otherwise." Cassia catches on before I do, clearly on the same wavelength as Elias, and slips off her coat and hands it to me. I slip mine off without questioning it then wrap hers around me, relishing the warmth that I feel from her body.

Elias looks at Eric. "You two go up and around the mountain, it's the only other way out of here."

"What about me?" I ask.

"You won't be able to make it. But they should follow Cassia and Eric if she's wearing your coat."

"We'll take the bags," Eric says, slinging one over his shoulder and handing the other to Cassia. She shoves one last book inside before throwing the hood of my coat over her head and putting the straps over her shoulders. And then they exit the cave. I stare at Elias; he's rifling through the bookshelf.

"Is he here? Is Charles here?"

Elias turns to look at me. "Are you scared?"

"Is it that obvious?"

He drops the books and moves toward me, eyes holding mine. "If he's here, he won't get you. I promise."

"What about Cassia and Eric?"

"They're more than capable of taking care of themselves, they'll be fine. Come on. We'll try to make our way down."

I catch his hand. "Ana . . ."

"She'll be okay." He pulls away. "I'll find her."

He turns around and walks toward the end of the cave. My entire body shakes but I follow, lifting Cassia's hood over my head in an attempt to keep my face concealed. Elias halts me at the exit before guiding me around the perimeter of the crater, along the rock face. The snow is cold, blasting us from all directions. We walk down the mountain in silence until he grabs my arm and pulls me flush against him, into a rock. Then, footsteps.

I see them, then. Two hollowers silently trudging up the mountain. "Most of them followed Cassia and Eric, the rest seem to be coming up," Elias says. My stomach clenches as I wait for him to tell me what to do. "When I tell you, I want you to run. Try to get down the mountain as fast as you can, don't worry about following the track."

"You're not coming with me?"

"I'm going to get Ana."

"I want to stay with you." The words come out before I can think them over. He turns to look at me, hard expression softening.

"Milena, you have to trust me."

"I do, but I . . . what if there are more of them farther down? They'll follow me."

He reaches out, surprising me, the tips of his fingers brushing where I'd been punched. I have to keep myself from flinching—his touch is so gentle it's like a breeze and not that of a creature who could so easily destroy me. "If they do, they won't hurt you because they need you."

"I don't want them to take me."

His eyes burn like a candle in a dark room. "They won't. I'll find you. I can always find you, Milena." It's not the first time he's said it, but it's the first time that it comforts me. "Go, now." He draws away. "You remember what I told you?"

"Run. Don't stop."

He nods, steps away, looks out at the path, and ushers me forward. It's clear. There's silence, just the muted sound of falling snow and the gentle whisper of the wind. I almost don't move, but Elias nudges me and I dash out from behind the rock, tripping into a pile of snow. I pull the coat over my head and push to my feet, reaching for the dagger in my pocket and gripping it tightly.

My mind races but I don't turn back—I weave through the trees, maneuvering around rock faces. I run and run and run. The sky shifts to an ugly gray as the snow hardens, twisting around in the wind and pricking my face. Adrenaline fuels my body, but in the back of my mind the fear screams—for Eric and Cassia, for Elias and Ana, but most of all, for myself: That I'll run into Charles waiting at the bottom of the mountain. That he'll stand over me again with a machete and I'll be too paralyzed to even attempt to protect myself. That I'll let him kill me, that I won't even fight back.

Ahead, sparse clusters of trees are scattered across the track leading down. I propel myself around the corner without even watching where I'm going. Big mistake. I see him before he sees me, skidding to a stop as my heart pauses. A middle-aged man I don't recognize leans against one of the trees, studying his fingers. The hairs rise on the back of my neck. *Go, Milena, run.* My feet skid in the snow as my breath attempts to catch up with me. But I'm a second too late.

"Hey!" The earth thumps behind me. I gasp for oxygen, the air like tiny shards of glass stabbing at my throat. Haggard breath fills the air; a hand latches around my ankle and sends me three feet into the air before I land face first in the snow. I shove myself up, limbs flailing as hands grapple my ankles and drag me back along the ground. Dirty snow chokes me. I kick one of my ankles free to collide my foot with my captor's chest. It gives me enough time to flop over onto my back as I scramble to reach for the dagger a few feet away. The man drags me closer and takes hold of both my ankles, a wicked grin lighting his face as he restrains me, lower body on top of mine.

"Got you." The greedy look in his eyes, the wicked set of his grin. I don't know this man. "Stop struggling."

I bite down on my lip to suppress a scream and squirm beneath him, afraid the one who comes to my rescue will be the one I'm most afraid of. My fingers brush the hilt of the dagger. When the man puts a hand across my mouth, I bare my teeth and bite it. It tastes of dirt and sweat. He curses, jolting back. I slash the dagger across his arm. He screams, leaping away and giving me time to scramble back across the ground. Fear threatens to shut my body down but I force myself to my feet and stumble farther down the mountain, hobbling on my nontwisted ankle and holding the dagger tighter. The wind howls but my mind screams, half of it calling me to keep going and the other begging me to give up. Voices bounce off the trees as the ground flattens. I don't know where to go—noise echoes all around me; it's difficult to tell what's coming from where.

Down. Go down. I can always find you. Elias's voice is the only thing that propels me forward. I burst into a clearing, but I'm not alone. There are at least five of them standing guard, machetes in their hands but faces concealed by dark hoods. I almost turn and run in the other direction until I see past them. In the circle created by their bodies, a figure is hunched over. My heart thumps. *Ana.*

"Don't move," a woman threatens. Ana's head darts up. Her face is gaunt and pale but her eyes are wide.

I hold my hands up. "Wait. Please . . . what do you want with me?"

The hollowers laugh and murmur mocking words that I can't make out. I weigh my dwindling options, my confidence weakening as I stare at their long, sharp machetes. Run and leave Ana. Stay here and get caught. Both options are terrifying. Before I have to make a decision, a buzz fills the air, a power so radiant even the hollowers hesitate. Gold flashes through the forest so fast it's a blur. *Elias.* He appears an inch in front of me, between me and the hollowers.

"Let her go," Elias warns.

"Give us the girl and she's all yours."

I tense. Ana raised him, and I'm just some human he picked up a few days ago. The decision isn't hard. But Elias doesn't waver, he stands his ground and lifts his chin. Even though I'm inches away, it's like I can feel his body starting to burn.

"Let her go," he says lowly, "or I'll have to get her myself."

"Elias, *no*," Ana calls. One of the hollowers turns around and smacks her across the face.

Elias flinches. "Don't touch her."

"What're you going to do, creature?" the hollower laughs. "You can't take on all of us. Without your moon, without your *beast,* you're *nothing.*"

Elias half turns to look at me. "Run." He steps forward and closes his eyes. I shudder, and stumble backward. The hollowers shout after me, starting to move. And when I'm only steps away, I can't help but glimpse back. Even though the sky is a muted gray, Elias glows like he's bathing in the sun's rays.

"Elias!" Ana calls. "Elias! Stop!" She leaps across the clearing toward him but gets caught in the crossfire. One of the hollowers reacts on instinct, the hooded figure plunging their machete into her stomach. She doubles over, gasping for breath and Elias's eyes open. He stumbles forward to catch her. I don't stick around to watch any longer. Turning around, I run in the other direction, the earth grumbling beneath my feet as footsteps clamber after me. Elias's shout turns into a cavernous roar that disturbs the birds high above.

A hand hooks around my ankle and tackles me to the ground. I land with a thud on my back, a hooded figure looming over me. Tears blur my vision as their nails dig into my wrist. But they're small, smaller than me. I buck my hips and roll over so we've switched positions, and with Cassia's words in my mind, press the dagger to their neck. My fingers shake uncontrollably. I press harder and squeeze my eyes shut. I can't kill them.

Do it, Milena. They'll kill you if you don't.

Blood prickles where the knife presses, seeping over my

fingers. "Stop!" they gurgle. "Millie, stop!" I open my eyes. His hood has fallen off, wide blue eyes filled with horror. A drop of blood runs from the small incision on his throat. "It's me!" He scratches at my wrists desperately. "It's *me!*"

The distant shouts fade into the background. Ana's dead, Elias is stuck with the hollowers, and there have to be more of them hidden within the forest, but all those thoughts get pushed to the back of my head. All I can focus on is the boy who lies beneath me with familiar eyes and inky black hair. He looks older than I remember, less innocent. His hair has been cut to his head, and there's a faint bruise over his left jaw.

Darius. The boy who was kind to me when nobody else was, whom I chased around the walls and tickled until he laughed so hard he cried. The Darius I'd sneak extra bread rolls to during soup nights. His eyes fill with relief as he stares at me. "Don't hurt me, I want to help you. I want to—"

His voice tunes out as my body numbs. I remember the last time I saw him. When he joked with me one day and then went on a hunt and treated me like the dirt beneath his feet the next. This is Darius, who watched with a wicked smile as Charles stood over me with a machete, ready to end my life. Darius did nothing; he encouraged Charles, he *wanted* me to die. I press the dagger harder against his throat.

"You were going to kill me. You stood there and watched him try to *murder* me."

"I'm sorry, Millie, please, I'm sorry. I want to help you! I didn't understand. Please, let me explain." Everything inside of me wants to believe him, to scoop him into my arms and take him with me back to the castle. I want to have a piece of home that doesn't hurt. "I miss you."

My grip loosens slightly on the dagger. "Why should I believe you?"

His eyes soften and I see the old him, the one who used to jump in puddles when it rained. But before I can blink, his knee goes into my stomach as he flips us around so he's once again on top of me. "You shouldn't," he says, grinning as he pulls me to my feet and pushes me forward, into the forest and away from the screams. "Help! I have her!"

I kick from behind and he releases me, glaring at me as we stand staring at each other in the forest. He reaches for me again with newfound strength and presses me into the tree, my hands trapped between us as I fumble to keep the dagger from slicing my own stomach.

"Stop! Darius, why are you doing this? Please, let me go!"

He grabs my head and pounds it so forcefully against the tree that the world begins to spin. "Shut up, Milena!"

"Darius, *please*. Please don't do this, let me go. They'll *kill* me."

"You don't even know the half of it," he says.

I succeed finally in pushing him off me, adjusting the dagger, positioning it in front of me. Darius doesn't see it, though, and presses his body into mine so forcefully the hilt of the knife goes into my stomach and winds me, making bile rise to my throat. Darius's grip loosens; there's a sudden suction of air and he releases me and stumbles backward, his hands to his stomach.

He's wearing a thick wool shirt, his coat pulled open. But the clothing does nothing to stop the blood from seeping from the stab in his stomach, the dagger on an upward angle, lodged in his body. I should run and not look back—Darius can't be alone. But when Darius falls to the ground clutching his stomach, eyes filled with fear, I catch him. "No, no, no, no. Darius? *Darius?*"

GRACE COLLINS

He gasps for air, chest rapidly rising and falling. I press my hands to the area around the dagger, blood coating my fingers, seeping across my legs. "*Darius.*" I lean over him, pressing my face to his chest as I hold him to me. "Darius, please, I'm—I'm so sorry."

He doesn't look at me, I don't even know if he can hear me. His eyes are vacant as they stare at the sky, mouth hanging open. His body goes limp in my hands. An iron fist wraps around my throat and restricts my breath. *I killed a thirteen-year-old.*

My voice is low and quiet, between a cry and a moan as I try to stop the blood from seeping out. I can barely see him, tears streaming down my cheeks and mixing with the scarlet that coats his body.

I know Elias is there before he speaks; I can feel his energy, his warmth. But it feels so distant, the cold in my chest too overwhelming. I can't look away from Darius.

"*Milena.*" My eyes snap up at the desperation in his voice, blinking to clear the tears. "Are you hurt?" He moves in a flash— one second he's far away, the next he's kneeling right next to me, hand on my forearm. His clothes are stained red. "You're covered in blood."

"I killed Darius. I *k-killed* him. He's dead."

"Hey." His hands pull at mine. "Look at me." I can't. Darius was a kid. I *knew* him. I liked him. "Hey. You're okay."

"I *killed* him."

"It's okay," he says, fingers swiping at my cheeks and coming away red. "It's okay. Let him go, Milena."

"I can't."

"You can," he says softly. He pulls me closer, dragging me across the ground so that Darius's body drapes across the forest floor, blood staining the snow. "I've got you." His arms wrap around me, holding my head against his shoulder, hand on the back of it. I can hear the steady thumping of his heart, the rhythm barely matching my own. And we stay that way, my body wrapped in his warm embrace. I don't know how much time passes—it could be seconds or hours—but we soon hear shouts. "We have to go."

I know he's right. I know we aren't safe. But I can't speak and I can't leave Darius here. His blood covers my hands—it buries itself beneath my nails and works its way into the crevices of my fingerprints. "Milena." He shakes me so that my gaze is on him again, eyes uncharacteristically warm. "Milena, I'm sorry."

And when he looks at me, fingers supporting my head and holding the back of my neck, I can't look away. A fire burns in his eyes, so hypnotizing everything around us fades away. Until I can't see anything anymore.

CHAPTER TEN

I wake up tangled in bedding, forehead damp and body wrapped in the warmth of the light streaming through the window. The room spins as I twist in the sheets and stretch my arms above my head, noticing Cassia. She sits on the edge of the bed, legs folded beneath her and a book in her hands. I'm back at the castle, but I can't remember how I got here.

"Cassia?"

She jumps. "Hey."

"You're okay. Is Eric—"

"He's fine," she says, uncrossing her legs. "How do you feel?"

I catch a glimpse of myself in the mirror opposite the bed. My hair is a frizzy mess and my eyes look dark and sunken. I brush the bruise on my cheek. My skin feels tender—like it's been scrubbed. "How'd we get back here?"

"Elias said you passed out. Again." She frowns. "He carried you back and I bathed and changed you. I hope that's all right— you were just covered in so much blood, and I assumed you'd rather it was me instead of Eric or Elias."

Pictures stitch together in my mind, bile rising in the back of my throat. I scramble from the bed and rush to the bathroom door, throwing myself over the sink as my stomach empties itself. My mind flashes with pictures of Darius's body, dead on the forest floor.

"What happened, Milena?" Cassia sweeps my hair back from hanging in my face.

"I killed someone."

"He would've killed—"

"I knew him. He was my friend. He was just a kid."

It didn't feel real last night. But now, leaning over the sink, I feel it—the heavy weight of both grief and guilt pressing on my organs. It doesn't matter how hard Cassia scrubbed my body, blood has found its home in the lines of my palms, and it's not the kind that can be washed away.

"The first few times are hard." Eric appears in the reflection of the mirror over the sink. He lingers in the doorway, a solemn look on his face.

"What?"

"It gets easier with time."

"*Murder?* It's not a hobby I intend to continue."

He raises a brow. "You think any of us do? You think we wake up in the morning looking forward to that sort of stuff?"

"I wouldn't put it past you."

"Get over yourself." His voice is so low it's nearly a growl. "They aren't people, they're hollowers, and they kill us all the time. You'll kill again and you'll get to the point where you won't even care."

"Stop it, Eric," Cassia says.

"You know I'm right, Cassia. Don't think I've forgotten how you didn't talk for days after you first hurt a hollower. Now you can do it in your sleep."

"What is wrong with you?" I spin around to glare at him. "Why do you hate me so much?"

"I don't hate you."

"You could've fooled me."

"Ignore him." Cassia glares at him. "Did you come here to antagonize her or is there something you wanted?"

"Elias wants you to get a message to the elders," he says. "He's going to see them."

"He's planning on *leaving*? So soon after what happened?" She moves to the door. "Let me talk to him."

"Cassia—"

"Why is he going to see them, anyway? Which, by the way, he still hasn't mentioned what Ana wanted to talk to him about before we had to leave so abruptly."

Eric stops her in the doorway, uncharacteristically gentle. "Leave it, Cassia, you know he won't want to talk about it."

"He *never* wants to talk about it."

"Contact the elders." He puts a hand on her shoulder. "Please."

She sighs. And for the first time since I met her, vulnerability peeps through her hard exterior, silver eyes shimmering in a way that reminds me of a child—of Darius. Eric steps out of the way to let her past, looking at me over Cassia's shoulder with something other than distaste for once. A question presses at the back of my mind, one that, deep down, I already know the answer to. "Is Ana dead?"

"Yes."

I remember last night very clearly. Ana leaping across the clearing, Elias holding her body in his arms. The same way he held me when he came across Darius lying dead on the forest floor, his blood coating my arms. But in the pain I felt after what I did to Darius, I forgot all about Elias's wounds. How could he hold me that way when his Ana was murdered because of me? How could he even look at me? I blink back the blurriness in my eyes, wanting more than anything to find Elias and apologize, because there must be some part of him, deep down, that knows this is my fault.

I don't hear Eric leave, but soon I'm all alone in the bedroom, deserted to be with my thoughts, and my heart aches. I don't know what it's like to have a proper parent, or what it's like to feel unconditional love, but I know what it's like to look up to someone so much you see them as a father. And even though Charles never cared for me, even though he's hell-bent on murdering me, the thought of watching him die the way Elias had to watch Ana makes me waver on my feet. You can't easily force yourself to hate someone you grew up trying so hard to gain love from. Emotions don't work that way.

~

When I was eleven, Flo and I tried to climb a tree guarding the village because we thought we'd be able to see the hunters. We snuck out of the kitchen and hid behind a tomato patch, tearing our dresses on the rough bark as we tried to tug ourselves up to straddle the top. With blooded knees and scratched arms, we slung our legs over the top of the branches and gazed out into the forest. The wind tossed our hair around our faces. The forest was a never-ending sea of green.

I still remember the look on Flo's face. Her freckle-covered cheeks were tinged pink, her hair lit from the sun, burning like a flame. We were *invincible*. Nothing could touch us. It was Cynthia who found us and screamed at the top of her lungs for us to get down, threatening to confiscate the board games that we so dearly loved. But we didn't come down; we didn't want to. With Charles and the hunters gone, there was no authority. We could do what we wanted.

It turned out to be a bad choice. When Charles got back just before nightfall, Cynthia was about ready to hack the tree down herself. Flo climbed down first, head hung in shame as Cynthia shouted at her, but my descent wasn't so elegant. When I was halfway down, my legs slipped off the stick jutting out and the foundation beneath me snapped. My arm broke when I hit the ground, an excruciating pain shooting from elbow to wrist.

I remember screaming, scrambling across the ground as I held my arm to my chest. But the clearest memory of that day is of Charles standing over me, eyes mossy and lips tight. I begged him to help me, to carry me to the tunnels and tuck me into bed. But he only stared and stepped back. He told me that I had to suffer the consequences of my actions—my *disobedience*. And now, in the castle with the very creatures Charles taught me to fear, I can't push the memory from my mind. The prospect of seeing him again calls up bitter memories, painful indications from my past that alluded to the idea that he never loved me at all. Signs that were so blatantly clear and scattered all through-out my childhood, that I cast aside, chose to ignore. And I can't help but wonder if I am partly to blame for the position I'm now in. It's not the only thing that I'm to blame for.

The library door is already open when I reach it, the stone transitioning to a worn carpet. I had spent the remainder of the morning in my bedroom, knees to my chest and back pressed against the wooden headboard, as I thought of Elias, Darius, Charles, and Ana. I peer around the door. Elias leans against the wall by the fire, his eyes on the flames. He looks like some sort of painting that should be hung next to the extravagant artworks lining the castle walls.

"You can't say anything." At the sound of Eric's voice, I leap back, gripping the door. Eric paces behind him, pausing when Elias doesn't answer.

"All this time . . . why did she lie to us?"

"You know why."

"But now we know the truth. I can't keep this to myself."

"Yes, you can." The fire crackles in the silence that hangs between them. "Elias, you *have* to."

"But—"

The door creaks and they both spin toward me. I freeze, blood running cold.

"Milena?" Elias calls.

"Oh, sorry, I was . . . I was looking for you and—I just got here." From the looks on their faces, neither of them believes me. "I wanted to talk to Elias."

The air is thick with tension. "Eric, can you see how Cassia's getting on?" Elias asks. Eric opens his mouth to protest. "Please." With a sigh, Eric brushes past me and leaves the room. I stare sheepishly at Elias, stepping farther into the room and taking a seat on the burgundy sofa. The bookshelves trap us in a cocoon of warmth. Elias picks up the book on the couch beside me so he can sit down, holding it tightly in his lap. I peer curiously at the cover—it's old and musty.

"How are you feeling?" he asks.

"Better."

If he notices my lie, he doesn't point it out. "Good."

Silence stretches between us. I have so much to say but I don't know where to start, because any sort of apology gets stuck half-way down my throat. It doesn't feel like enough. Nothing I say could ever be enough. "I wanted to thank you."

"You don't have to thank me for bringing you back here. I told you the hollowers wouldn't take you."

"That's not what I was going to thank you for." With a surge of courage, I shift closer, watching closely for any signs of irrita-tion. But he makes no effort to move away, his eyes softer than I remember. I don't have the courage to say what I really want—that I'm sorry about Ana, that I'm thankful he held me together when he must've felt like falling apart.

"You don't need to be afraid of me, you know."

I hold my breath at the tilt of his head, the slight lilt of his mouth—a nearly there smile. "What?"

"I see the way you look at me, Milena. The way you talk to me. You're afraid of me and you don't need to be."

I don't know how to respond. What he's said is both right and wrong. There's something about Elias that makes me feel secure, like nothing could ever touch me, and at this moment I trust him to protect me. But I know the reality of my situation—I saw what he did to those hollowers in the forest. Elias protects me because he needs me, and the second he discovers information that implies he doesn't could be the moment my life ends. I'm not afraid of Elias. I'm afraid he'll stop protecting me. "I'm not scared of you."

"The pounding of your heart suggests otherwise."

"Maybe you do scare me, a little." A lie. But it's much better than the truth.

"I won't ever hurt you," he says.

Sounds from the village waft through a gap in the windowpane. Laughter and joy swirl in the wind and fills the air. And as I stare at Elias, I believe him, despite the fact that I watched him tear a head from a body. And that terrifies me.

"Before we left the mountains, Ana wanted to talk to you, and then you wanted to leave straight away. Did she say something?" I ask.

"Ana couldn't help us like I hoped," is all he says. I watch him as he talks about her, noting the way her name rolls off his tongue while his eyes remain vacant of feeling. It irks me to see how well he can hide his emotions.

"Cassia told me that Ana raised you."

"She took me in when my parents were killed."

The revelation doesn't surprise me, but in a way, it makes me feel less alone. He was an orphan, just like me. "I'm sorry that she died."

"People die every day," he says, voice hard and cold. I frown, staring at him. He's careless with his words, seemingly unaffected by the death of the woman who raised him.

"That's an awful thing to say."

"It's true."

"That doesn't mean you don't get to be sad," I tell him, shifting so that I'm facing him. "Elias, I—"

"Don't say it, Milena."

"You don't even know—"

"You're going to apologize like it's your fault."

He can read me like a book while I can barely decipher one thing from his expression. "Elias," I start, "she raised you and they killed her because—"

"It isn't your fault."

I swallow the lump in my throat. "They wanted me."

He shifts closer and puts a hand on mine. My first reflex is to flinch, but his hand is warm and gentle as it smooths out my fist until my palm is laying flat. He opens the ragged book in his lap and places it in my hand.

"Here," he says, drawing away as I hold the page and smooth out its edges. On one side, is what appears to be some sort of list—a combination of words I can't read. The other is a drawing of a woman with long, wild hair and eyes that seem to shine even through the drawing. "This was an old, spare book Ana gave me. She had a few drawings in here but let me use the rest of the pages. I didn't know she still had it."

"This is amazing. Did you draw it?"

He stares at the drawing through half-lidded eyes, nodding.

"It's beautiful, Elias."

"She was beautiful, *incredible*. She taught me everything I know today. She protected me when I had nobody else." His eyes seem distant, like he's not sitting in the library with me but is somewhere with Ana, in his childhood. Lost in a world that's not our own. "And then she grew old and I became strong, and I vowed to protect her the same way that she protected me when my parents were killed." He looks away from me, to the window. "This is my fault, Milena. This isn't on you and it never was. Ana is dead because I didn't protect her, and that's on me."

He's wrong. He had an opportunity to trade my life for Ana's and when he didn't, they killed her. The fact that he's blaming himself for her death shakes me—that's too much of a burden for somebody who doesn't deserve it. "You can't mean that."

"I do. And I mean it when I say that I won't let the hollowers get to you as they did her."

"Until you realize the reason they want me doesn't affect your village, right? It wouldn't be logical to keep me safe when so many others are dying in my place."

"No. It wouldn't be logical." He didn't say it, but he may as well have. I was right: my protection is conditional.

I look back at the book in my lap, eyes slightly blurry as I try to make out the words on the second page. "What's this?" I pause in thought. "They key . . . *ingrebiance*?"

His smile is so warm it transforms his entire face. "The key ingredients."

"Oh. I've always confused the *d*'s and *b*'s. They look really similar."

"I think I like ingrebiance better, anyway."

This time, I can't hold back my smile. "You must think it's pathetic I can't read at twenty."

"I don't think you're pathetic at all. Did nobody in your village know how to read?"

I shake my head. "Most of them learned in school but Charles pulled me out and got me to work in the kitchen when I was young. I wonder if it was because he didn't want me to read about everything he was hiding from me," I say, leaning back so that I'm not so close to him. "Flo could read really well. She would always read the ingredients out to me when we made stuff together."

"Who's Flo?"

The thought brings an acid taste to my mouth. "I thought she was my best friend. Who she really was? I don't know." The fire crackles in the corner, embers spitting out onto the stones around it.

"The one with the red hair?" Elias says. "The one you protected that night, the one you risked your life for? *That* was Flo?"

"That's the one."

"Did they treat you well?" he asks. "Was your childhood . . . okay?"

"I don't have anything else to compare it to."

He shifts closer, just a whisper away. "I'm sorry all this happened to you."

His apology feels so sincere, filled with emotions I can't interpret. "It's not like it's your fault."

I know that I should lean away, that I should remove myself from the situation before I get even more tangled in him, but at this exact moment, the only thing I can think about is how close we are and how warm I feel. Because even though our lives are different, when he looks at me, it's like he understands what it's like to not belong anywhere.

"Elias, I wanted to thank you for last night. If you weren't there . . . if you hadn't . . ."

"Don't thank me."

"I want to." My eyes go down to his hands, clenched in his lap, then back up to his face. "I've never felt so safe in my whole life, and I know you're just doing it because you have to, but I—"

"Milena—"

"—I needed someone last night, and you were there. Even after what happened with Ana, even though it was *my* fault—"

"Stop." I freeze as his fingers brush my chin, tilting my head up to look at him. "Stop it, you don't owe me any apologies."

Goose bumps rise along the back of my neck. He's so close—if I leaned in, our noses would brush. And even though I know he could give me to the hollowers at any second, I want nothing more than to be closer to him. But the reality of our situation is like a slap to the face. Elias's guardian died in place of me; it doesn't make sense that he doesn't resent me, even just a little bit.

"How don't you hate me?" I whisper.

"I couldn't hate you." His eyes search my face, expression desperate. "I *can't*. Even if they did kill her because of you, I couldn't hate you for it because—" There's a cough at the door. Elias leaps away from me so quickly a whoosh of air blows my hair around my face. Over his shoulder, Eric stands in the doorway.

"Am I interrupting something?" He shoots a pointed look at Elias.

"Nothing."

Eric looks at me and I shrink into the couch. "We should talk, Elias."

"About what?"

"You know what."

Elias doesn't even look at me before getting up and exiting the library, brushing past Eric and leaving as fast as he can, like he can't think of anything worse than being here with me. His departure stings, his absence allowing thoughts I'd tried to repress back into my mind. I try to keep my face straight as Eric watches me from the doorway.

"Do you know where Cassia is?" I ask.

"Milena." His voice is softer than usual. "It'd be better for everyone if you kept your distance."

He turns and leaves the library and I slump back, the strange energy Elias filled me with feeling as if it's seeping from my fingertips and dripping to the floor. And when I'm alone again, the thoughts I'd tried to silence crawl back in my head and the weight on my chest returns, the book discarded beside me. The cover is orange and tattered, a stark contrast to the small, paper books we had in my village—books I'd read with Darius when we were both learning.

If my knife hadn't plunged into his stomach, what would have happened? Would I be with the hollowers right now or would I be dead? Or would Elias have saved me before they got to me? Did I really kill Darius for nothing? Does that make it worse? Thoughts race around my head, justifications and accusations that I can't seem to organize or pull apart, but Darius floats at the center of them. Because even though he's gone, his presence is heavy.

~

After wandering through the castle halls, I find Cassia in Elias's office. She's sitting at his desk, drowning in paper, and doesn't look up when I open the door. "I was just going through Ana's books and I thought—oh, it's you."

"Sorry. I thought maybe I could help you."

"That's all right." She waves me closer, and I take the seat across from her. "I was supposed to meet Eric and Elias here. I'm just going through Ana's books to see if there's anything more about the sacrifice. We must be missing something."

"You think that might help?"

"I don't know, but it's all we've got right now."

She flicks through the pages, intensely focused. My mind brings me back to the mountain, when Ana had taken Elias outside to cover the paths. I hadn't thought much of it until Cassia mentioned they were already covered, and then Elias's abrupt decision to leave—it didn't feel natural. "Do you know why Ana wanted to talk to Elias?" I ask. "When she took him outside."

"They hadn't seen one another for a while." She shrugs.

"But didn't you find it a little weird? You said yourself the tracks were already covered by the snow."

"If I were Ana, I wouldn't want to talk to my son with a bunch of strangers around either." She looks up at me with narrowed eyes. "Milena, what's this about?"

"The way she looked at me before they left, Elias's decision to leave as soon as they'd finished talking . . . don't you find it all a little weird?"

"Look, Elias is a mysterious guy, he always has been. It's easy to think he's hiding things, but it's not always that deep. I trust him, and you should too. If he says Ana couldn't help, then she couldn't help." Before I can respond, Eric shoves the door open, Elias a beat behind him. They both look surprised to see me there.

"Good, you're here," Cassia says. "I'll send word to the elders that you'll be visiting. But I've been going through Ana's books. Have you heard of adrix?"

"Yeah, it's an antibacterial medicine. I told you those books are useless, Cassia," Eric says. "Even Ana herself said there'd be nothing in them."

"Well, what would you suggest I do? We still have to figure out what the hollowers want from Milena, and these are all we have."

"What we really need to talk about is what we're doing about the hollowers," he says. "They're getting more confident. Who knows how long it'll be before they try to infiltrate the village."

"We'll have to up security, maybe enforce an earlier curfew," Elias says, moving to stand behind the desk. He looks at me. "Was your colony ever in contact with other hollower groups?"

"I didn't even know there were others."

"It's strange," Cassia adds. "They've never worked together like this before. It certainly increases the risk for us."

"It's only going to get more dangerous as long as Milena stays here," Eric says.

Cassia raises a brow. "It's not like she has anywhere else to go."

"How long are we supposed to let this go on?" he says. "How many people are going to die if we keep her here?"

"You want to just give me to the hollowers?" I say.

"You want families to keep losing their loved ones because of you?"

"Eric, that's enough," Elias says coldly. "We're not giving you to the hollowers, Milena. Ever." Eric murmurs something beneath his breath about having to leave, and he twists on his feet, his shoulder knocking mine before he slams the door behind him. The room seems to shake. I wonder if I'm the only one who can feel it as guilt winds its way through me.

Cassia snorts. "And to think he could've been your second in command. You really dodged a bullet there, Elias. Why is he so worked up, anyway? He's so angry these days."

"Just ignore him," Elias says.

"Oh, believe me, I do."

Elias chuckles. Cassia's smile widens as she swings herself over his desk, mumbling something more about Eric's temper.

"He has a point, you know," I say.

"Who? Eric?" Cassia says.

"Maybe he's harsh in his delivery, but he *is* sort of right. The longer you keep me around, the more everyone here is at risk."

Cassia leans against the desk. "You're saying we should give you to the hollowers?"

The last thing I want is to go back to the hollowers, but the thought of more people dying in my place is almost more frightening. "I don't want to go with them. But I would understand if you didn't want me to stay here anymore."

Elias sighs, stepping forward. "Eric *is* wrong. You have a place here, Milena, no matter what anybody says." I can't look away from him, because for the first time in so long, I feel a sense of belonging. And the feeling is indescribable.

"What should we do?" Cassia asks quietly.

"We'll have to enforce a lockdown. Make sure nobody leaves the village territory without permission."

"What about the night of the First Run? We can't enforce a curfew then."

Elias pauses in thought. "We'll celebrate inside the village this year. It's too dangerous to do it outside, even during the night."

"What is the First Run?" I ask.

Cassia scribbles something on the paper on the desk. "Shifter tradition, all the kids shifting for the first time go on their first run. We celebrate beforehand with a bonfire and music with the entire village. It's the biggest event of the year."

"When is it?"

"End of the week," she says, looking at Elias. "I'm going to arrange something about the lockdown. Do you want me to get back to the elders to let them know when you'll be there?"

He shakes his head. "That's all right, I can do that." Cassia nods, bustling for the door with an armful of paper and books. She smiles as she passes me and pulls the door shut behind her much more delicately than Eric had.

"Don't worry yourself over Eric," Elias says without looking up, continuing to fiddle with the papers on his desk. "He's just doing what he thinks is best."

"I know," I say. Eric's perpetual bad mood doesn't affect me anymore. The moment I accepted that he doesn't like me it stopped bothering me. But that doesn't stop me from thinking about all the reasons why he doesn't like me. And honestly, it's getting harder and harder not to agree with him. "Is the First Run compulsory?"

"Compulsory?"

"Like . . . do I have to go?"

He smiles and his entire face brightens. "Not if you don't want to. But it'll be safe. The hollowers won't get in."

"It's actually not the hollowers I'm worried about."

"The shifters?"

"I don't exactly fit in."

"You say that like it's a bad thing."

"Isn't it?"

"Not always."

I step forward and rest my hands on his desk. "What are you doing?"

"Paperwork," he says. "Nothing you'd find interesting."

"You'd be surprised. Anything is more interesting than sitting around doing nothing." I pause. "Not that I don't appreciate being here or anything, I didn't mean it like—"

"Do you have any hobbies?"

"Hobbies?" I don't know why, but the thought of carrying out regular tasks is unfathomable. I'm in a different world now, a world where none of that stuff exists.

"Hobbies. You know, activities done regularly in one's leisure time for pleasure—"

"I know what a hobby is."

"That's a relief," he says. "I was starting to think the hollow-ers banished you to cleaning in every spare second you had." I notice the look in his eyes, the slight tilt of his lips. He's *teasing* me. "So?" he asks again. "Is there anything you'd like to do while you're here?"

"What sort of things? Like painting or writing?"

"Painting is all right. Though I'd suggest reading before you get to writing."

Blood rushes to my cheeks and I let out a nervous laugh. "Good idea. Reading then? It would be nice to learn."

"That could be arranged. Anything else?"

I remember racing down the mountain face, feeling utterly useless as that man grabbed my ankles and dragged me along the ground. Though the idea of having to fight for my life petri-fies me, I know it's important. It's possible that Elias won't pro-tect me one day, and when that day comes—

"I want to learn how to defend myself," I decide. "In case things don't work out here."

Elias's smile slips away. He turns around, opening his desk drawer and fiddling with the contents.

"What're you doing?"

"I'm getting the key to the training room."

"What, *now*?"

He looks up at me with a grin and my stomach somersaults.

Elias has always been beautiful to me, but before, he was unreachable. Now, standing there and smiling at me, he's beautiful in a whole new way—where I don't have to worry about him snapping my neck. "Why not?"

~

The training center, as Elias called it, is underground. And though I spent half my life hiding from supposedly ravenous creatures in a dark tunnel, I don't think I've ever seen anything more terrifying. The center is an area larger than the courtyard of my old village, an elaborate obstacle course stretching around the perimeter of the room—ropes, rock walls, and bars line the course, with soft black mats beneath each obstacle. Everything is black—the walls, the obstacles, the mats on the floor. The only color is the silver of the blades on the weapons lining the walls, too many for me to count. Machetes, daggers, swords, bows and arrows—a collection I couldn't dream of ever needing to use. And staring at them now, I wonder if this is a good idea after all.

"Why do you have so many weapons?" I leave Elias by the door to walk the length of the wall. "Can't you just shift?"

"We can't shift when we're kids, so we have to learn how to fight. And even after that, we need to be able to protect ourselves during the day, when shifting isn't an option."

"And the extensive obstacle course? You plan on climbing mountains too?"

"Purely for endurance. Most battles are lost because you don't have the strength to keep up with your opponent."

I remember how my lungs burned as I sprinted down the mountain, the way my legs threatened to give out on me. The thought that this is my reality now is hard to swallow. Back in my village, I thought the most physical activity I'd get to do was hunting a few animals to bring back for a meal. I want to learn to protect myself, but actually being here in front of all these weapons and obstacles is overwhelming. And Elias being here doesn't help to calm any of my nerves.

I look at the weapons again, eyes landing on the smaller ones. "Should I pick one?"

"Eager, aren't you?" Darius's cold, lifeless body flickers on the backs of my eyelids. "No weapons for now." He puts his hand over mine and guides it to my side and away from the weapons. "I don't want you to accidentally trip and shoot me with an arrow."

"That's fair."

"First, you need to work on your endurance."

I don't even try to stop my groan from escaping. "You want me to practice *running*?"

"Most of the people you'll come up against will have had a lot more training than you. Your best bet is always going to be running away, even if you do have a weapon."

"And what if they still catch me?"

"We'll get to that later. For now, try this endurance course," he says, nodding toward it.

A wooden ladder leads to a platform about five feet off the ground. My stomach plummets when I put my feet on the first few rungs, memories of climbing trees with Flo filtering through my mind. Finally reaching the platform, I cling to the wooden pole for support, trying not to seem nervous when I look down at Elias. "That wasn't so hard."

The left side of his mouth tilts up. "You haven't even started yet."

I face the course, rubbing my hands on the black pants Cassia loaned me as I stare at the first obstacle. It's some sort of rope swing, multiple strands of rope hanging from the ceiling and no other way across to the next platform aside from swinging. "Can't be that difficult, right?" I reach for the first rope, my feet leaving the platform, and dangle in midair, trying to use my body to swing to the next one. I get three ropes in when I completely miss and drop to the black mats with a thud. Elias appears above me, slightly blurry.

"You have very poor upper body strength," he says plainly. Cynthia used to say the same thing to me when I would be scrubbing pots and she would tell me to use elbow grease. Elias leans down and pulls me up by my forearms. "You can take a break if you want."

"No. I'm fine, really. I need to finish."

Taking a deep breath, I clamber up the ladder again, this time making sure to properly swing myself to create enough momentum and reach the next rope. I successfully make my way to the next obstacle, a balancing pole, from which I promptly fall twice, making my abdomen burn. And then the next one, a speed run to avoid getting whacked by a swinging pendulum that knocks me to the ground. By the time I reach the end of the course, it feels like hours have passed. I collapse onto the ground, arms like jelly.

"That wasn't so bad," I say, a smile crossing my face as Elias appears standing over me.

"How does your body feel?"

I laugh, flipping over so that he's no longer upside down. "Never better."

"Good. Do it again."

The smile immediately drops from my face. I wait for him to laugh—he doesn't. "What?"

"That was only the practice round, Milena. You've still got three more to go."

My legs are weak and my arms feel like they'll give way simply holding a glass of water above my head. I want nothing more than to lie in a warm bathtub, close my eyes, and succumb to fatigue. But there's a gleam in his eye, something that stops me from walking right out the door and going to sleep. Like he's *daring* me to try it again. And so, with shaky arms and quivering knees, I push to my feet and hobble back to the beginning.

~

My nightmares are filled with red. Darius's hands scratching at my throat; my stained fingers at his chest, widening the gaping hole there. He screams and cries. His eyes roll back in his head. His family stands over his body, wailing. Bodies press down on top of me. My fingers scrape at skin, drawing blood. And then my dagger is lodged in their chests and they're falling over, blood seeping into the white of the snow. Over and over and over.

I wake in a layer of sweat. My legs are tangled in a rope of sheets and I clutch at my throat, twisting at the red painted against my eyelids. Stumbling from the bed to the bathroom, I knock my head on the doorway and lean over the sink, pushing my sweat-drenched hair from my face as voices echo in my head. My hands shake as I turn on the tap and splash icy water on my face.

There's a knock on the door.

"Milena?" I freeze, then splash my face once more, trying to compose myself as I pat it dry. When I open the door, Elias is standing there with a fist raised as if he's about to knock again. He enters, eyes immediately darting around the room as if surveying for some type of threat. "What happened?"

"What?"

His eyes scan from the tip of my head to my feet. "I heard you screaming."

I fidget with the hem of the shirt I'm wearing, feeling incredibly uncomfortable as I stand in front of him, my hair a wild mess and my mind still shaken up. "I'm fine. I had a bad dream, that's all."

"About Charles?"

"Darius." I sit on the edge of the bed, pulling the sheet up over my bare legs before looking back at him. "Eric says it gets easier with time . . . killing. But I don't want it to get easier. I don't want to kill enough hollowers that it has to get easier."

Elias snaps to, coming to stand in front of me. "Don't listen to Eric."

"But—"

"It affects him the same way it affects everyone else. It never gets any easier, you just get better at dealing with it."

"That's horrible."

"That's life."

"I don't *want* that life. I don't want to kill anyone."

He lets out an exaggerated breath and rubs the back of his neck. "And I hope you don't have to. But it isn't that simple; sometimes life chooses for us." The silence that fills the room is comfortable, any awkwardness stolen by the hum of energy that follows Elias wherever he goes.

"What're we going to do if the other elders can't help?"

"Don't worry yourself over that."

"Of course I'm *worried* about it. Do you have a plan? If they can't help?"

"I don't know, Milena." He shakes his head. "But we'll figure something out."

It's unreasonable of me to expect Elias to provide me with all the answers to my questions, but that doesn't stop me from wanting him to.

"You should get some sleep," Elias says, letting go of the bed frame. "You must be tired from your training today." My body aches and my muscles cry, but I know that I won't sleep, not again. "Good night, Milena."

I don't want to be alone. But my pride is greater than my fear, so I bite my tongue to keep from asking him to stay. "Good night."

~

I don't see Elias or Eric for the next four days. The hollowers don't make any moves; Cassia spends half her time organizing the First Run ceremony and the other half helping me train. Each morning she comes to my bedroom, brings me breakfast, and instructs me to meet her in the training center. Apparently, Elias signed me up to the class of fourteen-year-olds that Cassia usually teaches. And despite the brutal consequences felt after that first training session, a small part of me hopes to see him there again.

But he never comes.

"Try to punch anybody with that and you'll break your hand." I face Aliyah, a petite brunet with impressively muscular arms—the exact kind of upper body strength Elias taunted me for lacking. There are three instructors for this class: Cassia leads it, and her shifter friends Aliyah and Bastian help out.

"What's wrong with it?" I ask.

Aliyah steps toward me, nodding to the group of kids standing in front of Cassia, all making identical fists. "Do it like that."

Since Cassia leads the group, she's usually busy with the kids, and Aliyah or Bastian gets stuck with me—the least competent in the group. But I don't mind—the welcome I got from the two of them was much warmer than the whispers and stares I got from the kids.

"Knuckles folded over your palm, thumb crossed over your fingers," she reminds me, demonstrating with her own fists. I copy her movements, flashing a smile as I mimic the kids in front of Cassia. I lead with my hips and throw my fist at Aliyah, aiming for her throat—the soft parts of her body, just like she taught me. She catches my fist before it hits her, lowering it and smiling. "Better."

"Better than what?" Bastian says as he comes toward us with a glass of water, wiping his hand on his forehead. "A six-year-old? Because that's not much of an accomplishment."

Bastian is a mousy-brown, stocky man with a large nose and a very strong jawline. He's the polar opposite to Eric—I don't think I've ever seen Bastian without a smile.

"*Hey*," I say defensively. "I'm trying."

"Trying to give a high five?" I punch his arm but he doesn't even flinch.

Cassia comes over to us, wiping her hands on her pants. "Everything all right?"

The kids are packing up their things and starting up the

twisting staircase that leads to the foyer. Bastian flicks my cheek with his thumb. "I'm just giving Milena some helpful tips."

"You and I have very different definitions of helpful." I laugh.

"You guys want to get some lunch? I'm starving," Aliyah says.

Bastian stretches his arms above his head and starts for the exit. "I'm in."

Aliyah looks at Cassia while putting her hair into a messy bun atop her head. "Cass?"

"Can't. Elias has me running all over the place trying to organize the First Run tonight. Maybe next time."

"Milena?"

I hesitate. Honestly, the thought of going into the village petrifies me. I know what people here think of me, and I can ignore it so long as I stay in the castle. But venturing outside means immersing myself in the judgment and hate. Thankfully, Cassia comes to my rescue. "Milena's helping me," she says. "We'll see you at the ceremony tonight."

Aliyah sighs, mumbling something about Cassia always being too busy before disappearing from view. "You really want me to help you?" I ask.

Cassia nods. "I'm getting bored out of my mind all alone in that office. Your company will be much appreciated."

"Where is he, anyway?"

"Elias? He and Eric went back up the mountain. They'll be back tonight in time for the ceremony."

"Back up the mountain? What? Why?"

"They went to get Ana's body, to bury her." She pauses. "There were also more books there. They might be important."

"When will he leave for the coast?"

She shrugs, brushing her hands on her pants. "We're trying

to plan his trip to the elders but we have to be careful. We don't want to lead the hollowers to them and get more people killed before we get there."

"What do you think?" I ask. "Do you think the hollowers are just mistaken?"

"I don't know." She sighs. "All I know is, it's a lot of fuss over someone if you aren't one hundred percent totally confident."

I mull over her words as we clamber up the stairs and spill into the foyer, following her as we make our way through the labyrinth of rooms toward the library. I know she's right. I might not be a wisper, but that doesn't mean the hollowers have made a mistake. Why go through twenty years of raising someone you're only going to kill if you aren't positive that you need them? It seems like a lot of hassle over a maybe.

Once we've settled into the sofas in the library, Cassia gives me a few mindless tasks that don't require reading. I can't keep my mind from drifting to Elias. Right from the beginning, he was mysterious and filled with secrets. But the more time I spend with him, the more I feel like I know him. Little fragments of his personality shine through his hard exterior, and each little piece I hold close to my chest, afraid he'll close off for good, like how I thought he might when he snapped at me in the forest.

You don't need to know me and I don't need to know you.

And now I'm afraid of Elias for a new reason. I'm not scared because I know he can rip my head off, or because he might stop protecting me. I'm scared because the more I think about him, the more wrapped up he gets in my heart. And just like those hollowers in the forest whose hearts lay separate from their bodies, I'm giving him the opportunity to rip mine right out of my chest.

CHAPTER ELEVEN

After spending most of the afternoon scouring pages of books I can barely read and coming up empty, I finally give in to Cassia and agree to go to the First Run. The entire village dresses up for the celebration, which is why I'm wearing a silky, long-sleeved blue dress that reaches just past my knees. It's soft against my skin and shimmers when I move. When Cassia first pulled it out, I was entranced by the way it flowed through the air. I'd never seen a piece of clothing so beautiful.

"Will you stop fussing?" Cassia swats at my hands. "You're going to ruin all my hard work."

I follow her through the castle halls, pulling at the pins stabbing my head. "It's just so uncomfortable." One comes loose and my hair tumbles around my shoulders. "Oops."

"Oops? You *definitely* did that on purpose." She continues

down the hall, the bottom of her dress swaying elegantly with her every step. I never thought I'd see her in one, but the loose, black dress she wears looks stunning. As we descend the staircase, distant music wafts through the foyer. "Hurry!" she says. "It's starting."

She pulls me around the side of the castle.

As we round the corner, the celebration comes into view, red pulsing from a large fire, reaching to the sky. There are clusters of people around the fire, all barefoot and dressed in similarly silky garments. A group gathered on the far side of the clearing hold instruments, poised and ready to play as the villagers gather around them. And then I see Elias. He stands on a raised podium on the other side of the fire pit wearing dark pants and a long-sleeved white shirt, the top of it open, revealing his toned, scarred chest. My stomach flips as his eyes scan the crowd. Cassia pulls me through the gathering of murmurs and sour expressions until we reach the fire, the warmth biting back at the cold air.

"Welcome to the First Run!" Elias calls, his declaration evoking cheers. "We're here to celebrate those shifting for the first time this year. Due to unavoidable circumstances, the run will be inside our territory and led by the guards. But don't let this stunt our festivities." He turns and nods at a group of people at the front. "And now, to the runners. I present to you Maria!"

A young girl dressed all in white steps up to the podium, her cheeks stained pink as the crowd cheers in triumph. Elias continues to call names and one by one they gather on the stage to equal fanfare. The crowd chatters as the runners bounce eagerly on the balls of their feet. I watch as they head off the podium toward a group of men and women who wait at the forest edge.

And then they disappear from view. I turn to Cassia. "That was anticlimactic."

She laughs. "The celebration hasn't started yet. We wait until they get back to start celebrating. This is all for them, after all."

I step closer to her, moving away from the fire. It's so hot it's nearly unbearable to be so close, and the smoke makes my throat constrict. More murmurs capture my attention, but when I glance at the group of girls responsible, they simply giggle and dart their eyes away, turning their backs to whisper among one another. Cassia tugs on my arm. "Ignore them, Milena."

"I'm trying, but—"

"But nothing. They're bored and have nothing better to do than gossip." She glares over her shoulder at the group of giggling girls and they all look down. "Oh look! There's Bastian and Aliyah!"

She yanks me through the crowd. With Cassia's words in mind, I hold my chin high and avoid looking around me, painfully conscious of the stares that follow us.

"Milena?" Aliyah looks gorgeous in a silver, floor-length dress that displays her enviable, muscular arms. "Elias said you were thinking of staying back."

"Staying cooped up in a room gets old after a while."

Bastian nudges me with a bright grin. "We're glad you're here."

"It seems like you're the only ones."

"Ignore them," Aliyah says.

"Easier said than done," Bastian says, rubbing the side of his head. "I know how you feel, Milena. I was the talk of the village a few months back because I spent a glorious night with a beautiful woman."

Aliyah laughs. "You deserved to be the center of gossip for a while. She was *married*, Bastian."

"I didn't know!"

"They never do."

Bastian opens his mouth to retort but he's interrupted by the call of a loud horn. My immediate reaction is to stumble backward, my heart thumping in my chest. But Cassia presses her fingers to the inside of my wrist. "Calm down. It just means the shifters are back."

The group emerges from the tree line, their clothes dirtied, torn, and pulled haphazardly over their heads. But it's hard to focus on their clothes when their eyes are alight with joy, smiles stretched to their ears. The crowd around me cheers, throwing their arms into the air as the musicians start to play. The joy is contagious. I can't stop grinning as the crowd around me dances and those who have newly shifted embrace their friends and family. "That was fast," I say.

Cassia nods. "It's hard to stay shifted long when you first do it."

I scan the crowd until my gaze lands on Elias. He stands with a group of people by the fire, laughing at something, his entire face illuminated. He looks ethereal.

"What now?" I ask absentmindedly, staring at Elias. His eyes catch mine and he tips his head, smile widening.

"Now," Bastian says, "we dance."

He takes my wrist and pulls me toward him, Cassia and Aliyah trailing behind as he spins me in circles and flips me under his arms. Laughter bubbles up from inside my chest.

I love to dance. Sometimes, while the hunters were gone, Wilhelm would play his rickety ukulele in the village center. Flo and I would spin in circles, dipping under one another's arms until we were laughing so hard our stomachs hurt. Dancing fills me with euphoria. It makes me feel like nothing could ever go wrong. As Aliyah grips my hand and spins me under her arm while Bastian dips her backward, heat spreads all the way to my fingertips. Next, Bastian spins Cassia so hard that she stumbles over his feet and lands on her hands and knees on the ground. I don't get to laugh for very long because soon he's spinning me until my squeals die and my insides hurt from laughing.

Nobody else matters then. It doesn't matter that people here don't like me. When the music plays and people dance, it all fades into the background. And then, in my seemingly endless spin, I trip over my own feet and bump into someone. I gaze up at the culprit, familiar eyes burning into mine.

"Hey, sorry."

Elias puts his hands on my forearms to steady me. "I see that your balance hasn't gotten any better."

"I'll have *you* know I've been training very hard, thank you very much."

"Cassia did mention that." He holds me steady.

"I bet I could take you on now."

"Is that so?"

I swing my fist toward his throat. He catches it before it reaches him, and in one swift movement, twists my arm behind my back and spins me around so that my back is to his chest. With one arm he holds mine securely against my back while the other snakes its way around my throat. My heart stutters to a near stop. "You sure about that?" His breath sends tendrils of anticipation through my body.

"You just wait until you see me take on that obstacle course. Maybe you've met your match."

His hand loosens around my neck and he spins me back

around. His smile is less teasing now, transforming into something soft. He steps closer, fingers trailing my arm, looping around the strap of my dress. "Maybe I have."

He's so close it makes my head spin. After days of not seeing him, playing his words over and over in my mind, it doesn't feel real to stand in front of him right now, to have a night that's so perfect when my life is so filled with chaos. A bloodcurdling scream fills the air and the hum of energy abruptly halts. The music cuts off and silence spreads over the villagers as the joy and euphoria that filled the air immediately evaporate. Elias wraps a hand around my arm and pushes me behind him. He faces the forest, shoulders rigid, head held high. The village holds a collective breath, our eyes on the forest.

Eric and Cassia appear beside him, standing a fraction ahead of me.

"Get ready to shift!" Cassia yells.

Someone emerges from the tree line, gasping. Elias steps forward, giving me a proper view of the man stumbling toward us. He wears dark clothes but his pale skin, peeking out from underneath his sleeves, is stained red. "Smithe." Elias puts a hand on Smithe's shoulder. "What happened?"

Smithe gasps, resting his hands on his knees as he tries to catch his breath. "*Hollowers.*" The crowd vibrates and Elias's eyes fall on me. "It was a small group, maybe six or seven. I killed most of them but two of them got away, and they took Nella with them."

Beside me, an older woman hobbles forward. "Was she alive? Was Nella alive?"

"She was alive when they took her but she wasn't conscious." The woman is silent, her face falling as someone comes up behind her and wraps their arm over her shoulders. My insides tighten with guilt as they lead her away. "Why are they out at night?" Smithe's voice cracks. "Why are they risking it? Why'd they take Nella instead of killing her on the spot?"

Because of me.

Concern etches Elias's face as he exchanges glances with Eric. My head spins, the world unsteady beneath my feet. The voices start around me again as I meet Harrison's stare, in among the others. He glares, eyes sending a clear message.

It's all because of me.

"Everyone, go home. Those of you who live beyond the forest, we'll house you in the dining hall in the castle. I don't want anybody to leave the village until it's safe." Elias turns to Smithe. "Where did the rest of the guards go?"

"They went after the hollowers, to get Nella back."

Cassia and Eric disperse the crowd, ushering everyone back. Somebody grips my arm. I turn to find Bastian. "Are you all right?" I nod, slightly shaken. "Come with me and Aliyah. Cassia will be busy for a while." I let him pull me through the chaos, the night air filled with shouts as people rush to get back to their homes. Aliyah leads the way through the crowds of people.

The streets, while lit with lanterns, feel dark and sinister as we move away from the others. Shadows lurk at the edges of the forest, waiting to snatch unsuspecting victims. I shiver, grateful when after a few minutes we reach a small wood cabin. Bastian ushers us in, moving to start a fire as Aliyah slumps down at the table and stares blankly at the wall. The room is cluttered with books and pieces of paper scattered over the floor, and the bed in the corner is covered with mismatched articles of clothing.

"Do you want anything to drink?" Bastian asks once he's lit the fire.

I follow him to the kitchen bench and glance back at Aliyah. "Is she okay?"

"She and Nella are good friends." He reaches for a pot and fills it with water before grabbing three mugs from the cupboard above his head. "Tea?"

"You sit down, I'll make it." He opens his mouth to protest but I shake my head. "Really, I mean it."

I pull the pot of water over to the fire and place it on top, my hands burning from the flames. How many of Elias's people have been affected by the hollowers since I've been here? Did they have attacks like this before I came? My mind races with guilt. I know what I should do, that I should leave the castle without telling anyone. And maybe if I was brave, I would.

But my heart begs me to stay. The small feeling of belonging I get when I'm laughing with Cassia or talking to Elias keeps me rooted here—a deep desire from within that just wants somewhere to fit in. But the longer I stay here the more innocent people are going to die, and yet fear kills all logic. It paralyzes me, keeps me in place, and like a coward, I keep my mouth shut and shove down the guilt.

Pathetic.

"Milena?"

I jump at the sound of Bastian's voice. "Huh?"

"The water has boiled."

"Oh." Embarrassed, I take it off the fire and distribute it into the mugs. "Right, sorry."

I bring the mugs to the table and place them in front of Bastian and Aliyah, staring at the one in front of me. The thought of drinking or eating anything makes me nauseated, so we just sit in silence as steam spirals in the air between us.

I swallow and shift in my seat. "Maybe I should get back."

"No." Aliyah's voice is barely a whisper. "Stay. It's not safe for anyone out there alone." Silence stretches on. I wish I was anywhere but here, having to witness the painful consequences my presence has had on the people in this village. "Why would they come out at night? They would have known they would likely die. Do they not value their lives?"

"They want me."

"Don't try to pin this on yourself, Milena," Bastian says. "Cassia explained the situation. It's not your fault they're delusional."

Before I can protest, there's a knock on the door. Aliyah and Bastian exchange glances and Bastian gets up and opens it, revealing Elias. "Is Milena here?" he asks.

I step around the corner so he can see me. "I'm here."

"Come on. I'll take you back to the castle."

He doesn't have to ask twice. I stride toward him, desperate to escape the tension, and match his pace, walking beside him. The emptiness of the streets fills me with an eerie feeling.

"Do you think they took her for the sacrifice?" I ask. "Nella, I mean."

"Maybe. The other guards followed so it's likely they'll get her back like we did Eric."

I ponder his words. Would they really have killed Eric that night? Wouldn't it have been better for them to use him for the sacrifice seeing as it was so close to my birthday? I never really thought about it, but catching a shifter must be much harder than catching a human.

"What *was* Eric doing there, anyway?" I ask. "Why did he go into the tunnels? We'd never had a break-in like that before."

"He didn't go into the tunnels," he says. "They set a trap to catch him. For the ceremony, I assume."

"As sorry as I am for what they did to him, I don't think I'd be alive if he wasn't caught."

"You wouldn't be," he says, voice low.

At the castle, Elias steps ahead and pulls the doors open for me. "What now?" I ask, stepping into the foyer.

"I have to organize more search parties to go after the guards."

"Well, thanks for walking me back."

He smiles and steps past me, heading for the staircase. "I'll walk you to your room."

Honestly, the last thing I want to do is to go to sleep. But I don't bother offering to go with Elias because I know my presence would likely cause more turmoil. The guards don't want to see me, especially if Harrison has already filled their minds with stories about me.

"Did you enjoy tonight?" Elias asks as we walk the maze of halls.

"I liked dancing. It reminded me of home. Or what I thought of as home, anyway."

"You seem happy when you talk about that place." Elias looks down at me, his expression strange. "Were they kind to you?"

"Most of them were indifferent. The younger ones were always nicer, but after they went on their first hunts, they didn't want to associate with me anymore. I always thought it was because they thought they were better than me, but Darius said it's because that's when they learned the truth about me."

"That you weren't like them?"

"I guess."

"That doesn't seem like a valid enough reason to go from liking you to hating you."

"Maybe Charles told them about the sacrifice too. He can be very persuasive, and our people basically worship him. Despite everything, he's a good leader." We reach my bedroom door. I wish Elias didn't have to leave, that we could go to the library and talk for hours.

"Did they hurt you?"

I shake my head. "Charles was never loving, but he never physically harmed me. He had to at least pretend to tolerate me, I guess."

"That must've been lonely."

"I never knew any different. It wasn't so bad."

"I'm sorry, Milena. I'm sorry you had to live through that."

His words make me hold my breath. There's always been something intense about him, and this is no exception. It feels like he carries the burdens of all wrongdoing on his shoulders, like it's his fault. "You don't have to apologize for the way they treated me."

He turns away, his jaw clenching. "What about your friend? You mentioned her before—Flo? You had friends, right?"

"Flo is . . . she *was* my best friend. We got on so well, we did everything together and there was never one moment that I felt she wasn't being genuine. I just . . . I don't understand her." My voice cracks. "Of everything that has happened, that hurts the most. Sometimes I wonder, maybe she didn't know, maybe she did care about me like I cared about her." I tuck a strand of my hair behind my ear self-consciously. "I know it sounds stupid."

"It doesn't. You didn't deserve that. You shouldn't have lived like that."

My back presses against the door. I don't want him to leave and I don't want this conversation to end, but I know he has much more important things to do than stand here talking to me. And yet, he stays. "What about you?" I ask. "Your childhood with Ana, did you have many friends?"

"It's not all that interesting. You don't want to know about all of that."

"Yeah, I do."

He sighs. "It was mostly just me and Eric."

"Eric?"

"Back when all the elders lived up there, there were more kids. But he was the only kid I hung around much."

"What a joyful companion he must've been."

"He's not all bad, Milena." He laughs.

"I know. He's looking out for those he cares about. I just happen to not be one of those people."

Elias leans forward, his hand on the door frame. "Don't concern yourself over that."

"I don't."

The air between us buzzes with that same magnetic tension, urging me closer. A comfortable silence falls over us, his warmth wrapping around me like a blanket. Despite the events of the night, Elias still fills my head like nothing else, filling me with a sense of security, and I know I'm not the only one. The villagers orbit around him like he's their sun. "Do you miss the mountains?" I ask, voice low. "Where you grew up?"

"I miss the summer. There's a lake up there we used to swim in. Maybe I can show you sometime, when this is all over."

"I never learned how to swim."

He leans his arm against the door frame, dangerously close. "I can show you that too." In this hall, it feels like we're the only two people in the world. The outside pressures seem minuscule, trying and failing to penetrate the walls. I can almost forget the events of tonight, or the constant fear in the pit of my stomach, but a shout wafts from the foyer and snaps us from our daze.

Elias sighs and takes a step back. "I should go."

"Of course," I say. "Maybe tomorrow I can help you go through some of Ana's books to see if there's anything that might help us. Maybe you won't have to go see the other elders."

"Milena." He considers his next words carefully. "There's something I need to talk to you about. I'll come to see you later."

"Okay," I say, trying to mask my excitement. And as I watch him leave, I have to convince myself it would be a bad idea to follow.

~

After he leaves, sleep is the last thing on my mind. My body buzzes and I can't stop fidgeting. So, I make my way down to the empty training center and let my energy loose on the endurance course. The more I do it, the easier it becomes. Repeating the movements over and over, I wonder if Elias is going to come at all. And then Eric appears, passing along the message that Elias has decided to go to sleep and wants me to do the same.

I can't help but feel disappointed as I wander back to my bedroom. Elias said he wanted to talk to me, and it had sounded important. My arms and legs ache from my training over the past few days, but I'm wide awake still, and the thought of seeing

Elias certainly played a part in that. I stroll down the halls, running my finger along the stone walls as I climb the staircase and pass the slightly ajar library door. There is a shuffle of feet.

Elias is hunched over the table next to the fire, a collection of books spread out on the wood in front of him as he brushes his pencil across the pages. I know that I should turn around, that I should walk away before he sees me, but instead, I stand in the doorway and try to ignore the pressing weight of betrayal that has settled atop my chest. He doesn't owe me anything, and yet, the fact that he got Eric to lie for him so he wouldn't have to see me stings more than it should. I take a step back but the floor creaks beneath my feet before I can escape.

"Milena?" I freeze when his eyes flash to me. "Didn't Eric talk to you?"

"He told me you'd gone to sleep." He shifts at the desk so that his hand covers the book in front of him. "You said you wanted to talk to me."

"I thought you could use some sleep."

I try to read his face but it's indecipherable. "What did you want to talk to me about?"

"It's nothing."

"It didn't sound like nothing before. What're you reading?" I move closer, trying to get a glance at the books in front of him.

"Milena—"

"You said I didn't have to sit around doing nothing, and I'm grateful you're letting me train and learn to read and not have to work as hard as I did at home," I say. "But none of that matters when I still don't know why the hollowers want me."

He looks pained. "I know."

"You promised you wouldn't keep things from me, so don't."

He doesn't respond at first, and it makes me want to scream. A few hours ago, I could've sworn he felt the same pull that I did. The way he stared at me made me feel like we were the only two people in the world. Now, though, he's apart from me, staring at me like he did all those nights ago when he brutally shut down my line of questioning.

Useless filler, he'd called it. *You don't need to know me and I don't need to know you.*

This confusion is so frustrating, and these mixed signals almost make me turn right around and leave, but curiosity forces me to persist. I close in. "What are you reading?"

I don't look at him as I lean over the books strewn across the desk, squinting to see what is scribbled beneath his arm. "I'm not *reading* anything," he says eventually. When I realize what he means, my heart drops to the pit of my stomach. The books aren't written by Ana, they're books *of* Ana—pages and pages of sketches of her.

"I'm sorry." I bury my face in my hands and groan. "I shouldn't have jumped to conclusions."

He pulls my arm away from my face. "Don't apologize."

I look at the drawings again. "You're really good at that, you know."

"Ana taught me before she passed."

He mindlessly flips through the pages. I'm both confused and disturbed by how casually he refers to Ana's brutal murder. She raised him, yet I feel like her death has affected me more than it has him. "She was beautiful," I say as he pauses on a drawing of Ana and another couple laughing. "What was she like as a parent?"

The shadows in the room make his eyes seem almost brown

when he looks at me. "The same as any. She taught me all I needed to know."

"Did she love you?"

"She took me in when I had nobody else."

I know from experience that taking someone in means nothing in terms of love. "What about your parents? Your biological ones?" He shifts uncomfortably at my question. "You don't have to say if—"

"My mother killed my father."

"That's awful. I'm sorry."

To my surprise, his lips rise at the edges. "You're not the only one with a messed-up family life."

I look out the window. The village looks like a ghost town, the streets between cabins deserted. Compared to the usual liveliness at night, it feels wrong.

"This is them," Elias says. He pauses on a page with three people: a smiling couple and a baby held in the woman's arms. But the drawing cuts off just before their feet. "Ana drew it, one for her and one for my parents. I don't remember much about them, but I remember this moment. My mum was so annoyed because I wouldn't sit still long enough for Ana to complete the second drawing. That's why this one is half finished."

"They look really nice."

"Ana said she was a really good mother."

"But she killed your father."

"It was an accident."

"An accident?"

"Yes." The fire is dying down, the charred wood chalky black. "It's getting late. You should get to sleep." I wait for him to elaborate but he doesn't make any effort to. He stands up from the table and collects the books.

"I'm sorry. About Ana and your parents."

He doesn't look at me as he places a book back on a shelf. "People always end up suffering because of me."

"Elias, you can't seriously think that." He doesn't say anything, nonchalantly stacking books. "That's not fair."

"Don't worry about me, I'm used to it."

"What? So you just stop caring?" I scoff, taking a step closer. "I don't believe that. I see the way you lead your people; you care about what happens to them."

"I'm their leader. I keep them safe. Caring about them isn't part of the job description."

I put a hand on his arm to halt him when he moves past me. "And what about Cassia and Eric? You expect me to believe you don't care about them either?"

"You can believe what you want."

"You care about what happens to them and they care about you." There are only inches between us now. "Is that really so bad?" He shakes free of my arm as he turns to extinguish the fire. "And Ana, you cared about her. And you care about what will happen to Nella, and all the others the hollowers have killed." He continues to ignore me while I stand there blabbering away like an idiot, the voices of insecurity warning me to stop talking as the fire hisses and dies. "You have nothing to say?"

His eyes meet mine, cold and hard. "Go to bed, Milena."

One part of me wants to listen, to run to my room with my tail between my legs and bury my face in my pillow in shame. But the other part of me replays the past few days. It reminds me of the way he stared down at me during the bonfire, of his light and warmth.

"I care about you too."

He freezes. He turns and looks back at me. "You shouldn't."

"But I do." I take hesitant steps toward him, afraid he'll turn and walk the other way. His face is devoid of emotion. It's so different from what I saw at the bonfire, even different from the past few days. It's the expression he wore the first few days I knew him. But I don't back down, because in the midst of all this chaos, Elias is the only one who makes me feel like I can breathe. With the hollowers coming after me, murdering shifters every chance they get, I have nothing to lose. I reach him and put my hand on his arm, searching his eyes. "And I think you might care about me too."

Flecks of amber ignite in his eyes. He's silent, his body rigid in place as he towers over me and stares. It takes everything within me not to step away and cower in a corner.

"I care about you, Elias."

"Milena, you can't." His voice is low, husky. He steps back so that my hand falls between us.

"Why not?" He has nowhere to go, his back to the bookshelf behind him as I inch closer. He grips my forearms but I can't tell if he's trying to pull me closer or push me away. His eyes blaze, our noses touch, and his hands drop to my lower back.

"Why do you push everyone away?"

"*Milena—*"

"Tell me you don't feel it."

He doesn't. His face dips closer. My eyes flutter shut when his lips brush against mine. A burning sensation spreads from my lower back, where his fingers touch my skin, to my chest. He's so gentle, but the mere grazing of lips is enough to set my stomach on fire. I want to wrap my arms around his shoulders; I want him to hold me to him like he did that night with Darius, but before I can even fathom what's happening, Elias spins us so that my back is against the bookshelf and he's a few feet away, not touching me.

His eyes are a hundred shades of a storm, a roaring blaze ready to be unleashed. "You're wrong."

"What?"

He leans forward, his body close but eyes so far away. "I don't feel *anything* for you." He's gone from the room before I can blink.

CHAPTER TWELVE

I wake up to a pair of silver eyes and white hair in my face. "What in the world are you doing sleeping in the training room?" Cassia asks. I shoot up so fast we bump foreheads. She steps back with a groan and I rub my throbbing head as memories of last night sift through my mind.

After Elias left me humiliated in the library, I stormed back to the training center and tried to do anything to distract myself from what had happened. As a consequence, my body now aches, and cuts and scratches litter my arms from badly handled daggers. If I stopped moving, thoughts of Elias crept in and made me want to hide in a corner.

"Milena?"

"What time is it?"

"Early morning." She frowns and looks around the room at

the various mannequins with knives in their chests. "How long have you been here?"

"I must've fallen asleep here last night."

"Have you seen Elias?"

My eyes sting but I blink back tears. I refuse to cry over what happened. "No."

"You were with him last night—"

"I said I haven't seen him, Cassia. Just leave me alone." She takes a step back, her eyes flashing hurt. "Cassia, wait, I'm sorry. I'm just—"

"Tired, I get it. I wanted to invite you to lunch with me and Bastian, but I can see that you'd rather be alone."

"Cassia, wait." But she's already storming up the staircase, leaving me with my thoughts in the cold and dark training center. I follow her, burying my hands in my hair in frustration as unwanted thoughts creep back into my mind. To my complete horror, I run into Eric and Aliyah in the hallway.

"Milena!" Aliyah calls. I force a smile before turning to continue upstairs. "Where are you off to in such a hurry?"

"I was just going to have lunch in my room."

"Don't be silly, come with us."

I look at Eric. "I don't know if—"

"Come on." She ushers me to the door. "We're going to be late."

The village looks different in the daylight, the sun beating harshly on the stoned path. Aliyah pulls me toward multiple circular tables lined up just outside the castle, platters of food placed in the center of each.

"What's all this?" I ask as she has me sit beside her.

"Elias organized it. It's sort of a continuation of last night's celebration, since it was cut short." I glance around at all the people taking seats. They embrace one another and offer each other warm, comforting smiles. The smell of food rises in the air, but it only serves to make me feel nauseated. "Do you want soup?"

"Sure. Thanks." Elias stands on the other side of the clearing. I avert my eyes to the bowl in front of me, my cheeks burning with humiliation. Cassia sits at another table with Bastian, but she doesn't look at me. I don't know if she doesn't see me or if she's intentionally ignoring me, but it only makes the guilt expand.

The air in the village is filled with chatter as people share food and smiles in the aftermath of last night's chaos. Aliyah tries to make conversation with me but I can only manage one-word answers. The fleeting comfort immediately evaporates when the tree line begins to rustle. I tense in my seat, looking at the trees as chatter turns to silence. Four men appear dressed in the same clothes Smithe had worn last night, all torn and covered in dirt. But it's the body draped over the man at the front's shoulder that causes me to shudder.

Aliyah slaps a hand over her mouth as people stand from their tables. When the group reaches us, the man gently lays the body on the ground in front of Elias. It's a woman with fiery red hair fanning around her, and skin stained red. Nobody breathes a word as the older woman from last night stumbles through the tables and stares in silence at the body on the ground. "*Nella.*"

"We didn't get to her in time." The man who was carrying her lowers his head. "They left her hanging in the forest. They—they carved into her skin." He kneels down to lift her shirt. Bile rises in my throat at the marred sight of her skin, the bloodied marks all curved into the shape of the letter *C*.

C *for Charles.*

The older woman falls to her knees, her body collapsing as her haunting wails fill the air. "*My Nella.*"

"Why now?" the guard asks. "Why all this torture?"

From the crowd, Harrison steps forward and looks at me. "Because we're keeping—"

"Harrison." Elias's voice is low, a warning that makes my stomach flip in fear.

Harrison snarls. "This is a democracy. That means we should get a choice in what happens around here." People listening begin to nod. "It means we should get a choice in whether or not *she* stays here."

People turn and look at me with tears in their eyes and murder written on their faces. I hold my chin high and clench my fists so they can't see me shake. But I can't stop my eyes from watering. "We offer refuge to all humans, Harrison," Elias says. "We always have and we always will."

"At the expense of our own people? At the expense of our children's lives?" Harrison raises his fist in the air and some shout in agreement. "When does it stop? Why is her life valued above the lives of so many others?" Harrison's expression is terrifyingly calm as he meets my gaze. "I think someone has overstayed their welcome."

Elias steps forward but I don't give him a chance to reach me—I turn and race toward the castle. My mind screams as I shove the wooden doors open and head upstairs, stumbling over the uneven surface and scraping my knees. When I burst into my bedroom, I head right to the closet. The people here hate me, and they have every right to—people are dying *because* of me. And Charles will never stop.

"What're you doing?" I jump. Eric stands in the doorway. He

watches me as I fumble through the closet, tugging out coats and shoving them into the backpack Cassia left.

"What does it look like?" I snap. "I'm leaving."

I need to get to the training center and then the dining hall—I need a weapon, food, and something to carry water in. My mind races but I try my hardest to organize my thoughts into coherent ideas.

"All because of some rumors?" Eric says.

It's the death, it's the rumors, it's the rejection. I can't stand being here any longer. I can't stand being ostracized, I can't stand being around Elias, I can't stand being the reason for people's unhappiness. I need answers.

"Leave me alone, Eric."

"Or is it because Elias rejected you?" he says. I glare at him as my cheeks begin to burn. I thought Elias's rejection couldn't sting any more than it already did, but I was wrong. "If so, you're more pathetic than I thought."

"Why do *you* care? You've wanted me gone from the moment I got here."

"You can't leave."

"You can't stop me."

"You're being stupid." He steps in front of the door, blocking my exit. "You stab a kid once and suddenly think you can take on an army of hollowers?"

"What is *wrong* with you? You're nothing but cruel to me, begging me to leave, but when I try to actually go, you threaten to stop me?"

"Where are you going to go?" he asks.

I don't know. I have nowhere to go; I have no one to go to. The only person I trust anymore is Cassia, but her kindness isn't enough for me to justify staying here when each day someone new dies and being around Elias stings even more. I can't be here anymore; it isn't good for anybody—not even me. "*Away.*" I sit on the backpack to try and zip it up. "Away from here."

"And what are you going to eat, huh? How are you going to look after yourself?"

I try to think of anything I might be forgetting. Aside from getting a weapon, food, and water, there's nothing else from this place I need to bring. Taking a deep breath, I sling the backpack over my shoulder. But when I try to get past Eric, he doesn't move. My memory flashes, remembering Eric tied to that pole, Charles stabbing a stick into his chest as Eric roared in agony. The shot Darius gave him. How we drugged and tortured him. And still, he's standing here, defending me, wanting to keep me safe. "Eric, move."

"No."

I shove him with my shoulder. He's only a fraction taller than me, so we're nearly eye to eye. "*Move.*"

"You're not going through this door." Tears of frustration prick at my eyes. I hit his chest so hard my fist aches. He doesn't care; doesn't even flinch.

"Eric. . . . *Please.* I can't be here anymore."

"Not everything is about you, Milena. Toughen up."

"This *is* about me and that's the damn problem! Everything keeps happening because of me, and the only way I can stop it is to get the hell out of here. That's what you want, isn't it? For this to stop. Isn't that what you all want?"

He clenches his jaw. "You're not leaving, Milena."

I glare at him, anger burning inside me. Eric isn't tall, but he's solid and can shift into an animal, whereas I'm nothing but a human with a week's training. There's no way I'm getting past him. "Or what? Are you going to physically restrain me? Chain me to the castle so that I can't leave?"

"Unlike the hollowers, we're not barbarians."

"You've got nothing but your words then. And you call me pathetic."

He snarls. "You're not leaving through this door."

Raising my chin, I step toward him, so close that I barely have to speak above a whisper for him to hear me. He's completely unintimidated by me. But I don't care; I wrap my hand around the door handle and get right in his face. "Then leave me the *hell* alone."

I step back and slam the door with as much force as I can muster. Eric doesn't try to open it, but I'm not foolish enough to believe he would just leave it unguarded. When I try the window, it doesn't budge, the lock on the hinge still rigid from the last time I tried to escape. I go to the bathroom, snatch the soap holder off the basin, and throw it at the window, shattering the glass all over the floor.

Slinging the backpack over my shoulders again, I clamber out the window and carefully use the uneven stones in the wall to climb down. A reckless idea, but I don't have enough time to create some sort of rope. The sky is still bright though the sun retreats behind the hills. I have hours before it disappears altogether, and though my natural instinct is to hide from the night, I know now that it's my very best friend.

Making my way around the side of the castle, I reach the entrance and wind down the staircase to the training center, freezing in the doorway when I see the figure perched by the wall. Cassia stands against the endurance course with a book in her hands. She looks at me before I can escape.

"Milena? What're you doing?"

"I'm leaving."

"*What?*" She drops her book. "Where?"

"I need to see Charles. I need to talk to him."

"He won't talk to you, Milena. He'll kill you."

I stare at the weapons lining the wall and reach for the dagger— the only one I know how to actually use. Cassia puts her hand over mine. "Stop, think about this for a few moments. You're being impulsive."

"I've been thinking about it ever since those children died."

"That wasn't your fault."

I march over to the weapons on the wall. "Maybe I didn't kill them, but they'd be alive if it wasn't for me. So would Ana, and so would Nella."

"That's not—"

"What would you do?" I turn to face her, a dagger in hand. "What would you do, Cassia? If you were me, if people kept dying because of you, if someone was after you and they kept killing your friends until they had you, what would *you* do?"

"That isn't—"

"What would you *do*?"

Her eyes meet mine. "I'd give myself to them."

"Exactly. You can't stop me from doing the same."

"Does Elias know?"

"That doesn't matter." I turn and head back up the staircase, taking them two at a time and barging out of the entrance to reach the forest. A shiver trills through me, the daylight warning me to turn around. Swallowing my fear, I press on, ducking my head to avoid branches.

"I hope you have some sort of plan because I really value

GRACE COLLINS

my life." I nearly fall face first into a tree, spinning around to find Cassia staring at me with amusement. She holds two large knives, similar to the ones Charles held against my throat that day in the forest. "I can't stop you from leaving and you can't stop me from coming, so don't even try."

And even though I know it's selfish, I don't. I try to convince myself that it's because I know that I can't stop her and that if she gets hurt, it won't be my fault. But deep down, I know that isn't true. Despite the deaths, the ostracism, and Elias, the selfish seed inside of me wants to stay and hide in that lavish room forever. But with Cassia by my side, facing Charles doesn't seem so scary.

~

A frigid wind trails after us through the forest. The air bites at the exposed skin of my wrists. Cassia's a silver flash in front of me, all animal. Though walking with her while she's a wolf is a lot lonelier, it's safer for us both as her senses are heightened.

As soon as the sun disappeared, she told me to turn around. When I faced her again, a silver wolf stood in her place, her weapons on the ground. I scooped the knives up, shaking as I remembered the way the creatures closed in on me as I lay in front of the kitchen shack that night in my village. The night I met Elias.

We walk for hours. My feet ache and my knees tremble but I don't stop. The silence gives my mind room to scream, to run over scenarios in my mind, to play out situations that keep ending with my blood draining from my chest and painting the forest floor. I don't even realize how much time has passed until the sky begins to lighten again and birdsong bounces off the trees. My stomach rumbles but I push on until the sun rises and Cassia pauses.

"How do you feel?" Cassia asks.

I stop moving and Cassia crouches low to the ground. She's been talking in my head now and then, telling me to walk quieter, to go more to the left or to stop walking altogether. This time, however, her tone is wary. "I'm okay. You?"

"I'm starving. Hold on."

She walks behind a tree and seconds later comes back as human, her clothes rumpled and dirty. She grins as she fixes her hair. "I tried to stay that way as long as I was able but that sun is really getting to me."

"It's all right. Maybe we should take a break, anyway. I could really use something to eat."

"Good idea." She walks over to me and takes the knife from my hands. "I'll be back in a moment."

"Where are you going?"

"To get breakfast."

While she's gone, I gather some sticks, figuring whatever she's going to bring back is going to need to be cooked. When Cassia returns, she's holding two dead rabbits. I don't hesitate. Working in the kitchens meant that I skinned and cooked a lot of the animals that the hunters brought back. The first time Charles brought a bunch of dead rabbits back, I fainted. After a couple of months, skinning animals became as mindless a task as peeling potatoes. Cassia helps me prepare them and then moves over to the flames. She stabs her rabbit through a stick and then holds it over the fire, and I do the same.

"How long should we wait?" I ask as the fire spits between us.

"It's not exactly safe during the day, but there isn't anywhere for us to stop and rest."

"We should put the fire out as soon as possible. The hollowers could see the smoke."

"Does that really matter? We're going toward them anyway. Speaking of which, what's the plan?"

"It's not very elaborate."

"Fantastic."

"I know that I want to talk to Charles, but I'm not sure how. I don't exactly want to give myself over to him, but I need answers."

"So you'll come back to the castle afterward?"

"No," I say darkly. "I'm not going back there. He'll keep killing people. It isn't fair."

She takes a bite of her rabbit and licks her lips. "You think you'll just waltz in, talk to him, and then he'll let you go?"

"He won't let me go. But I've been thinking . . . I know he seems like an awful person to you, but if I can somehow get someone from the village and hold them hostage, there's a good chance he'll talk to me without trying to kill me."

She tears a leg from the rabbit and hums in thought. "You're sure he won't just let you kill them?"

"If there's one thing he loves more than plotting against me, it's protecting his people and making life better for them."

"Don't you think he would've protected you, then?"

"Not if killing me benefits his people. Besides, he was always distant with me. I never understood why he was so neglectful, but now it makes sense—he never saw me as one of them."

"Okay, so what do you want to do?"

"Do you think you can get me to the village? We'll take the first person we see."

"And if he doesn't care? Kill the hostage?"

"No." I wrap my arms around my body, the chill in the air creeping beneath my skin. "I won't kill anyone, not again. If something goes wrong, you have to leave me." She scoffs. "I'm serious, Cassia. I don't want you caught up in this mess because of me."

She stays silent and stares at the ground, digging her stick into the dirt. "Elias won't be happy with me if I come back without you."

I tense at the mention of him and stare past her head. "Elias doesn't care about me, he only cares about what it could mean for his people."

"You're joking, right?" she says. I turn around and busy myself stamping out the fire, trying to ignore my hurt. Cassia doesn't move to help.

"I saw you guys at the First Run, you know." She shifts slightly. "You were like . . . I don't know, pressed against one another or something."

Blood rushes to my cheeks. "It was nothing."

"You don't expect me to believe that, do you?" She shakes her head. "He's different with you."

"He's not."

"He is. I've known Elias for a long time, I would know." The air is so cold it hurts to breathe. The reminder of Elias's rejection stabs like a knife in my heart. "And I won't leave you, Milena. I won't let them kill you, and if everything goes accordingly and we leave in one piece, I won't let you go off on your own. There are so many hollower colonies in this area, it isn't safe for you."

"What does that have to do with Elias?" I say, irritated.

"It would hurt him, too, if something were to happen to you. He deserves to be happy after everything he's been through, and you make him happier," she says.

I wish I could believe her. She speaks with such conviction and confidence, but I can't forget what Elias said in the library. And hearing Cassia talk about him this way, with such passion and devotion, makes me ache for a relationship like theirs. For someone who'd do anything to ensure my happiness like Cassia and Eric would for Elias.

The irritation I feel fizzles out. "You really care about him."

"Because he's *good*, Milena. And he only ever seems to suffer." She casts the rabbit bones aside before turning to face me. "But you're my friend too. And I promise you, I won't go back to Elias unless you're with me."

You're my friend. Her words echo in my mind, making my eyes water, but I look away.

There's no point arguing with her. She has made up her mind just as I have made up mine. I can't go back to the castle, not when Charles kills innocents, not when the villagers hate me, not when Elias doesn't want me. I don't belong there and I won't overstay my welcome. So, as we pack up our things and cover the embers from the fire, I promise myself that if it comes down to it, I'll make the decision that she won't.

~

We walk for hours, until the sky turns dark. The last time I made this journey, running on fear and adrenaline, I hadn't realized how far it was or how long it took. Cassia shifts into her wolf form the second the sun disappears, leaving me alone again with my thoughts. The closer we get to my village the higher my anxiety climbs.

I know my plan is the only way this could potentially go right, but it's already so weak that with every step we take, the knot of dread in me grows. Because deep down, I fear that I'm not strong enough. Not strong enough to follow through if the first villager is Flo, not strong enough to stand tall in front of Charles. What will they think of me, after what I did to Darius? And the thought of something happening to Cassia is nearly enough to make me turn around and walk straight back to the castle.

A few feet ahead, Cassia pauses. "Stop."

My heart drops. I hold my breath as I wait for her to tell me what to do, fingers wrapping around the hilt of the dagger in its sheath. Cassia's eyes turn to me, wide with alarm. I hardly have time to register our surroundings before red flashes across the clearing and Cassia is pinned up against the tree by a black wolf.

"Cassia!" I pull the dagger from my pocket, reaching for her before the wolf on top of her flashes its eyes at me. I freeze in place. *Red eyes. Eric.* But he's not alone.

Elias appears in front of me and reaches for my arm. "Leaving without saying good-bye?"

"How did you find us?"

"You make it sound like it's hard." I clench my jaw and walk away from him. The sting of his rejection still lingers, but seeing him now, when I'm so close to getting away, only makes me want to leave more. It's another reminder of why I don't belong in his village. "What're you doing?"

"What does it look like?" Leaves crunch beneath my feet as I stomp away from him. "I'm leaving."

I don't know where Cassia and Eric are or if they're even

following us, but the forest doesn't frighten me, not when the one who rules it is right on my tail. "You're not thinking straight," he says. "Just come back and rest. We can talk about it all tomorrow."

"Leave me alone, Elias."

A burning hand wraps around my arm. "Milena—"

"Don't touch me."

"Nella's death isn't your fault."

"That's not true and you know it." Despite the cold that digs at my spine, my cheeks burn. "I can't deal with this anymore, Elias. I can't *be* there anymore. I'm nothing but a burden to your people. The villagers hate me, Charles keeps killing innocents, and you—" I stop myself, the burn from his rejection still hot. "I have to see Charles."

"He'll kill you."

"You don't know that."

"I *do*." He continues forward until I'm pressed up against the tree behind me. "Trust me."

"If he doesn't have me, he's going to keep killing your people. Is that what you want?"

Shadows move across his face, the light of the moon illuminating the scar on his jaw. "Nobody's saying you have to leave."

"They don't have to. They're going to start hating you too. You realize that, right?"

He stays silent. I'm right, and he knows it. His duty is to protect his people, and by keeping me around he's not fulfilling it. Pretty soon, his people will begin to resent him for it. "They trust me to make the right decisions." He takes another step. We're nearly touching yet he feels so far away. "They might not see it now, but they will later."

"See what? That giving me to the hollowers may be more detrimental to you than hiding me from them? Then help me find somewhere to hide, away from your village *and* the hollowers. Because I'm not just some puzzle you can't figure out; I'm a *person*. I have feelings, I can make my own decisions, and I'm not going to stick around a bunch of people who hate me just because it *might* benefit you."

He catches my wrist to keep me from going any farther. "That's not how I see you. I know you're a person. Please come back, Milena, it isn't safe."

"You don't care about me, you just care about what I mean to the hollowers."

"That's not true." He uses his hold on me to pull me closer. "Milena . . . please."

"Let me do this on my own," I say, more a plea than anything else. "I know you have to do what's best for your people, and I know you want to keep them safe, but they don't want me there. The longer I stay, the more people are going to die. We're getting nowhere with the hollowers and I can't keep feeling like such a burden to—"

"Milena, wait."

"Let me talk!" I tug against him. Somewhere in the distance, a howl spirals through the trees, a reminder that the night is ticking away. "Just let me go, I need to—"

"Stay because I want you to." He steps closer and the forest fades into the background; all I see is him. "I *want* you to stay. Not because of the hollowers, and not because I should protect you but because . . ."

"Because what?"

He brushes the inside of my wrist. "Because I care about you."

All the energy in my body focuses on him, my mind racing. "I care about you, Milena. I feel it too."

I falter. "You're only saying that so I'll stay."

"I'm not. I wouldn't do that."

"You said you didn't feel—"

"I lied to you." He reaches out to caress my cheek, his calloused fingers rough against my skin. "It's not in your head, Milena, I want you too."

"*Why?* Why did you lie?"

"There's a lot I've kept from you—who I am, things I've done. Things that might make you hate me. And I want to protect you. After everything you went through . . ."

"We've all done bad things." Darius trips through my mind, the feeling of his blood as it seeped into my skin. "That doesn't make you a bad person."

He smiles sadly as he brushes some hair from my forehead. "You don't know how hard it is. To have you so close but so far away—someone I want but can never have."

The stars are completely insignificant compared to his eyes. I feel feverish as I stare at him, my skin hot as he holds my face. I press my palm to his cheek. "I'm right here."

"You don't understand."

"Then explain it to me."

"Don't leave," he pleads. "I'll forbid anyone from leaving the village—the hollowers won't risk coming in, people will be safe. You don't have to leave. You belong there."

"You once told me some of us weren't meant to belong."

"I wasn't talking about you."

I make a fist in his shirt to pull him closer and I can feel his breath on my lips. Our eyes meet, and it's like he can see right through me—every thought I've ever had, every fear, every desire. And the vulnerability that accompanies it is strangely comforting. "Stay," he breathes. His lips touch mine as I lean my head against the tree. "Promise me you won't run."

I don't know if I'm in my right mind; I don't know if his confession is clouding my better judgment, all I know is that Elias feels the same way about me that I do him and I never want that feeling to go away. "I promise."

The world melts away when he kisses me. Nothing matters anymore—his initial rejection, Charles's plan to kill me, the betrayals of Flo and Darius—it all evaporates and now there's only Elias and me. And with my face cradled in his hands and his lips pressed against mine, I've never felt so at home. My arms tangle around his neck, our bodies molded against one another. His touch sears my skin. Energy pulses between us. I can't breathe, but this time I don't care.

"*Elias!*"

Suddenly he flies across the clearing, away from me.

I try to catch my breath as I wait for the burning to fizzle out, but it never does. My heart stutters—the air around me burns hot and gold. Flames wind their way up my legs, gasping for oxygen and singeing the bottom of my pants. I scream as a force throws me across the clearing, the breath knocked from my chest when I land on my back, Eric hovering over me. Almost as quickly as he launched me across the clearing, he rolls off me enough so that I can scramble backward.

Smoke fills my nostrils. Cassia stands with her jaw wide open, her hands hanging limp at her sides. Fire spirals into the sky. The spot where I'd been standing is engulfed in flames, but the tree isn't what's burning. Elias stands in the middle of a flame spiraling high into the sky, his clothes ash at his feet but his skin glowing gold, completely unscathed.

"You're a—but that's . . ." Cassia is the only one who can speak. She stumbles toward Elias. "*How?*"

Elias stares at me. It isn't hard to read the horror in his eyes. Dots connect in my mind as the blazing fire separates us: Elias doesn't shift, he's more powerful than other shifters, he's private and filled with secrets. Elias is a *wisper*.

Cassia reaches toward his shoulder and she leaps back with a hiss of pain.

"Don't touch me." He closes his eyes and puts his hands in front of him. "You can't touch me right now."

Eric marches toward Cassia and pulls her back. She's so caught off guard she stumbles and falls over. "You need to leave, Elias," Eric says. "Now."

Elias's eyes land on me. "Milena . . ."

"I can deal with it." Eric steps in front of him so that I can't see him anymore. "*Go.*"

Elias doesn't need to be told a third time; he flees from the clearing. I rub at my ankles where the fire licked my skin. Eric takes his jacket off and throws it over the flames still lingering in the clearing.

"You *knew*?" Cassia asks.

He ignores her, making sure to stamp out the remainder of the flames. "We need to go back to the castle."

"You think I'm going to ignore what just happened?" she scoffs. "Elias is . . . he's a *wisper*. They're *supposed* to be extinct."

"If you care about Elias, you will." Eric marches over to me and pulls me to my feet. "Are you hurt? Did the fire burn you?" My throat is dry. I stare at him dumbly. "*Milena.*"

"I'm okay. He just . . . Elias . . ."

"Drop it." The forest around us is still, a coldness seeping into the air with the departure of the flames. But my blood still burns beneath my skin.

"Elias is a wisper. He nearly lit me on fire."

"Come on," Eric says, "we're going back to the castle."

His words snap me out of my trance, and I retreat into the darkness, remembering how I got into this situation in the first place. I was supposed to be leaving. With Elias gone, I have more clarity. His presence was intoxicating—he clouded my judgment. "Wait."

Eric glares. "Don't make this difficult."

"This doesn't change anything." The conviction in my words isn't there, my desire to leave as weak as my body. "The hollowers are still going to kill your people. If I come back, I want it to be on my own terms."

He raises an eyebrow. "And they are?"

"You have to help me come up with a plan to get Charles alone so I can talk to him. And if the hollowers attack before then and somebody gets hurt, you have to let me leave." I look at Cassia but she's still pacing the clearing, her mind somewhere far away. "Do we have a deal?"

"Fine. But you're going to have to get on my back."

"Are you joking?"

"Does it look like I'm joking?" He scowls. "I don't want it to happen any more than you do, but if I let you walk, we won't get back until tomorrow." I bite my words as he disappears behind a tree, tugging Cassia with him.

Elias wants me just as much as I want him. Elias is a wisper. Elias almost lit me on fire. Despite what I told Eric, this changes *everything.* Nobody knows about him, and it has to stay that way. If Charles found out, if he discovered that the man offering me refuge is the one who could grant him immortality, there's no telling what he might do. I shudder, the forest whispering threats in my ears. The skin at my ankles stings from the fire.

Eric and Cassia wander back to me, both wolves. I swallow nervously as Eric steps toward me, shifting from foot to foot as he pulls his lips back and snarls in annoyance. I awkwardly climb onto his back, burying my hands in his rough fur before taking a deep breath. "Here goes nothing."

He shoots off through the forest before I can even throw my leg over the other side. I tighten my grip and bury my face in his fur as we head back to the very place I just ran from.

CHAPTER THIRTEEN

Nerves creep up my spine as we stand in front of the looming castle, the green vines snaking into the crevices between the stones and choking the towers. The journey back was treacherous; Eric didn't accommodate for me at all, trying to keep up with Cassia, who stormed ahead a few hours into the trip. I'm relieved to be on my own two feet when we reach the castle, but my body still buzzes from the speed at which we traveled.

Inside the foyer, Cassia appears at the top of the staircase leading down to the training center, her cheeks dark, lips twisted into a scowl. She doesn't look at me as she passes, but Eric catches her arm.

"Let go of me, Eric," she hisses and tears her arm away. "I don't want to see you." I watch her stomp through the wooden doors and slam them shut behind her, metal rings rattling in her departure.

"Great," he says. "Just what we needed."

"She's just hurt."

"Wow. Amazing observation."

I choose not to rise to his temper, and instead move toward the staircase Cassia just came from, but Eric puts his hand on my arm.

"What do you think you're doing?" Eric asks.

"I want to talk to Elias. He's down there, isn't he?" Eric doesn't let go of my arm. "Can you let me go? I think I deserve some answers." I turn from him before he can respond and descend the staircase, my insides twisting with nerves as I gently push the door open and step inside the training center. Only one of the lanterns is lit, so it takes me a few seconds to adjust to the darkness. But when I do, I spot Elias. Weapons lie on the floor in front of him. He's midway through putting them back on the wall when he turns.

"Milena?" He straightens up, standing taller. "Cassia said you were coming with Eric, but I was afraid you'd run off."

"You never *did* say how you found us. Cassia said she was covering our tracks."

"I told you,"—the ghost of a smile crosses his face—"I can always find you."

I step into the room, my shoes pattering against the padded floors. "Was Cassia okay?"

"She's hurt I didn't tell her. She thinks it means that I don't trust her." He sighs and reaches around to rub the back of his neck. "I have to ask . . . did I—are you—"

"I'm okay. I'm just shocked."

"I know you must be mad I didn't tell you."

"I'm not. I understand why Cassia is, but I'm not mad. You

don't owe me anything." I pause. "What are your gifts? Is it just the fire?"

"I can also put people to sleep."

The first time I'd met him outside that kitchen shack, the day I tried to escape the castle, the night I held Darius's limp body in my arms—each time consciousness slipped through my fingers when Elias looked at me. "It was you. All those times, it was you?"

He grimaces. "Would you believe me if I said no?"

"It's a relief, actually."

"A relief?"

I lean closer so that our arms touch, and smile. "I kept passing out around you. It definitely wasn't helping me with my show these people you're not weak plan."

"I don't think you're weak."

"Maybe you don't know me, then."

"I know you." He looks at the floor, the scar on his jaw catching in the candlelight dancing on the wall. "When I first saw you, huddled against that crummy building with that hollower, I thought you were stupid. You put your life on the line for a hollower who didn't even care about you. I didn't understand why you would do that, and I pitied you for it. I thought you were all beauty and no brains."

Heat creeps up my neck. It's stupid—his statement was filled with insults—but nobody has called me beautiful before. "In hindsight, it was pretty stupid."

"I understand it now. I understand *you*. You're annoyingly impulsive, but you're not stupid; you're loyal, brave, and compassionate. You would've given your life for that hollower whether or not she deserved it." He pauses, warm fingers tilting my chin so I'm forced to meet his eyes. "You're many things, Milena, but weak isn't one of them."

Blood pounds in my ears as the space between us hums with energy. "I'm sorry for being so impulsive."

"It's your emotions; they control you."

The moment in the library enters my head, when I'd been transparent with him and he'd completely shut down. "Is that such a bad thing?"

"In this world, it certainly won't do you any favors. But it makes you *you,* and I wouldn't change that for anything."

Silence stretches between us, the only sound the creaking of the foundation behind him. His words feed a part of me that lay dormant for so long. The idea that someone could like me for me always seemed out of reach. I never concerned myself with the idea of love. In my village, none of the boys I was interested in would touch me with a ten-foot pole. I quickly got used to being avoided; I learned to shrug it off when people snickered about me in the shadows. But I can't shrug this off.

"I never should have kissed you in the forest."

His words are like a slap to the face. "What?"

"I've done bad things."

"What does that have to do with anything?"

He turns his head to look at me, lips pressed in a firm line. "At first, I thought you were my punishment for all the bad things I've done—someone I want but can never have. But I've made things worse. Now, I'm not the only one being punished."

"I don't care what you are, Elias. You could be a shifter, a wisper, or a human. It doesn't change the way I feel about you."

He turns so that I can't see his face. "You don't understand."

"Then *explain* it to me. Tell me the truth."

"The truth? If I could go back and erase what happened in the forest, I would."

"Is that how you really feel?" My voice hangs limp in the air as I wait for him to answer, but he just stares at the ground. "Fine."

"Milena, wait."

I don't listen. My walls of composure are crumbling, the pride that keeps them up slowly evaporating. I can't fall apart in front of him, not again. I can't let him see that side of me, and I need to get out of here fast if I want to avoid it. A hand wraps around my upper arm and spins me back around. I have no choice but to stare up at him. "I don't want to hurt you."

"You're doing a really bad job of that."

"I'm sorry, I'm not . . . I'm not good at this."

"Your mood swings make my head spin," I say. "One second, I think you feel the same way I do, and the next you're saying stuff like that. How do you expect me to feel?"

"I do feel the same. I *do* care for you, Milena."

"Then why would you say those things?" I ask. "Why would you say that you want to erase what happened?"

"I wanted to protect you from *this*." He's so close my thoughts trip over one another. "This torture of knowing that we can never be together."

"You're the only one pushing me away."

He sighs and lets his hand fall away. "Do you remember when I said my mother killed my father?"

"You said it was an accident."

"It was."

"How did it happen?"

"My mother was an orphan who grew up thinking she was human; her parents died when she was a baby and Ana took her in. When she met my father, a shifter, she got pregnant. They were happy until . . . when she got upset once she . . ."

"She lit him on fire."

"It *ruined* her. She wasn't the same afterward and she killed herself. Ana raised me as her own and taught me everything I needed to know about being a wisper. I spent all of my childhood training to hide who I really was and learning from Eric how to mask myself as a shifter."

All his life, he's had to hide who he is. He's lived with the burden that his mother killed his father, and the knowledge that the same power runs through his veins. "I'm sorry that happened."

"It was a long time ago."

"That doesn't make it any less painful. But that was your mother, Elias. That's not you."

"You don't know that."

"I know you." I swallow my hesitation and step closer. "I know you'd never hurt me."

"I'm just like her. I've killed innocents before, and it wasn't on purpose. I burned them like she did. I couldn't control it and I couldn't stop it. It just happened."

"But that was so long ago, maybe if you learned how to—"

"Were you not there in the forest when I kissed you? Did you not see the way flames surrounded us?" He pulls away, creating distance between us. "I've been trying to learn for the past six years. There *is* no controlling it."

"So what?" I stare at him from across the room, hopelessness stabbing at my chest. "Are wispers just supposed to be alone forever?"

"Wispers are immune to other wispers' powers. That's why the race died out so easily—it wasn't safe to interbreed." I want to tell him that I don't care, that I've never felt like this and I don't know how to stop it, but I can't. "I didn't mean to care about you. Not like this."

My vision is glassy. "That's it then? You won't even try?"

"It's because I care about you that I won't."

He faces the wall. I hold myself as if I can somehow keep all the broken parts of us together. When Elias held me in the forest and said he felt the same way that I did, I felt like I could fly. But it didn't last long—nothing good ever does.

"I'm leaving to visit the elders tonight," he says. "Please stay until I get back."

"If the hollowers—"

"There's a permanent ban on leaving the village." He walks to the door. "They won't risk coming in. People will be safe."

My chest stings. I want to be around him. I want to talk to him and know more about him. But being around him with the knowledge that nothing will ever happen between us is more torture than not being around him at all. "When will you be back?"

"A couple of days, maybe."

"Be careful." I blink back tears. Elias is slipping through my fingers and all I can do is stand here and let him.

"Good-bye, Milena." He steps out of the training center and leaves me in a screaming silence. I want to chase after him and beg him to stay, but I stay rooted in place and stare at the ground. I don't follow him because deep down, I know he's right.

~

I don't see Elias before he leaves; I'm not even sure if I want to. Instead, I launch knives at the mannequins and practice the endurance course. My body burns with adrenaline, but no matter how much energy I exert, the ice in my chest doesn't thaw.

I can't remember the last night I felt properly rested. Ever since I left the village, my schedule has been all over the place. But even now, in my sleep-deprived state, energy thrums through my body. I need to devise a plan. It's futile staying here and just waiting for the hollowers to attack. And while Elias might find something in his travels, I refuse to sit around and do nothing. I owe it to the people here to try and figure out a solution. So after a quick bath, I wander the halls of the castle to find Eric. He sits at the desk in Elias's office with a stack of papers in front of him and his chin perched in his hand, looking up at me when I step inside. "Elias has already left."

"I'm not here for Elias." I move to the chair opposite him. "I'm here to talk about Charles."

"I'm busy right now."

"We had a deal."

He stares at me a few moments before pushing the papers to one side. "Fine. You want to talk to him, right?"

"Something like that. I just need answers, and he's the only one who has them. Charles is convinced he needs me to complete the sacrifice, but I can't figure out why."

"You think he'd tell you even if you did talk to him?" he asks. "It's too dangerous to go to their village, and not worth it."

"What if we try to do what they keep doing and ambush them?"

He raises an eyebrow. "You want to kill your old friends?"

"*No.* We don't have to kill them, just hold them hostage or something."

He laughs. "And then what? Charles tells you what you want to know and you just let them go?"

"What would you suggest?"

"I would kill them all."

"Are you serious?" I stare at him, slack jawed, as if waiting for him to laugh. "We don't have to stoop to their level, you know. Killing people would make us just as bad as them."

"They're not people. You really have no idea how any of this stuff works, do you?"

"Unlike you, I grew up learning how to cut vegetables, not throats."

"I pity you."

"Don't you want to know why they want me too? Why don't any of you seem to care anymore?" He looks up, eyes cold. And for a moment, something flickers across his face. Because it's true; it feels like ever since we got back from the mountains, our investigation halted. And now, I'm the only one who seems to really care. It doesn't make any sense. "Eric?"

He opens his mouth to respond but is interrupted when the door is roughly shoved open. Cassia stands there, eyes wide, breath ragged. "I think you guys should see this."

"What's wrong?"

"See for yourself."

She hurries out, and I'm right on her heels, Eric not far behind. We skid through the halls, coming to a stop at the top of the staircase that leads down to the foyer. Cassia leans over the edge, waiting for some sort of reaction. I can't yet see past the banister but voices rise up from below. I take a deep breath and step forward, peering over the staircase and down to the front doors. Two guards restrain a squirming prisoner.

She's almost unrecognizable, mud in her hair and torn fragments of her dress revealing scratched and bloody skin. She struggles in their hold, her legs thrashing as her eyes shoot around the foyer. They meet mine and an invisible force hammers violently against my back.

"Millie." Her voice is no more than a whisper as she falls still in the guard's arms, a strangled sob escaping her throat. *"Millie!"* I inhale sharply and stagger backward until I hit the wall, my childhood flashing against my eyes—red hair and tear-stained, freckled cheeks fill my vision. *Flo.*

~

"We should kill her and leave her at the gates of her village, send a message to the hollowers that we're not afraid of them."

"Don't be stupid, Eric." Cassia paces in front of us. "She might be useful."

Eric scoffs. "You don't want to make them pay?"

"You know Elias wouldn't want that."

"Elias isn't here."

"Exactly. Which means I'm in charge. We're not killing her, not yet."

Their voices fade into the background as I stare at the ground, mind rattling with the haunting sound of Flo calling to me from the castle foyer. She sounded so desperate and hopeful, but all her words did was twist the knife of betrayal deeper. The moment she started screeching, Cassia ordered the guards to take her to the prisons. Flo let them take her, my name echoing through the halls as she was dragged away. I could only stare after her in shock—I barely even registered it when Cassia took my arm and dragged me into the office with Eric.

"Milena?"

I look up. "What?"

Eric and Cassia are both staring at me expectantly, but Cassia opens her mouth. "I asked how you knew her. She called you Millie."

"She is—*was*—my best friend. My only friend."

Their bickering turns to silence as they watch me. I keep my eyes on the ground.

"Don't talk to her," Cassia says.

"What?"

"It could be a trap. Maybe Charles sent her on purpose to shake you up."

I hesitate. "She might be able to help."

"If she cared about you, she wouldn't have been your friend knowing that they planned to kill you." Eric looks at me pointedly. "I agree with Cassia, you shouldn't talk to her."

I know he's right, but it doesn't make it hurt less. The others never pretended to like me, but there was never one doubt in my mind that my friendship with Flo was real. But just like everyone else, she watched as Charles nearly killed me and she didn't do anything to stop it.

"What should we do, then?" Cassia asks. "Should I talk to her?" I stand, scraping the chair against the wood and capturing their attention. "Milena, don't talk to her."

"I'm going to bed."

Cassia and Eric exchange glances. "Are you sure?" she asks.

"I'm really tired."

Before either of them can comment, I turn on my heel and make a quick escape out the door, heading up to my bedroom with a vendetta. It wasn't a complete lie. I *am* going to my bedroom, but even though my head pounds and my knees feel like jelly, I don't plan on sleeping.

Seeing Flo hurt more than I expected it to but hurt isn't the only emotion I feel. Anger floods through my body like wildfire. I'm mad that she's here, that she watched Charles try to kill me, that she had the audacity to call me Millie. But worst of all, she pretended to be my friend. And I'm not going to let her get away with it.

~

After waiting an hour in my bedroom, and then creeping past the office to make sure Eric and Cassia aren't still in there arguing, I sneak through the halls in search of the prison cells. It takes me three different attempts, turning down the wrong hall each time, before I reach them.

The prison cells can barely be called rooms. The roof is so low I'm convinced someone as tall as Elias would hit his head against it, and the interior path is a stark contrast to the lavish castle. The walls are a grimy green, the stones covered in moss and condensation. There are no windows; the only light comes from the lanterns strung up outside of each cell. A pungent smell of steel and blood forces me to breathe through my mouth. All of the cells I wander past are empty, my feet padding on the wet stones as water drips against the floor.

I see Flo before she can notice me. She sits huddled in the corner of the cell at the end of the corridor with her arms wrapped around her knees. Her skin is paler than usual and her entire body shakes in the icy prison. She looks so small and innocent there, curled around herself in the shadows of the cell. She looks afraid, too, and I almost forget why I'm here.

"Millie?" She unfolds her arms from around her legs and drags herself across the floor of the cell until she can wrap her hands around the bars. "You came. I was so scared."

I notice the slashes on her arm, oozing with blood. "You lied to me."

"Millie, please—"

"Don't call me that." Her breathing is ragged and uneven, her freckle-covered face contorted with pain. "Why did Charles send you?"

"They didn't tell you?"

"Tell me what?"

"*I* came here." She coughs as she tries to stand, but her knees buckle and she slumps back to the ground. "I wanted to find you; I wanted to see you. I've missed you."

"Stop lying to me."

"I'm not lying." She grips the bars. "I'm sorry about what happened, it was so wrong. You're my best friend."

"Best friends don't plan to murder one another and then lie about it. Best friends don't do what you did!" I snap. I'd kept it pressed down for so long I was almost able to ignore it, but in front of Flo, the wall tumbles down.

"I'm sorry," she cries. "I'm so, so sorry."

"*Why?* Why did you pretend to care about me?"

"I never had to pretend." She pulls herself to her knees. "I swear, Millie. I promise, it was never a lie."

I wipe the tears from my cheeks. "I don't believe you."

"You don't understand how hard it was! When I turned sixteen and found out the truth, I didn't know what to do. I wanted to tell you, but it would have ruined everything. I couldn't bear to be your friend but Charles made me."

"He *made* you be my friend?"

She nods, her bottom lip wobbling. "He said if everyone treated you badly you might run away." I wrap my arms around myself. I know it's foolish, but there was always a small seed of hope inside me that prayed she didn't know, that she was just as in the dark as I was. But that seed is now crushed. It hurts more than I thought it would. "It was so hard for me, Millie. I never—"

"It was hard for you? Hard for *you*?"

"I didn't mean it that way. You don't know what I went through!"

"I would *never* have done what you did. I would never do that to my friend."

"Please, let me make it up to you."

I don't want her to know that I still care about her, that there's a part of me that wants to scoop her into my arms and cry. She can't know that my heart aches to laugh with her again. I want her to hurt like I am. "I will *never* forgive you."

She falters. "Are they going to kill me?"

"I don't know. And I don't care."

"I can help you," she says quietly.

"Tell me why Charles wants me."

"You haven't figured it out yet?"

"It's impossible. There's nothing."

"It's obvious. You're a wisper. He needs a wisper."

"Is this why Charles sent you? To fill me with more of his lies?"

"He didn't send me and I'm not lying. The *immortalia sacrificium* needs a wisper, a creature, and a human."

"I know that. But there are shifters and humans everywhere, and I'm not a wisper."

"You're wrong, Milena." She leans forward, scrambling for the pocket of her dress. "Your parents didn't die in a raid as Charles said. Your parents weren't even human." I take a step closer when she brings out a crumpled slip of paper. "Everybody thought wispers were extinct until twenty years ago, but then Charles heard of a wisper who'd killed their family," she explains shakily. "When he got there, they were already dead, but there was a child—*you*. And so he took you." Her eyes meet mine, so bright in the dark cell. "You're a wisper, Milena."

"Do you think I'm stupid? Stop lying, Flo."

"I'm not." She puts her arm through the metal bars, holding out a crumpled paper. "Look. I stole this before I left because it might help. Charles took it from the cabin where he found you." Tearing the paper from her hands, I frantically unfurl it until sketched lines are visible. And when they are, my stomach tightens. "You see?" Flo says. "It has to be—"

I don't hear the end of her sentence because I'm already out of the prison cells and in the halls. When I reach the library, I find the stool and climb atop it, frantically pulling books from the shelf in search of the one with the same gray cover Elias had been looking at when he rejected me that night. It's beneath a stack of books. I pull it from the pile and smack it down on the desk, flipping through the pages with shaking hands. The sixth page is the one I'm looking for, the sketch staring me right in the face as my shaking hands smooth out the edges of the paper Flo had given me. I place them side by side.

Elias's voice fills my mind. *Ana sketched two—one for my parents and one for her.* I examine the pictures, heart picking up.

The woman's lips are curved into a smile, the father has his arm around her, and the child looks halfway between crying and laughing. *I remember this day. Ana kept getting annoyed because I wouldn't sit still.* My entire body shakes and I step backward. The images lie side by side, like in a spot-the-difference picture book Charles let me read when I was younger. But there are no differences because the sketches are identical.

~

Eric has no shirt on when I burst into his room. He quickly snatches his shirt off the bedpost before scowling at me. "*Ah!* Did the hollowers not teach you how to knock?"

"Where's Cassia?"

"You came here to ask me where Cassia is?"

"Where is she?"

He shakes his head, irritated. "In her room, why?"

"I went to see Flo."

His expression turns from annoyance to anger. "You did? We told you not to talk—"

"Meet me in the library. I'm going to get Cassia."

I'm gone before he can say anything else, bursting into the room three doors down. Inside, Cassia is sprawled across her bed, book in hand. "Uh, hi?"

"Come to the library," I say. "I have to show you something."

She scrambles off the bed to keep up with me as we head down the hall to the library. When we get there, Eric is standing by the fireplace with a less-than-impressed scowl, dark shirt crinkled and crooked. "This better be good," he says. "Because you blatantly lied to me and Cassia about going down to see that girl."

"You went to see Flo?" Cassia's mouth falls open. "Milena, we told you not to!"

I run a hand down the side of my face. "Guys—"

"I told you, she never listens," Eric complains.

"Oh, come on, Eric." Cassia plants her hands on her hips. "Just because it happened this one time doesn't mean—"

"*Guys!*" My voice is so loud that they both shut up. "Flo told me that Charles thinks I'm a wisper."

"She's lying, we already know that's not true," Cassia says.

"That's what I thought at first. But then she told me *why* he thinks that, and it all makes sense."

Eric steps closer, eyeing the desk with the sketches. "This is Elias and his family. Where did you get the other one?"

"Flo gave it to me. She said Charles heard of a wisper who'd killed her family. He went to look for her and found me in the house. He took this drawing too."

"Elias's mother killed his father," Cassia says.

"Exactly." I watch as Cassia pushes past Eric and snatches the sketch, holding it in front of her face to check for imperfections. "For some reason, I was in that house and Elias wasn't. Charles thinks I'm the one in the drawing, he thinks *I'm* the one whose mother was a wisper but . . ."

"But it was really Elias." Eric doesn't look at either of us. "He should have been looking for Elias all this time."

His words fill the air with a bitter chill. I was never the one Charles wanted; he was raising the wrong person the entire time. He's been after me when the one he really needs is Elias. But Eric doesn't seem surprised, he speaks matter of factly.

"You *knew*?" Cassia gapes.

Eric looks at me, his expression void of emotion. "Yes, Elias too."

I step back like he's struck me. "How long? How long have you known?"

"Since we saw Ana in the mountains."

"And you didn't think to say anything?" Cassia demands. "We've wasted all this time trying to figure out what they want with Milena and you knew all along?"

"I won't apologize for not telling you. We couldn't risk revealing Elias's secret."

The ground feels unsteady with betrayal. The entire time they've known that I was the wrong person, that I was just in the wrong place at the wrong time. They let me believe that I'd done something terrible to warrant the hollowers coming after me, when all along, they were actually looking for Elias.

"Why on earth has Elias gone to see the elders, then?" Cassia asks. "Or is that trip fake too?"

"He was never going to the elders. They wouldn't have told us anything we didn't already know." He pauses. "He's going to the hollowers, to kill Charles."

My blood runs cold.

"What? Is he crazy?" Cassia demands.

"I tried to talk him out of it, but you know how he is."

Eric's loyal to a fault, even when he doesn't agree, even when it goes against everything inside of him. And now Elias is going to reveal himself to Charles. "We have to leave now. We have to stop him. Charles can't know that he's a wisper."

"He wouldn't want us to leave the village," Eric says. "We're staying here."

"Cassia?" She looks away. I frown and step toward her. Cassia is always so sure of herself, so confident. But the look in her eyes now is something unfamiliar. She's standing right in front of me but seems worlds away. "You know I'm right. We have to get Elias before Charles finds out and gets to him."

Cassia looks at the fire. "We have to go now."

Her voice is a whisper but we both catch it. Eric scoffs. "Elias wouldn't want us to risk going out there."

"Elias isn't here."

"Cassia—

"I'm in charge, Eric. We're going."

Tension lingers in the air like a thick cloud of smoke. "We should bring Flo," I say. "Just in case we run across some hollowers."

"I'll go get her. You two go down and get some weapons." Cassia snaps into motion, spinning and staring at the door. She grabs my arm on the way. "Get two daggers—one in your pocket and the other in your boot. Always have one in your boot, do you hear me?" I nod, but she shakes my shoulders. "Promise me, Milena."

"A knife in my pocket and one in my boot, I swear."

"Good. Flo and I will leave first so we're ahead of you."

"What? No." Eric catches her arm before she can leave. "We should stick together."

"Eric, listen to me."

"No. What's going on with you? Splitting up is the last thing we should do."

"I *am* doing what's best." Her jaw clenches and she tears her arm from his grip, voice so sharp that Eric actually shuts his mouth. "I'm going to walk ahead of you two. If I come across any hollowers, I'll send you a signal. It's the safest way."

They stare at one another, the tension between them like a rubber band stretched to its limit. I shift from one foot to the other, the battle of wills between the two of them setting me on edge. Eric looks away first and scowls at the fireplace. Cassia takes the opportunity to dash from the room, leaving me alone with Eric. "Shall we get some weapons?" I ask.

He snarls and heads for the door. "I want you to know that I disapprove of this."

"You disapprove of everything."

~

We fly down the staircase to the training room. My head spins as Eric eyes the weapons lining the wall. I remember the last time I was here, with Elias, and a familiar ache rocks my chest.

"You learn how to use any of these bigger weapons yet?" Eric asks.

"I could probably use the machete if I had to, but I feel more comfortable with the daggers. Besides, I promised Cassia."

He pulls two daggers from the wall, sliding them into cotton covers and handing them to me. I put one in my boot and the other in my pocket, like Cassia instructed. After scanning a little longer, Eric chooses knives similar to those that Cassia used when we were heading to the village, before Elias and Eric stopped us.

"You ready?" Eric asks.

"Shouldn't we wait until Cassia goes ahead?"

"She'll be long gone by now." He puts his knife in the sling over his shoulder and moves to the staircase. "Stick close to me and don't go off on your own."

"I won't."

"I'm serious. If you even have a scratch on your head when we get to Elias because you didn't follow my instructions, I might just have to kill you myself." Eric disappears through the door and into the castle entryway. I follow him into the foyer and out through the creaking wooden doors. The trees crowd in clusters, darkness weaving throughout the branches in the absence of the moon. "Are you coming or not?" Eric stands at the edge of the forest, his eyes the only light in the night that surrounds him. I swallow my fear and nod. And together, Eric and I begin our trek into the forest.

CHAPTER FOURTEEN

Paranoia creeps up my spine as we walk through the forest; I feel like someone's watching us. Eric walks three steps ahead and I stick close to his heel, shivering. His knife glints each time he moves, a dangerous reminder of where we're heading. The farther we walk, the harder my heart pounds. We're leaving safety but getting closer to Elias, and for that reason, I can't turn around. It's barely been a day since I last saw him but he dominates my thoughts all the same. The possibility that Charles might figure out who he is terrifies me.

Whispers and distant howls haunt the night air. I stare at Eric's back and pick up my pace. "Won't Elias be there already?"

"He went to scope out another colony on the way, to see if they're collaborating. We should intercept him on the way to your hollowers."

Sticks crack loudly beneath my feet while Eric somehow walks through the forest without making a sound. "What if we accidentally miss him?"

"We won't."

"What if—"

Eric swings his arm backward, shoving me sideways and perching protectively in front of me. Where I was standing, there's now a knife on the ground. I fumble for my dagger as Eric darts away. One second he's a blur and the next he's standing in front of me, his arm a sleeve of blood and a limp body beside him. I blink in horror. "We need to go *now*," Eric says.

I scramble to my feet but it's too late—shadows lurk behind him. Eric sees the look on my face and turns around, holding his arm out to shield me as he crouches low to the ground. Two dark shapes scatter through the trees, coming toward us. The closer they get, the easier they are to make out. Crooked smiles play on their faces as they step forward, mere inches away.

"Stay back," Eric growls. "I'll cut your throats out."

The one on the left laughs. "I'd like to see you try."

Instantly he appears beside the man. I stumble backward, nearly tripping over the dead body lying on the ground, and grip my dagger. Icy fingers scratch the back of my arm and wrap around my wrist, spinning me around before I can run. I've never seen the man before, but the smile that spreads over his face makes my skin crawl. His eyes gleam with danger and he tightens his grip. "Hello, Milena."

My wrists erupt with pain when his fingernails break skin. I wince and try to wrench my arm free, but his grip is too tight. Alarm flashes through my mind as he reaches for my other

GRACE COLLINS

hand, the one without the knife. Aliyah's words float into my mind: *Thumb across fingers, go for the soft parts of the body.*

Before he can get a hold of it, I swing my fist back and launch it at his throat, my knuckles crunching when they collide with his face. Pain blossoms in my fist. The man staggers back, a gurgling sound erupting from his mouth as he clutches at his cheek. I take the opportunity to put my hands on his shoulders and bring my knee up between his legs. I don't waste time watching him fall; clutching my dagger as I turn, I see Eric slash his knife across the throat of a woman trying to hold his arms. The woman falls to the ground and Eric faces me. The color drains from his face. "What's wrong? Eric?"

I turn, following his gaze, and step back when I see what he sees. The shadows, scattered in a circle around us, outnumber the trees. I stumble back, knocking into him. He wraps his hand around my wrist to steady me, but I don't miss the shaking in his fingers. A dark shape steps into view and holds their hand toward Eric. She wears a torn, yellow shirt and dark pants ripped at her ankles. "Give us the wisper."

Eric tightens his grip on me. "Over my dead body."

"Oh, how I would love that. But unfortunately, it goes against our agreement, and I'm not one to break my word."

"Agreement?" I glance at Eric. "What agreement?"

The woman laughs. "Didn't you hear, little girl? The creatures are trading you for their safety."

"Don't listen to her, Milena." Eric doesn't look at me, his eyes focused on the hollowers. "She's trying to get in your head."

"What agreement is she talking about?"

"I haven't made any damn agreements with the hollowers!" He turns to the hollower. "If you want Milena, you'll have to kill me first."

"You really think you can get out of this? Stick with the deal, creature."

Stick with the deal. The shifters made a deal.

"I told you, I didn't make any damn deals! Get out of here before it's too late."

The woman frowns. "You can't kill all of us."

"Maybe not." A wicked smile lights Eric's face. "But I can sure kill you." He moves then, and is halfway across the clearing, knife raised, when somebody steps in his path and he skids to a stop, so startled he loses his balance and topples over.

"Eric, *stop!*" She stands between Eric and the hollowers. Cassia.

Eric pushes up again, a growl reverberating through his chest. "Cassia, get out of the way."

She steps forward, hands in front of her body. Shadows wrap around her like an embrace. "I can't."

I feel the knife before I see it, a sharp pain blossoming in my chest as her eyes meet mine. Connections form: Cassia went on ahead, took Flo with her. She wanted to split up. The hollowers made a deal with a shifter. My knees buckle, the tree behind me the only thing keeping me steady. But I don't look away from her. And for the first time since meeting her, tears flow in a steady stream down her cheeks. I should feel something—the warmth of the blood against my skin, the stinging wrist. But the only thing I feel is betrayal.

"*Cassia.*" Eric steps back in shock. "Cassia, what have you done?"

"I'm sorry." A sob echoes through her. "I'm sorry, Milena. I'm so sorry."

My entire body trembles. The hollowers fade into the background, the shadows of the forest crawling toward me, scratching at my brain. It's just me and Cassia in the clearing, a knife in her hand and a stab wound in my back. "How could you?"

Cassia flinches. "I'm sorry."

I want to believe her but actions have spoken louder than anything she could say. "You have to run." Eric starts toward me, reaching out. "Milena, go—"

His eyes roll to the back of his head before he falls over, a hollower standing over him holding a rock stained with Eric's blood. "Stop it!" Cassia leaps in front of Eric to catch him before he hits the ground. "You agreed you wouldn't hurt him!"

"Relax, he's still breathing," the woman says. "You really think he would've let us take the girl?"

Cassia falls silent and holds herself. I take small steps back, eyes on Cassia as I try to comprehend what she's done. Eric wanted me to run, but as I look around, figures stand in a circle around me, lining the perimeter in dark shapes. There's nowhere for me to go.

"No point in running, wisper." The woman notices me peering around. "You're completely surrounded."

She nods at Cassia. "Grab her."

"But—"

"We had a deal. You're the only one she won't try to kill."

Cassia reluctantly approaches me, hands stretched out. I hate that the woman is right, that Cassia walking toward me now is more frightening than any hollower. My hands shake uncontrollably, my dagger pointed at her chest. "Don't, Cassia." I move away. "Please. It's not too late." Her face scrunches up, tears cascading as she gasps for air. But she doesn't stop moving. "*Please.*"

She grabs my wrists. Her hands are cold. It takes nothing for her to disarm me; my body weakened, disorientated. With a flick of her wrist, my dagger falls to the ground and my knees buckle. Once again, the betrayal of someone close to me has stripped me of any fighting ability I thought I had. She pulls me so close our noses nearly touch. I try to pull away, refusing to look at her, but she holds me in place, glassy eyes meeting mine. Her breath brushes across my face, eyes rimmed red. She whispers, "Don't forget the dagger in your boot."

"Why are you doing this?"

"I'm sorry." Tears trickle down her cheeks. It's only when my wrists tremble that I realize she's shaking as much as I am. "I have to protect him."

With what strength I can muster, I bring my arms down toward my knees in an attempt to break from her hold. But before I can do anything, her fist flies toward my face and everything goes black.

~

A dull pain throbs in the back of my head. I roll over, bones cracking against the hard floor I lie upon as I try to open my eyes. Images immediately come to mind: wandering through the forest with Eric, coming across the hollowers, Cassia stopping Eric from hurting them.

Cassia. I sit up so fast my head spins. Pain flourishes in my wrists as I try to pull them apart, but both my ankles and my hands are restrained by thick rope. I groan, bones aching as I roll over. But opening my eyes does nothing. The room is dark, the ground beneath me like ice, and somewhere down the hall water drips methodically against an iron pipe. There's only one place this could be. The tunnels where I grew up.

I cough into the silence and struggle frantically against the restraints.

"Hello? Is someone there?"

I hesitate, peering around in the darkness, trying to locate the voice. My vision is blurred, head still spinning as I adjust to the deep abyss. "I'm here."

"You've got to help me," they say, "I'm stuck, and the chains are silver and I'm so tired."

"Are you a shifter?" I try to sit up properly but my hands and ankles are tied together, which makes it difficult. "Did the hollowers bring you here?"

"Yes."

The ache in my head worsens as I try to sort through my thoughts. Fear and paranoia sit at the forefront, but betrayal lurks closely behind. Cassia gave me to the hollowers. And the worst part is that I understand why she did it.

"Where are you? I can't see you."

A body presses against mine. I blink, my eyes wide as he blurs into view—a scrawny body littered with blood and raw skin. Chains weave around his limbs, the skin beneath angry with blood. My stomach flops; he can't be older than thirteen.

"How long have you been here?" I ask, awkwardly maneuvering myself across the floor without using my hands or feet.

"I don't remember. Are you the one they keep talking about? The wisper?"

I'm not a wisper. I'm just a regular human mistaken for someone more important—mistaken for Elias. But I keep my lips pressed tightly together. Cassia betrayed me to protect the one she cares for, and I'm not about to out Elias to anyone else. I want to protect him too. The longer I look around the more I can make out. We're where Eric was held, deep in the tunnels. But being locked away here isn't all bad; I know how to get out. I try to roll myself over to get closer to the boy, but my elbows clank painfully against the floor.

"We have to get out of here."

"If you're a wisper, can't you use your gift to save us?"

We're both tied up. I'm too weak to escape and he's wrapped in silver. "Can you shift?"

"What?"

"I need you to shift. I'm tied with ropes, maybe you can tear them with your teeth."

"I can't," he stammers. "These chains are wrapped around me."

"I know it hurts," I say, trying to sound more sympathetic. "But if you can somehow shift enough to tear these, I can help get those chains off you. It's our only chance of getting out of here."

His sob echoes around us. "I'm only fifteen. I haven't shifted before."

I squeeze my eyes shut, wishing the throbbing in my head would subside. There's so much going on it's hard to think. I was shaken up enough from Flo's arrival, and the knowledge that Eric and Elias kept hidden, but Cassia's betrayal put a greater spin on things. Flo and Cassia, the two people I'd known to be my friends both betrayed me. Aside from Elias, Cassia was the only one I could trust, the only one who didn't make me feel like a burden.

If the hollowers sacrifice me, nothing will happen because I'm not who they think I am. The hollowers won't become immortal, the sacrifice won't work, and they won't know why. Everyone will be safe from this, I'll be dead, and the hollowers won't have any incentive to keep targeting the shifters. It makes sense, but I know that isn't why she did it. Cassia doesn't want me to die. But when it came down to it, it was a choice between me and Elias. Cassia chose Elias, and I can't blame her because I would've done the same. But that doesn't make it easier.

"What was that?" The shifter's low voice brings me from my thoughts. "Hey, did you hear that? Someone's coming."

The pattering of footsteps makes me freeze. They tap against the floor like clockwork, echoing louder and louder in the tunnels. Anticipation crawls through me, and I drag myself across the ground, toward the shifter. Up close, he looks even worse: dark circles linger beneath his eyes and his black hair is clumped with grease. He's shirtless, the chains wrapped around him surrounded by red, and his ribs poking through his skin.

"They're coming," he whispers. "They're going to kill us!"

I want to be brave. I want to reach out and touch him, as if I could somehow make him feel safer through an embrace, but my arms are still bound, and I can't move. So I press myself against him, relieved that his skin still burns hot. We're so close I can feel him shaking. "I'm scared," the boy whispers.

He's just a kid, an innocent thrown into this mess because of me. I want to tell him that it'll be okay, that we'll make it out of this, but I don't want to make promises I can't keep.

The footsteps stop, and from where I lie, I can see two pairs of feet standing before us. I swallow, refusing to lift my eyes.

"I see you've made friends. How nice." The voice makes my stomach curl. Any bravery I'd bundled up inside dwindles away. It's the voice that's haunted my nightmares since the day he stood over me with a machete. And even though I knew this day was inevitable, I'm entirely unprepared.

"You're not even going to look at your guardian?"

I do. Though it hasn't been that long, I expected him to look different now. In my nightmares, his eyes are red, and his smile twisted; he looks more sinister. Now, he looks the way he did when he stood over me that day in the forest. Like Charles. It would've been easier if he looked like the monster he'd become in my head.

"You're not my guardian. You made that perfectly clear when you tried to drain me of blood."

"And here I was thinking you'd be happy to see me."

The shifter presses closer to me. That's when I realize I'm the one who's shaking, not him. "How could you?" I ask. "How could you do this?"

"You know."

"Because you're selfish. You want to be powerful and you were willing to ruin my life to do that."

"I'm not selfish."

"Maybe you're delusional, then."

"Watch your mouth," he snaps. "I thought I taught you to be more obedient than this."

"I should've stopped listening to you a long time ago. You were never kind to me."

"Would you have preferred that?" he demands, taking a threatening step closer. "Would it have made it better if I'd treated you like my own daughter? Would that have made this easier for you?" I know he's right, and it hurts. The only kindness Charles ever gave me was not pretending to love me. "Exactly," he says when I don't answer. "I made a choice. It was better for both of us that you didn't get attached to me."

My chest aches for something I never had, a family I always

GRACE COLLINS

wanted. He's wrong about that. I was attached to him, too much so—his lack of love made me strive for his approval. Now, all that's left are fragments of a broken, one-sided relationship. "You chose yourself over me."

"No," he says. "I chose between you and the fate of my people. Hollowers are dying out, Milena. Without the sacrifice, soon we'd be just like your species—extinct."

And the worst thing is, it doesn't make it right, but it makes sense. Betrayal hurts. It burns deeper, though, when you start to wonder if you would've done the same thing. "I hate you."

"No, you don't." He kneels so that we're eye level. "You still love me. You never stopped."

He stares at me, his eyes empty of emotion while I fall apart right in front of him. I hate that he's right, I despise that I spent my entire life looking up to him, loving him, wishing he would notice me. That my emotions can't be flicked off like a switch. I hate that, deep down, there's still a part of me that wishes he would untie my hands, scoop me up in his arms, and brush my hair from my face like a good father would do. I squeeze my eyes shut, sending tears down my cheeks. "All I ever wanted was for you to love me."

"I'm sorry I couldn't give that to you."

Charles always called me weak, and I'm proving him right. "Did you just come down here to antagonize me then?"

"No, I came to apologize." He rises to his feet so that I can only see his knees. "For what it's worth, I'm sorry this is what it has come to."

"If you were sorry, you wouldn't do this."

"Being a leader means making hard decisions, Milena. Sometimes, you have to choose the majority over an individual.

I'm sorry you had to be that individual, but I don't regret anything that I've done. I'm doing the right thing by my people, and I won't apologize for that."

Charles being here hurts more than I imagined. It would have been easier if he'd been hateful, if he'd spat on me and laughed in my face. But he apologized. He said he wished it wasn't me. For some reason, that makes it sting so much more. Charles has known me my entire life, sort of adopted me, and still chose them over me. Elias, who's barely known me for weeks, has treated me as an equal, like one of his own. And even in the face of death, he continues to protect me. Does that make him a bad leader or a good one? "I don't want to see you anymore."

Charles doesn't leave right away; the tunnel falls into silence as he stands there staring at me. "You control fire, don't you?"

"What?"

"Fire, it's your gift." He takes a step back, eyes narrowing. "We came across the remains of fire just outside the village the other day, and other hunters we've come across in the forest are nothing but ash. You burned them, didn't you?"

They know. *They know.* And when he asks me this, for a brief moment I understand what Cassia did. If they find out the truth, not only will they have the opportunity to actually become immortal, but Elias will die.

"Yes." I meet his stare. "It was me."

"I'll see you at the ceremony, Milena." He turns on his heel and thumps down the tunnel, whistling as he walks. The machete Charles used to nearly kill me has nothing on the dagger he just twisted into me. In another world, I might've been on their side—in another world, I might've wanted me dead too.

"Milena?" The shifter reaches for me. "Is that true? What he said, about the fire?"

No one can know about Elias. "Yes."

"Can't you free us? Can't you burn something?"

"No." My voice is flat and hopeless.

He's silent for a few moments. Then: "What if we made a dagger from the—"

A dagger. Keep a dagger in your boot.

"What's your name?"

"What?"

"What's your name?" I repeat.

"George."

"George, I'm going to twist my body around. I need you to reach into my boot."

"What? Why?"

"There's a dagger in there. Once you pull it out, cut my hands free and I can do the rest."

He doesn't need to be told twice. As soon as I've maneuvered myself along the ground with my feet toward him, he slips his fingers into my boot and brushes against my ankle, retrieving the dagger from its cover and holding the glinting metal in front of himself. And then he slices the ropes binding my hands and I'm free.

My bones ache in protest when I leap to my feet, but I push the pain away. Maybe we're going to die; maybe we'll be drained of blood and sacrificed to the hollowers. But it isn't going to be today, not if I have anything to do with it.

~

George is too slow. Even after I've untangled the chains from his body, he moves so slowly I could crawl and still beat him. I wrap his arm over my shoulder and put mine around his waist, ignoring the moaning of my own bones.

His ribs are so close to his skin they stab at my hands. Nausea rises in me at the way his bones move beneath his skin, like the smallest wrong move and they'll break through to the surface. "How do you know where to go?" George asks as I pull him forward.

We move slowly through the dark halls, listening carefully for any footsteps or chatter that might alert us to people coming toward us. But so far, it's only me, George, and the distant echo of water dripping from pipes onto stone. "I used to live here," I say as we creep around a corner.

"You lived *here*? With the hollowers?"

I pause when something clatters down the hall. "Did you hear that?"

"I don't hear anything."

I should trust him; he's a shifter, he has better senses than I do, but doubt swirls in me. I was so sure I heard a bang, a movement of some sort around the corner. What if the silver dulled his senses? What if he's too weak to hear things as he normally would?

"Are you sure? I could've sworn I heard—"

We skid around the corner. We're not alone. Flo stands frozen in the hall, her mouth half open, red hair tangled in knots atop her head and a tray of food in her hands.

"You're supposed to be chained up," she says.

"Does that disappoint you? Were you coming down there to laugh in my face about how you tricked me again?"

"What are you talking about?"

"You really expect me to believe you had nothing to do with Cassia making that deal? You must think I'm stupid."

"I didn't have anything to do with it, I swear." She shakes her head and steps forward. "She took me from the cell and told me she was taking me home."

I drop George in reflex. He falls to the floor but I don't have time to waste apologizing as I brandish the dagger in front of me. "You're such a liar."

She freezes. In the low light, her green eyes seem black. "Millie, I swear I came down here to help you. I wasn't lying about all that stuff I said. I left the village by myself to find you because I regret what happened."

"Even if I believed you, which I don't, your regret doesn't erase what you did. I still hate you."

She reaches for me, dropping the tray. "Millie, please—"

I spin her around so that my dagger is pressed against her throat. Flo stills in my grip. I swallow my guilt and hold her closer. "Get up, George. We have to get out of here before any more of them come. Can you run?"

He climbs to his feet and leans against the wall for support. "I'll try. What are you going to do with her?"

Flo's entire body trembles against mine. I can feel her chest rise and fall rapidly, the rapid beat of her heart. She's just as scared as I am. "I don't know."

We continue forward, Flo whimpering and George dragging himself along the wall. We're moving slowly, too slowly, but I can't risk letting Flo go. I pull her along with me, her body shuddering as we walk.

"Let me go, Millie," Flo says. "I can help you. You won't get out without me."

"Shut up." I press the dagger into her throat. "I don't trust anything you say."

"But I—"

"I said *shut up!*"

George looks at me, eyes wide, innocent, as he drags himself along the wall. We push forward, the living areas coming into view. The last time I was here, I was playing checkers with Flo. I was so oblivious to what was just ahead, so foolish to believe the people here actually cared about me. I don't want to hurt her. Just like Charles, part of me still loves her, but my brain knocks me straight. Flo pretended to be my best friend for years. I confided in her. We spent hours upon hours together, laughing, crying, and telling stories. And she stood by and watched as Charles tried to kill me. What Flo did is worse than all the others combined. I wish I could hate her for it. I wish I could stop caring, but I can't.

Shadows dance upon the wall as we move through the empty dining room. It looks strangely dark considering it must be day by now. I push the concern to the back of my mind and continue forward until we reach the entrance hall. "What time is it?" I ask.

"It's midafternoon. But people aren't around because they're preparing for the ceremony."

My heart hammers in my chest as we head down the hallway, toward the light of day. But when we reach it, my hope falls away—someone's there, guarding the opening.

George skitters back the way we came. I hold Flo tighter. "Make a sound and I'll slit your throat."

She gulps against the blade but doesn't call my bluff.

"What're we going to do?" George asks, frightened. "Find another exit?"

"There is no other exit."

Ideas run through my mind, but not one of them gets us out of here. I spent every night in these tunnels before I left; I know them like the back of my hand. The entrance to the tunnel faces the forest, so we could easily slip into the trees if nobody was watching, but we have to find a way out first. Our only option is forward, but it's blocked.

If I could somehow creep up behind the guard, maybe I'd have a chance of attacking him. But that means letting Flo go, and I'm not willing to risk that. Besides, he's broad shouldered and a couple of heads taller than me—it doesn't matter that I've been training, he'll still be stronger than me.

I make sure Flo is tightly secured, then walk toward him, and pray with everything I have that he's the only one guarding the entrance. George lingers a few steps behind, but when we're a mere three steps away he stumbles and scuffs his feet across the ground. The man guarding the entrance goes rigid. He spins around, eyes sharp.

My heart drops. Part of me was hoping I wouldn't know him, that he was some hollower from a village I'd never been to, but I'm not so lucky. Jack stands in front of me, a hunter a couple of years older than me, with dark hair and bright, blue eyes.

He glares at the dagger pressed against Flo's throat. "How did you get out?"

"Don't come any closer," I warn. He pauses, head tilting as if wondering whether or not to believe me. "I'm serious. I'll cut her throat."

"I don't believe you. You were always such a pushover."

"Yeah? Well, turns out constantly being the target of murder changes a person."

He steps closer. "You wouldn't kill your best friend."

"*Ex*–best friend."

Flo lets out a yelp when I cut into her slightly, enough that blood trickles across my fingers. I feel a flash of nausea. I hadn't meant to draw blood. "I'll stop! I'll stop!" Jack freezes and raises his hands in the air. "What do you want for her?"

"Put your machete on the ground."

"What?"

"You heard me." He doesn't move. "Now!" The machete clatters to the ground and he steps back. I shoot George a look. "George, pick his machete up."

He hesitates. "I don't know how to use it."

"Just pick it up, George. Please, trust me."

He hobbles forward, his eyes never leaving Jack as he tentatively picks up the machete and holds it with trembling hands.

"Great," Jack says. "You've got the machete, now give me Flo."

"I don't think so. I want you to go down the tunnels, all the way to where I was tied up. If you make any noise, I'll kill Flo. Do you understand me?"

"How do I know you're not bluffing?"

"Didn't they tell you?" I swallow, forcing a sadistic smile to my face. "I killed Darius."

I have to force myself to keep eye contact. But my words have the intended effect. Jack's eyes flash and Flo, who had been squirming in my hands, falls still. "You coldhearted witch. He was a kid."

I try to hide my flinch. "So was I, but that didn't stop any of you."

"You're never going to get away, you know. Charles won't stop, none of us will."

I take Flo with me and step back. "Go down the tunnel. *Now*."
He walks back, slowly, eyes on me until he's around the corner.
But I don't let myself relax. I spin around, grab George's arm
with my free hand, and pull both him and Flo forward.

"We need to get out of here." I tug them toward the entrance.
"It won't be long till he comes after us."

The brightness outside momentarily blinds me, and from the
way George covers his eyes with his hand, I know I'm not the only
one. I blink frantically, half concealing myself behind the jutted
metal. Rain pierces my skin like thousands of tiny knives. Flo's
red hair blows across my face but I swat it away. One hundred feet
away, the forest waits. The temptation to peer around the corner
presses at me, to see the vegetable patches and the kitchen shack,
but I can't risk being seen. The clearing between us and the trees
is empty.

I glance at George. "Can you run?"

"I can try."

I take the knife from Flo's throat and spin her around to face
me. Tears stain her cheeks. "You're coming with us," I say. "If you
scream or try to run, I'll hurt you. I'm serious."

"I told you I want to help you."

I look to George. "Run on three."

"I'm scared."

"I know. But we're in this together."

"What if they catch me? What if I'm not fast enough? What
if—"

"I won't leave you. Whatever happens, we'll do it together,
okay?" I turn and face the forest entrance again. "One, two—"

George stumbles ahead of me and I'm quick to follow. The
wind races through my hair and rain stabs at my skin, but we

push forward, across the clearing to the trees. I imagine the village behind me, the familiar gardens, the kitchen shack, but I don't turn around. I don't think about Flo being dragged behind me or George stumbling ahead.

All my life I hid from the trees. The night and its shadows were my enemies. I feared the pink hue of the sunset. Ravenous creatures haunted my nightmares, agonizing growls and blood-matted fur rattling my bones. My reality was distorted, twisted by a man who shaped my childhood, but I always knew monsters were real. Now I know that they can look human too.

CHAPTER FIFTEEN

Rain pelts my face. My fingers are numb as I drag Flo by the wrist through the trees, George lagging behind. Adrenaline helps me forward as the gray above claps with thunder. It's me, Flo, and George. No Cassia to lead me through the night, or Elias to make decisions, or Eric to scowl at me. George relies on me, peering up at me with fear in his eyes as he waits for me to decide each turn we take. Flo stays silent. But I have no idea what I'm doing.

If the hollowers have noticed our absence, they haven't found us, but it won't be long before they do. The rain has muted my senses. If they were close, I wouldn't hear or see them coming— yet another thing adding to the anxiety swelling inside me.

"Millie, please listen to me." I ignore Flo and scan the clearing. We've reached the bottom of a hill. Beside us, a cliff stretches high into the air. Boulders cluster at the bottom, the area sparser and not protected from the rain. I have no idea where we're going or what to do, all I know is that we need to leave. Flo tugs my sleeve. "Millie—"

"I told you twenty minutes ago, and I'll tell you again: I don't want to hear anything you have to say."

"I'm trying to help you!"

"You're trying to save yourself," I hiss, backing her against a tree. "You don't care about us. How long was George down there starving to death? You did nothing."

"He's a creature."

"And you're a hollower who betrays her friends. Who's the real monster here, Flo?"

Her eyes water. "I care about you."

"You're such a liar."

I let her go and she crumbles to the ground. "Are you going to kill me?"

"We don't have time for this. Get up."

She looks up at me with red-rimmed eyes. "I don't want you to hate me."

"You should've thought about that before you betrayed me. I said get up. I won't ask again, Flo."

She gets to her feet, movements sluggish and slow. Her hair looks like fresh blood where it sticks to her skin. "You should head in the other direction if you're trying to get back to the creature village," she says. "You're heading the wrong way."

"Why should I listen to a thing you say?"

"Because I loved you like a sister, I still do. It was supposed to be fake, but it never was."

"Get this through your thick skull, Flo." I stab her chest with my finger. "I hate you. I will always hate you. You mean nothing to me."

She stumbles back. "You don't mean that."

"I do." I get so close to her that she has nowhere to look but me. "I hate what you did to me. I wish you were dead."

The words tumble so quickly from my mouth it's too late to take them back. Her lips part. Her skin is ivory, brown freckles across her nose a stark contrast. I step back, unable to look away from her as she stares speechless. Eventually, her eyes drift to the ground. I turn and shut my eyes. I can feel George's heated gaze on me. What am I doing? What did I just say?

A scream bounces between the trees. I turn and look at George. "They're here."

"What do we do?"

I frantically search the clearing for an idea but come up empty. Flo steps forward and grabs my wrist. "Follow me."

"Let me go!"

She doesn't, and my knife falls from my fingers as she shoves me toward the boulders, grabbing George and pushing him after me. He falls into my arms and I tug him to my chest as I press against the rock face, scanning the direction the scream came from. I'm seconds away from sprinting in the opposite direction when Flo suddenly screams at the top of her lungs.

I press myself against the rock, the rain sharp without the protection of the trees. George pulls himself up so he can see through the gaps between the two boulders. Seconds later, four hollowers burst into the clearing, panting and gasping.

"Flo!" One of them takes her as she slumps to the ground. "Flo, what happened? Are you okay?"

"She tried to kill me," Flo sobs. "I was so scared."

"It's okay, where did they go?"

"That way." She points them in the opposite direction to where we're standing. "Quick, go fast, they're trying to get back to the village."

Three of them immediately dash in the direction she points, but one lingers behind, a hand on Flo's shoulder. Her eyes move past and I press myself hard against the rock face, but she doesn't see us. "I'm so glad you're okay." She pulls Flo closer. "I thought something—I thought she might've hurt you."

Flo buries her face in her chest and I have to look away. I've never seen this guard before, but the way she looks at Flo is so tender. And even though it's foolish, my chest feels hollow. We did everything together growing up—there wasn't one thing she didn't know about me and I thought I knew everything about her. But now, we have two different worlds; we care about different people. Flo has a different life and I'm not part of it. And no matter how much I try to convince myself otherwise, it hurts.

George starts slipping between the boulders, grazing his arms against their hard surface. A scream escapes his mouth—it doesn't go unnoticed. "What was that?"

"What?" Flo's voice shakes. "I didn't hear anything."

Footsteps approach. I see her before she sees me, peeking through the gap between the two boulders. Without a second thought, I slam my elbow into her nose. She groans, staggering back with a cry. "They're here! They're—"

I sling George's arm over my shoulders and wrap mine around his waist, and we stagger along the cliff face. My cheeks sting with the force of the rain, but I don't stop, and I don't retreat to the trees. "I'm sorry," George cries. "I didn't mean to."

"It's okay," I say and focus on moving faster, the muscles in my arms protesting. "We just have to keep going."

Shouts surround us. I can't tell if they're coming from in front or behind, all I can do is continue forward and pray that it's the latter. But my prayers aren't answered. We skid to a stop when two men intercept our path, standing against the cliff face wearing villainous grins. I turn us around before they can come after us, but my attempts at escape are futile—more hollowers stand behind us now as well, a group lurking by the boulders and another at the edge of the trees. Defeat sinks my heart like an anchor. We're surrounded.

"Where are you going to run to, wisper?" I recognize the man who steps forward from the shadows. It's the man from the forest, the one who'd grappled at my arms before I punched him in the face. "That's right. You have nowhere to go."

My entire body trembles as they close in on us. I struggle against their hold when they grab at me, trying to free my elbow so I can slam it into one of their faces, but three of them restrain my arms behind me. A woman picks up George and snaps his wrist like it's nothing more than a twig. He releases an agonizing roar. His back arches, bones protruding through his skin.

"Stop! What're you doing?"

A mouth presses against my ear, breath hot. "Stop struggling or it'll be his leg next." I fall still as George rolls around on the ground, clutching his arm to his chest. I cry as the woman drags him to his feet and forcibly restrains his broken wrist behind his back. "Good," she says. "A lot of people are waiting on you; it'd be rude to keep them waiting for long."

A sharp pain laces my head as a hand buries itself in my hair and jolts me forward; another hollower drags a groaning George behind as we're pulled around the corner. We're led around the cliff face and into a crevice where two cliffs face each other. My heart drops when we come to a stop in front of a figure concealed by shadows. Charles steps forward, gray hair plastered to his forehead and clothes stuck to his skin.

His eyes meet mine and he sighs. "I thought after we spoke you might be more willing to go along with this, considering what's at stake."

George whimpers beside me. "You obviously don't know me at all, then," I say.

"You didn't think we would let you go, did you?" My vision blurs, but I won't cry for Charles; I won't let him get to me, not now, when everything is falling apart. If I'm going to die, I'm not going to give him the satisfaction.

Charles looks over at George on the ground. "What happened to the creature?"

The woman scoffs and kicks him in the stomach. "Broke his wrist."

"We don't need him anyway." Charles nods at the woman. "Dispose of him."

"Stop!" The woman picks up a screaming George by his hair and presses her machete against his throat. "What are you doing?" The more I struggle the deeper my captor's nails dig. "You need him—for the sacrifice!"

"No," Charles says, "we don't."

She slices the machete across George's throat. My scream ricochets off the cliff face like a birdcall. Blood gurgles in the back of his throat, and then his body falls limp. The world screams in horror and my knees go weak. The only thing that keeps me off the ground are the arms wrapped tight around my waist. The woman carelessly drags George's limp body across the ground behind her, his blood leaving a trail behind him like red paint on white paper.

"You're a monster." I glare at Charles, trembling. "The man who raised me wouldn't murder a kid."

"The man who raised you wouldn't murder a kid worthy of living." Charles is unapologetic. His lips rise to a scowl as if the blood trail on the ground is a nuisance. "He's a creature. I did him a favor."

My mouth tastes of acid. Charles is deluded. I grew up believing every word this man taught me about the creatures of the night when the monster stood in front of me all along. "And what about me? Am I not worthy of living?"

"You're simply a means to an end," he says. He mutters something to one of the hollowers standing at the ready behind him.

"How are you supposed to have your little ceremony without him? You need shifter blood."

"Creature blood," he corrects sharply. "And I have something better."

"What?"

"Your little friend paid me a visit."

Elias. Thunder claps above us. George's blood trail fades with the hammering rain, fragments of what was once a person browning into clumps of dirt. Charles waves his hand and someone emerges around the corner, a knot of dread coiling in me. But it isn't Elias restrained by a combination of shifters and chains. Red eyes glare my way and a low growl reverberates from his chest. *Eric.*

Just like the first time we met, silver chains wrap around his body, the hairless patches of skin beneath searing red. His eyes are sharp but his body is completely limp as a hollower drags him across the ground and drops him at my feet. I struggle against the man holding me, my arm twisting painfully when he tightens his grip.

"Let her go." Charles waves his hand. "There's nowhere for her to run."

I fall to my knees, hands frantically tugging at the chains wrapped around Eric. But they've been done differently than George's; there's a padlock to keep them in place. "What'd you do to him?"

Charles studies me. "How ironic that you'd fall into bed with the very creature you once tortured."

"I didn't do that."

"You were a silent bystander."

"Don't you dare put me on the same level as you. You're a murderer."

To my surprise, Charles laughs. "You're not so innocent, Milena." The smile that settles on his face is anything but friendly. "I have someone who wants to talk to you."

My stomach seizes as he moves aside and a woman steps forward. Her lips are tight, eyes burning with hatred. Cynthia. Darius's mother. She never liked me. Especially when Darius started hanging around with me and Flo. Anytime she caught him following us around, she'd scowl at him and confiscate one of his favorite toys. But the look in her eyes now is different than it used to be—it burns so hot I almost feel my skin sizzle from its intensity.

She comes toward me, her sharp blue eyes strikingly similar to Darius's. "Hello, Milena."

"Cynthia . . ." Gray clouds thunder behind her, the sky accompanying her grief and rage. "I—I . . ."

"You." She wraps a hand through my hair and forces me to look at her. "Are a monster."

Pain prickles my scalp but I don't move. I see Darius then, lying in the dirt. I killed him. I signed Nella's death warrant. I led Charles to those shifters. In some twisted way, I've killed many people. But Darius is different. My knife killed him and my hands were wrapped around it when it did. Blood is in the crevices of my hands, but Darius's is the only blood that won't ever wash away.

Ever since I can remember, I've always been afraid of monsters. At first, it was the creatures of the night, and then it became the hollowers. But now, as Cynthia stands over me with excruciating pain lurking behind her eyes, I wonder if I've become the very thing I've been so afraid of. "I didn't mean to. Darius was—"

She slaps me across the face—hard. A buzz fills my ear. I fall back from the force, stumbling over Eric and landing on his other side, my feet in the air. Cynthia storms over to me. "Get that name out of your filthy mouth or the next time I touch you it'll be much worse than a slap." I can't speak. My body is numb as she stares at me with daggers in her eyes. "You're disgusting," she hisses. "A coldhearted killer."

"No. *No.* You're wrong." I push to my feet. "I loved Darius, too, and I wish he wasn't dead. But I'm not a monster. He tried to kill me!"

"You're a murderer." She spits in my face and shoves me backward. "You're a monster, and I look forward to torturing you. You're a sick, twisted murderer, and you deserve to—"

"Cynthia, that's enough." Charles's voice is cold and stern.

Her cheeks turn scarlet.

"Is that why you're here then?" When I find my voice, it doesn't sound like me. "To make me feel bad before you kill me?"

She comes closer, her bony finger scratching at my chin as she forces me to look at her. "You have no idea what you're in for, do you?"

"What do you mean?"

"We're not the only hollower village, Milena. It would be incredibly selfish of us to keep you to ourselves."

"What are you saying?"

"We're not going to kill you. What we're going to do to you is much, much worse."

And from the look in her eyes and her malicious smile, I believe her. "But you were going to kill me that day when I first went hunting. You were going to kill me right on the spot."

"That was before we realized that you could be much more useful to us. We'll kill the humans and the creatures, and keep using new ones, but there are many of them. We don't need them alive."

"You're going to keep me alive?"

"You'll barely be alive. We'll drain you until you're nearly dead, and then we'll bring you back to health. And then we'll drain you again, and again, and again. That way, all hollowers can live forever. Our children can drink from you when they're born. There will be no limited supply."

My stomach churns. "You're going to use me as a blood bag."

"We're not going to kill you." A sickening smile creeps across her face. "But I'll be there every step of the way making you wish we would."

She turns her back to me. I have to be smart. I can't let myself be ruled by my emotions, no matter what Elias says.

238

It's my weakness, and I can't afford any weaknesses right now. Something tells me if I choose now to retaliate, Cynthia will make sure I have no energy left to give.

"Is this what you want, Charles?" I call. He looks at me. "To torture me like that?"

"It's for the good of the people. Cynthia, check her for weapons and then chain her to the creature. We need to make preparations before the others arrive."

He steps around the boulder and disappears from view. Cynthia isn't gentle when she checks me. Her nails drag across my skin when she lifts my shirt and pats down my pants, but she comes up empty—the dagger from my boot was lost in the forest during our escape. Hopelessness stabs at my chest as she wraps chains around me, attaching me to Eric.

"You know," she says as she tightens them around my arms, "when I first brought the idea to the villagers, Charles was opposed to it."

She pulls them so tight my arm throbs. "You expect me to believe that?"

"I don't care whether you believe it."

"Then why tell me at all?"

"Because," she says, rising to her feet, "I want to remind you that no matter how much someone cares about you, you'll always be second. He'll never choose you over them." And then she steps back and follows Charles around the boulder.

Chains dig into my wrists, the cool metal rubbing my skin raw as I shift and try to pull my wrists free. "Stop squirming." Eric shifts beside me, a groan escaping his mouth. "You're pressing the chains into my skin."

"Eric! You're okay!"

Cynthia didn't do a great job of securing my legs, but she made sure that my wrists were tucked tightly beneath the chains wrapped around Eric's chest.

"I said stop moving." He has an oozing scratch on his forehead and his lips lift into a scowl. "Good to see you're not dead yet."

"They're not planning on killing me anymore. Didn't you hear?"

"I was sort of preoccupied with the excruciating pain of my skin literally burning."

My fingers are so numb I can't feel them. "They want to keep me alive so that they can keep using my blood, never letting me truly die."

"That's morbid."

A chill creeps up my spine. "Only, it won't work. Once they realize my blood doesn't do anything, they'll kill me." The wind howls around us, carrying the low murmurs from around the corner. "How'd you get here, Eric?"

He looks away, glaring at the rock face. "There was no way I was letting them take you without a fight."

"Cassia let you go?"

"No. She wanted us to find Elias. I was done letting her order me around."

"You came after me."

"I'm a man of my word, Milena," he says. "Elias asked me to protect you. You're not dying on my watch."

I blink back tears, thinking of Cassia. I thought we were friends, and aside from Elias, I thought she was the only person I could trust. And after discovering the truth about Elias, the reason for his distance, the only thing that comforted me was the fact that I still had Cassia. But Eric, who doesn't even like me, was more loyal than she was.

"She thought she was doing the right thing, you know." Eric's voice is softer than I've ever heard it; it's as if he's talking to a child. "I don't agree with it, but she did what she thought was right."

I let out a shaky breath, thinking of Charles. The way he'd looked at me while I was in that cell, when he said he was sorry; the fact that he's the only one who wants to use my blood and let me die instead of keeping me alive. Cassia betrayed me for her family and Charles betrayed me for his. "They all think they're doing the right thing."

It won't be long before the moon comes out and the shifters follow. But Charles doesn't seem afraid of the dark anymore, not like he used to be. Or maybe it's because the shifters are afraid of him now.

"Does Elias know?" I ask.

Eric's eyes meet mine. They're cold and hard. "Cassia went after him. If he doesn't already, it won't be long before he finds out."

"What're we going to do? They're going to kill you."

"When the moon comes out, I can try and shift. It won't be pretty but it might give us a chance."

"What if it doesn't—"

I don't get to finish my sentence. Cynthia slips around the boulder and stands in front of us. Her expression is startlingly still but her eyes are a maelstrom. "It's time."

I help Eric clamber to his feet. The smell of burning flesh fills my nostrils as the chains dig deeper into his skin and my knees buckle beneath his weight. But Cynthia's disgust-filled glare makes me sure of one thing—I won't fall in front of her. She grabs me and tugs forward, Eric coming with me around the boulder she and Charles disappeared behind. The crevice between the two cliff faces is narrow, a winding path hemmed in by walls towering into the sky.

Eric groans beside me. And though the rain has cleared, the sky roars with an echoing thunder. Dozens of eyes watch me, stoic expressions and straight mouths. They stand as a barricade, blocking the rest of the path and any exit. I gaze around the clearing, each familiar face stinging. Charles stands in the middle of the group with a chalice resting on a wooden platform beside him. In his hand, a machete. But of all the eyes on me, Charles's are the most piercing. "Let go of the creature, Milena."

I grip Eric tighter, blood staining my skin from where the chains create rigid, bloody lines across him. Charles motions to Cynthia behind me, and she kicks Eric's knees from behind. He clatters to the ground with a groan, his body thumping against the earth, the mud splattering around him. I almost fall with him, but Cynthia's fingers press into my skin and keep me standing.

My eyes remain on Charles as I struggle against Cynthia, but she doesn't budge, her grip iron tight. "Charles, what are you doing?"

When he reaches me, he puts his hand on my arm. "This will hurt."

"Stop!"

My elbow juts out toward Cynthia's nose but more hands grip my shoulders to keep me in place. A sharp pain erupts from my arm. Thunder hammers the sky, but the sound is secondary to my scream as the cool metal of the machete slices into my wrist. All defense strategies fly from my mind; the pain is overwhelming. Charles finally drops the machete and pulls me forward, holding my arm over the chalice as blood trickles from my skin and drips into the cup. As soon as he releases me, I fall backward.

He takes another step forward and hoists Eric up from the ground. They won't kill me. They want me. But they don't need Eric alive. "Charles! Stop, please! Don't hurt him."

He looks up at me, his eyes lingering on the cut in my arm. "I have no regrets about what happens to him; he's a creature."

Cynthia wraps her arms around me; I jab my elbow into her face and she stumbles backward. I start toward Charles and Eric but a man intercepts me and knocks me to the side, pinning me to the ground. I have no choice but to watch as Charles pulls Eric forward. The villagers crowd around, eyes trained on Eric as he's brought to the center of the circle. Charles stands over him, a long, silver pole in his hand.

"Stop!" I scream.

But it's too late; Charles thrusts the pole straight into Eric's chest. An agonizing roar mutes the thunder. Eric's body convulses, sharp teeth sprout from his mouth, and fur rises along the bare skin exposed on his arms. His fingers morph into claws and his bones crack. When Charles pulls the pole away, Eric collapses to the ground.

"Stop! Why the torture?" The person on top of me grips the back of my head and pounds it against the ground. Mud fills my mouth.

"He needs to be in his creature form!" Charles plunges the pole back into Eric's chest.

Teeth. Eyes. Snout. Hair. With the darkening sky, Eric's body breaks. A rancid stench fills the air as his bones crack and poke through skin. He's half man half wolf, flesh morphed with fur.

The moment the body on top of me shifts, I roll to the side, scrambling across the ground until I lie in front of Eric and stare up at Charles, who pauses, pole inches away from crashing into me. "Please!" Strands of mud-coated hair hang in my eyes. "Please, I'll do anything! Just don't kill him!"

His jaw clenches. "Get out of my way, Milena."

"I can't."

"Then you leave me no choice."

Hands grapple me from behind and pull me from Eric's body as Charles lifts his pole. But a scream from behind him fills the air. He flashes around, the pole falling to his side as more screams join the group. Hope stirs in my chest. Charles stumbles backward when something flies toward him. His body is thrown across the ground and orange lights the tree beside me, chaos erupting as the clearing is engulfed in flames. The fingers slip away from me. And though fire burns toward me and my lungs heave, my chest alights with something else. Hope. Hope and dread. Elias is here.

"Milena!" Charles's voice bounces through the fire, so distant I can't tell what direction it comes from. I lower my body to the ground, scrambling toward Eric's slumped body. Smoke assaults my lungs as it climbs the cliff walls. I tug the neckline of my shirt up to cover my mouth and nose and then tug at the chains around his fur. His eyes are open, red burning in the darkness, but the hole Charles created in his chest oozes red onto the ground. It isn't healing.

I unwind the chains from around him, skin searing as the fire around us burns closer. Thankfully, in the excruciating shift, the padlock securing the chain shattered. "Go." Eric's voice fills my head, weak and dull. "Get out of here. Find Elias. Go."

Putting my hand beneath his legs, I try to drag him across the ground. "I'm not leaving without you."

"Milena—"

"You protected me, so I'll protect you. I'm not leaving without you."

I tug him across the ground. My body aches in protest and my wrist stings, but I push on and drag Eric's body as quickly as I can through patches of clear ground until we reach the edge of the forest. I drop him, coughing and spluttering as I fall to my hands and knees. Smoke spirals into the sky like a tornado, but that isn't the biggest threat. A figure blocks our escape. Cynthia's eyes bear into mine; two men stand by her side. I leap up and take an uncertain step backward, but the flames behind us keep me from going any farther.

"You," she spits. "You lied. You're nothing but some dumb human. I saw him. And I saw you. The fire wasn't from you." Dread knots in my stomach. Cynthia nods at the men beside her. "Kill her and make it slow. I need to find Charles."

She escapes before the fire can get closer, and the two burly men edge nearer. The first one wraps a hand around my arm. I punch his throat and he stumbles backward. The other digs his nails into the cut on my arm and the pain paralyzes me. Our eyes meet; he raises his dagger and presses it to my neck. But before he can pierce my skin, his mouth falls open, a blade protruding through his chest instead. His body topples toward me and I duck to the side as he falls to the ground, relief and confusion flooding my mind.

Flo stands where he did, her eyes brimming with tears and shaky hands drenched in red. A second dagger is in her left hand, stretched toward me. "Flo?" I stagger forward as the second man pushes to his feet and moves toward Flo.

"I love you, Millie," she says, her skin ghostly pale. "And I'm sorry for what I did."

"Flo. Flo, no!" I'm too late—she buries her knife in the guard's chest at the same time that his knife lodges in hers, and they both stumble to the ground. The world burns around me but Flo is the only thing that matters. I fall to my knees in front of her, hands shaking uncontrollably as I bury them in her shirt. Her warmth covers my hand in a sickly red. "Flo, please! Flo, come on, please, stay awake."

She stares vacantly into the sky, her face so familiar but so far away. I shake her shoulders. I told Flo I wanted her to die. Blood. Scarlet red against dirt brown. Hair weaves in and out of the ground like roots of a dying tree. Her body feels cold. Her bones sag in her skin. Her skin is dull and pale, like the mannequins I threw daggers at in the castle. Blood seeps onto my fingers. Vacant green eyes stare into mine, her bluing lips and freckled skin so lifeless.

"Milena!" Night falls over us as the fire is extinguished. I know I need to move, to get out of here before Charles finds me. "Milena!" Eric's voice fills in my head. "We have to go!"

I look at him. He's still lying on the ground, eyes burning with urgency as the hole in his chest seeps red. My entire body is numb as I stare down at Flo, the bed of dirt around her mixing with her blood. I don't cry; the blood on my shirt seeps onto my skin. Laughter fills my mind, memories of skipping around the fire, climbing the walls, our hair billowing around us like kites. When Flo smiled, it brightened her whole face. I step toward Eric. "Let's go."

His breath comes in short, ragged gasps as his eyes flit from me down to Flo. Putting my arms under his body, I drag. I don't feel the iciness in the air; I don't feel *anything*. Eric's silent, his fur warm against my numb fingers as we move. I don't know where to go, all I know is that I have to get away from Flo. The rain washes her blood away. But it isn't enough. She follows me, whispering in my ear, chanting in my head. *I love you.* It's all I ever wanted, for some of it to be true, for some part of her to actually care about me as I did her. And she did.

Branches stretch toward us as I drag Eric through the forest. The smoke in the back of my throat chokes my vocal cords. When I lift my eyes, I halt. Elias stands between the trees opposite us, his white shirt slashed across his chest, speckled with drops of red. My knees buckle in relief when our eyes meet. I can't tell if he's real or if I'm dreaming. "What're you doing here?"

"You didn't think I'd miss all the action, did you?"

He scans me from head to toe, the small smile dropping from his face when I don't answer. He crosses the space between us. "You're bleeding."

"It's not mine."

"Yes, it is." His hand wraps around mine to lift it in front of my face. The cut Charles made seeps with blood, but I don't feel the pain. Elias curses under his breath and tears a section of his shirt off. He wraps the material around the cut so that I can't see it anymore, before looking at Eric on the ground. "What happened to Eric?"

Eric groans when Elias rolls him over. "You shouldn't be here, Elias."

"Is it bad?" I ask.

Elias examines the wound, his fingers combing Eric's fur. "They used a silver blade. This won't heal on its own—we need medicine, or within the next hour . . ."

His expression darkens and he looks away. My heart drops. *Or he'll die.* I scrape my mind desperately for a solution. Because despite everything, I've grown to care for Eric, and the thought of losing him. . . . A memory of when I met Darius in the tunnels where Eric was kept arises in my mind. *I have to give it this medicine to keep it alive,* Darius had said, *otherwise the silver will kill it.*

"There's medicine in the tunnels. I think it could help him."

Elias looks at me, eyes sharp. "What kind?"

"I don't know. But they used it on him when we first captured him. Darius said it was to keep the silver chains from killing him."

"Infumine," Elias murmurs. He looks at the sky; the rain has started again. "If I lead us there, can you find the medicine?"

"Yes. But the hollowers—"

"Cassia and I came through your village on the way; it's deserted. All the hollowers were at the ceremony."

"Cassia's here?"

He rises to his feet, so close and yet somehow feeling worlds away. "Yes."

Silence stretches between us, thick with tension. "It isn't safe there."

"It's our only option." He looks at Eric, face troubled. I know he's right, but that doesn't slow the terror racing through me. Eric came back for me and got taken because of it; I have to do this for him.

Heat emanates from Elias's body when he steps closer. And though his expression is soft, he doesn't reach for me. "We should get to the village before the hollowers." He pulls Eric up, balancing him on his shoulders. "He needs infumine to stop infection. Now."

I nod. Protected as we are by the canopy of the trees, the rain is merely a drizzle, but it chills me to the core as Elias steps ahead of me and starts in the direction I had run from.

CHAPTER SIXTEEN

The forest groans in the wind as we move through it, Eric's grunts ricocheting off the tops of the trees. We reach the forest edge, the village pitch black before us. But Elias doesn't hesitate to move forward; it appears to be deserted. The tomato plant climbs up the wooden sticks, absent of fruit in the winter air. From over his shoulder, I can see the kitchen shack. Memories haunt the air, an eerie wind passing through the village whispering words in a voice that sounds like Flo's. Her body was so pale and cold, and I just *left* her there.

"Milena?"

I nod toward the tunnel entrance. "This way."

The tunnels echo with Eric's groans as Elias carries him through the dark halls. Elias's eyes are the only source of light, so I loosely hold the hem of his shirt and instruct him which turns to take. When the tunnel widens into the gathering room, I rest against the wall as Elias deposits Eric gently on one of the sofas and places a blanket over his lower body. He turns back to me. "The medicine?"

"Charles keeps everything in his room. If you follow that hall, it's the last room at the end. I can show you."

"Stay with Eric." I jolt in fright when his hand touches mine. "I'll be right back."

He pulls away and I blink at Eric, my eyes somewhat adjusting to the darkness of the tunnels. He isn't conscious. Pain pierces through the numbness as my wrist starts to sting. We can't stay down here for long. Even though the hollowers aren't here, after what happened at the ceremony, they should be making their way back to regroup. Elias returns and kneels beside Eric.

"Did you find anything?"

"Infumine." He holds up a small, glass vial. Charles's messy writing is scribbled across the bottom, the letters linked together and difficult to read. "It should fight off this infection for now. But we need to get him back as soon as possible."

He inserts a needle into the fur at Eric's throat. Conflicted emotions race through my mind—grief, relief, affection. But at the forefront, betrayal lingers. Because every person I've ever come to trust has lied to me, and Elias isn't immune. I can't suppress the way it affects me. "You knew. This entire time, you knew."

He looks at me. "What?"

"What'd Ana tell you in the mountains, Elias?" My voice is low, quiet, but he hears it, and his expression falters. The familiar sound of water dripping onto metal echoes somewhere in the tunnels, filling the silence. "Tell me what she said."

"Charles never wanted you, he wanted me." His words dangle in the air, thick, like smoke. "When the elders found out the hollowers were going after my mother, they knew they had to do something to keep me from them. They found you at a human orphanage and switched us. Ana left my mother's body in the cabin because she knew the hollowers wouldn't stop looking till they saw that she was dead. The hollowers knew they had a child, so Ana left you. She fabricated the scene, made sure there were only pictures left of a baby your age and younger, made it look like my mother killed her husband, herself, and left her baby on its own."

I wrap my arms around my body, an attempt to hold myself together as more fragments of my identity fall through my fingers. "Why didn't you tell me?"

"I wanted to but Eric convinced me not to say anything. Ana sacrificed herself to protect my identity, I couldn't jeopardize that."

"Cassia and I found out you're a wisper and, still, you didn't tell us." Deep down, I want there to be a reason, something that justifies keeping the secret. But his excuse is weak; my heart sinks in disappointment. "You shouldn't have come here, Elias."

"If I hadn't, both you and Eric would probably be dead right now."

"If they tried to use my blood, they wouldn't become immortal and they wouldn't know why. This would all end. They'd think there was something wrong about the sacrifice. They wouldn't know it was my fault it didn't work. But Cynthia *saw* you, Elias, she knows I'm not the wisper and it won't be long till she tells someone else."

"I don't care."

"You don't get it. They'll never stop looking for you."

"I said I don't care." He steps closer to me, eyes burning. "Milena, I didn't want you to hate me. That's why I didn't tell you."

"Why would I hate you?"

"You lived a life that was meant for me—it was never supposed to be you. Your only fault was being an orphan and Ana used that to protect me. Everything that happened to you is on me, it should've been *me*." His eyes hold mine. "It was all a lie. Everything that happened to you was my fault. If I were you, *I* would hate me."

I want to tell him he's wrong, that nothing could make me hate him, but I hold my tongue. We've always been connected. The day his parents died and Ana plucked me from that orphanage an invisible string tied our fates together. But I grew to care for him all on my own. His fierce loyalty, the way he looks out for others, his otherworldly beauty—all aspects that helped him weasel his way into my heart. He makes me feel like I belong somewhere, like I'm *wanted*. But if I had known the truth from the beginning, would I still feel that way, or would my affection have turned into resentment? I don't know.

"Everything's so messed up."

"I know," he breathes. "I'm so sorry." His eyes are like an embrace, causing goose bumps to rise along the back of my neck. From the day Charles turned on me, I knew my life had been a lie, but I hadn't realized it was because this life never belonged to me in the first place.

"Whose blood is on you?" he asks.

"It doesn't matter."

"It always matters."

"Flo's dead. She saved my life after I told her I wished she was dead." I can't help but crumble at the softness in his expression. "I know you probably think it was stupid. She was a hollower."

"She was your best friend." I want to collapse against him but he simply grazes the inside of my wrist, a touch so comforting it could almost be an embrace. If I close my eyes, I can pretend Flo isn't dead. I can pretend that Elias and I can be together, that he isn't a wisper, that Charles isn't after him, and that he didn't lie to me. If I close my eyes, everything washes away and it's just me and him. I can't help but lean closer.

"How long do we have to wait?"

"He should wake up soon," Elias says. We're barely touching, but his proximity is comforting enough. "He won't be at his best but he'll be able to walk, at least. We'll leave as soon as he can shift back."

The silence between us is as suffocating as smoke. My mind plays wicked tricks on me, twisting sounds and echoes that resemble footsteps from above. I watch Eric's chest rise and fall. "They'll be here soon."

"And I don't intend to be here when they do. Cassia will create a distraction to lead them away from the village."

"Right."

His expression darkens when he looks at me. "Milena, I know what she did to you."

For some reason, the revelation stings. Elias doesn't seem fazed by what she did—he doesn't sound angry. I know it shouldn't bother me but it does. Cassia has known Elias for a lot longer than I have; their history stretches much further than ours. "And you're okay with it?"

"*Okay* with it? Are you kidding?"

254

"You don't seem fazed."

"*Fazed* would be an understatement." He looks offended. "When Cassia told me what she did, I nearly lost it. She not only betrayed you, Milena, but she betrayed me and Eric too. It doesn't matter why she did it, she betrayed our trust."

"Then why is she here?"

"She wanted to help and I wasn't going to say no."

I try to push Cassia to the back of my mind. I don't want to think about her because when I do, thoughts of Flo creep in too. And the guilt paralyzes me more than any betrayal ever did.

Eric groans, his body shifting. He lies in human form, bloodied body covered in nothing but a small knitted blanket. "Eric?" I kneel lower so that we're eye to eye. "Are you okay?"

"What do you think?" he snaps.

I can't help but smile in relief. His eyes brush over to Elias. "You idiot. You shouldn't be here."

"Just put these on." Elias throws a pair of pants at him. Eric mumbles profanities under his breath, wincing with pain as he shuffles on the couch to pull the clothes on. Once he's finished, Elias reaches over to help him up. "Let's go. Milena, you stay behind us."

The darkness provides a strange comfort as we venture through the halls. We reach the bolted doors and I move over to the lever, wrapping my hand around. *Thump.* I freeze. "Did you hear that?"

Tension lines Elias's shoulders as we stare at the doors, waiting. Hope stirs in my chest—maybe I heard wrong. But the shout carrying through the wood isn't imagined, nor are the rigorous pounds that follow. "They're here." I leap away from the lever. "Charles is here. Where's Cassia?" Elias doesn't move, frozen as he stares at the doors with Eric slung over his shoulder. His uncertainty sets me on edge. "Elias?"

"There has to be another way out."

"This is the only exit."

For the first time since I met him, panic burns in his eyes. He doesn't know what to do any more than I do. "Leave me," Eric says. "You have to leave me." He tries to unwind his arm from around Elias's shoulder. "I'll only slow you down."

But Elias doesn't let him go. "We're not leaving without you, Eric. Don't even entertain that thought."

I look at Elias. "Can't you burn them or something?"

"I can't risk that down here. If I light something on fire, I can't control it. And if we're stuck down here, I don't want to risk burning you both to death. Take this." He thrusts a dagger across the ground toward me. It hits my toe, the tip nearly piercing my shoe. "We have to open the doors."

I bend over to pick the dagger up. "What?"

"They're going to get in—it's inevitable." He unwinds his arm from Eric and lays him to rest against the wall before marching to the doors, his eyes on me. "You have to take Eric and get him away from here. When they're open, I'll cover for you so that the two of you can get to the forest."

Eric frowns. "We're not leaving you."

"I'll be right behind you."

I trust Elias with my life, but this time, I don't believe him. "Elias, if they see you use fire then—"

"You said that woman already saw me."

"But we don't know if she told them."

"I don't care." He looks directly at me, face darkened by the shadows. "You and Eric have to get out of here or they'll kill you."

"No, this is stupid. We should stick together."

"We can't."

I search for words but come up empty because I know he's right. If we want to get out of this, there's no way we can do it all together. He moves over to the entrance, the tunnels shuddering with each pound against the doors. Ducking behind the crevice, his hand rests on the lever. "You two wait here. When I open the doors and it's safe, I want you to run. I'll burn them the second you're gone." Anger lingers in Eric's eyes but he's too loyal to argue. Elias looks at me. "Don't fight me on this. It's the only way."

"Please." My voice is a whisper, carried through the tunnel like a haunting echo. "We can't lose you."

"Promise me that when you get Eric out of here you won't come back."

"Elias . . ."

"Promise me."

"Only if you promise to come back."

"I'll come back, I promise." His eyes search my face. "You know I can always—"

"You can always find me. I know."

A sad smile crosses his face before he looks at Eric, who hobbles toward me and slings an arm over my shoulder. Together, we creep over to hide in the crevice behind the entrance and Elias stands facing it. I have to keep myself from screaming at him to stop. "Ready?" Elias asks.

I nod. Metal grates against metal, a screeching sound that pierces my ears. But once the doors are fully opened, there's complete silence. The pounding stops, as do the shouts. They didn't think we would open the door. My muscles tighten as I recall

Aliyah's instructions in my mind, every second of my training important. Eric and I are pressed against the wall. All I can see is the side of Elias's face. I know they're there, inches from Elias—the one they've been looking for all this time. Elias takes a threatening step forward. "I'm the one you want. I'm the wisper."

Somebody steps into view, their body half concealed in shadows. I squint to make him out. It's Charles. "This is the one, Cynthia?"

Cynthia steps beside him. "I saw him light them on fire. It was him."

"And Milena?"

A sinister smile creeps onto her face. "Dead."

I think of the place where Flo lies in a grave that was meant for me. Charles's jaw twitches but he keeps his eyes forward and turns away from Cynthia. "What do you want, wisper?" he asks.

"I want you to leave my village alone," Elias says. "No more murders, no more coming after my people."

"And in exchange?"

"I'll go with you."

A strangled sound escapes me, cut off by Eric's hand slapping over my mouth. "Shhh."

"He *can't* go with them."

"He won't." Eric's voice is so low it makes my stomach drop. "He has to get them away from here so we can escape."

The prospect of Charles having Elias is terrifying but I have to trust Elias. Cynthia steps toward Elias with a chain in her hands but Elias puts his hand up to halt her. "I'll come with you on *my* terms," he says. "No chains."

Cynthia and Charles exchange glances. "How do we know we can trust you?"

"You don't."

Silence. When Charles finally looks up, his eyes are narrowed into thin slits. "Everybody, get back," he calls behind without turning around. "Gather by the kitchen shack."

Seconds feel like hours as feet shuffle backward. Elias stays rigid in the entrance, his eyes never leaving Charles, who stands inches away. He nods at Charles. "Your turn."

"I don't think so."

"If you don't move I'll make sure you're all burned to a crisp."

Charles pauses, his lips pursed before he takes a step back in defeat until he's finally out of view. The second Elias steps forward, Eric nudges me. "Go."

Making sure my arm is hooked tightly around his waist, I stagger away from the shadow and into the entrance. The moon peeks through the clouds. Charles still stands facing us, his eyes trained on Elias. But when I move, he looks at me. I freeze. Charles doesn't move, his mouth parts slightly as we stare at each other.

"Milena!" Eric knocks my shoulder.

At the sound of his voice, Cynthia turns to look over her shoulder. "There!" she shouts, bony fingers pointing at me. "Kill her!"

Her voice breaks both me and Charles from our trance. I stumble backward, gripping Eric tighter as I start toward the forest. Some of the hollowers behind Cynthia follow us, but they're too late. The second Eric and I are out of the tunnel entrance, the ground between the hollowers and us blazes in flames. "Go!" Beneath the sound of the roaring fire, Elias's voice carries through the sky.

Behind us, the fire gasps for oxygen. I hobble us into the trees, my arms aching from the weight of Eric. "Left," Eric coughs.

"What?"

"Go left."

We weave through the trees and over fallen trunks and branches. But I'm not stealthy enough, my foot catches on a root and I fly forward; Eric tumbles from my arms to the ground. A branch jabs into my back where I land and the world spins above me as I try to gather my bearings. It wasn't a root that I tripped on.

A woman stands above me, a glinting machete in her right hand and a smile on her face, and my stomach drops. I scramble back on the ground until my back hits a tree, but she simply steps forward to block me. Flo's mother. *Does she know about Flo?*

"Where do you think you're going, Milena?" Eric lies a few feet away, eyes burning into mine as he crawls closer across the ground. My hand slips into my boot, feeling for the dagger Elias handed me. "You're nothing but a weak human. Now nothing is stopping any of us from hunting you."

When she reaches down to grab me by the collar of my shirt, I throw my arm out and swipe the dagger across her chest. She hisses, pulls me closer, and presses the machete against my throat. I twist in her hold so that my dagger is pressed just as tightly against hers. "You kill me and we both die. Is that what you want?"

Her green eyes meet mine; they're so similar to Flo's. If I crack, she'll see right through me. She'll see that even if I could, I wouldn't kill her, that her cries would haunt me for the rest of my life. She releases me and I stumble back, holding my dagger toward her as I walk sideways to Eric. "Don't follow us," I say. "Go back the way you came." She says nothing, her eyes on me as I slowly reach down to help Eric to his feet, the dagger in my left hand trembling where it's pointed at the center of her chest. "I'm serious. Don't follow us."

I turn my body, trying to maneuver Eric beneath my arm. An arm knocks into my chest and I fly backward, pain flourishing in my back as I hit the tree. In front of me, Cassia stands, facing the hollower, with a knife in her hand. The hollower's machete is now lodged in the trunk of the tree I'd been standing before.

"Nice try, hollower," Cassia hisses. The hollower's eyes flicker with panic, mouth opening to shout for help, but she's too late—Cassia's knife plunges into her upper leg and she falls to the ground, a strangled cry escaping her throat. Cassia spins around to face us. "Eric?" She kneels next to him. "What happened?"

"They took his blood for the ceremony," I say. "Elias gave him something to fight infection, but I don't know how well it worked."

She looks at me. My hands itch to slap her, to scream at her, to make her feel the pain she made me feel. But then I remember Flo, and I clench my fists and stare at the ground. "Milena, I—"

"I have to get Eric out of here." I push to my feet and step toward him. "I promised Elias."

"Elias is still back there?"

"Yes, he—"

But she's already gone, weaving through the trees back to the burning village. I pick Eric up, my hands trembling and knees knocking together. Eric clears his throat, his breath ragged and sharp as the branches claw toward us. "Wait."

"It's going to be okay," I murmur. All I can think about is Elias. I don't know enough about his powers to have confidence that my statement is true.

"Milena," Eric groans. The fire is far away now, the forest dark. I don't know how far we've walked and I don't know where we're going. "Milena, stop." If I stop, I don't know if I can continue. "Milena!"

"Elias said—"

"We're far enough!"

"We have to get back to the village."

"Unless you want to be walking for three days, that's not going to happen."

"Then what are we supposed to do?"

He unwinds my arm from around him and stumbles backward, leaning against a tree to support his weight. "Leave me."

"Don't be stupid."

"I'm fine here for a while. I'll contact someone to come and get me." He pauses, lip pulling into his mouth. "I know I shouldn't ask you this, but—"

"You want me to go back."

For the first time since I met him, vulnerability swims in his eyes. "They're all I have." I don't have to ask to know who he's talking about. "I know I can't force you."

"I'll go back. For Elias." As we stare at each other, I feel a surge of affection. This is Eric—no masks, loyal to the grave Eric. I turn around and take a deep breath.

A hand catches my wrist. "Milena?"

I turn around to look at him. When I first met Eric, his red eyes scared me, but now, in the darkness of the night where it feels like there is no hope, they're my only comfort. "Thank you. I'll owe you forever." I squeeze his hand, and then turn around and go back the way we came.

~

Eric and I were running for longer than I thought, the forest a blur as we pushed through it in our desperation to get away. Now, I'm heading back with that same desperation. When I think of Eric, anxiety gnaws at my mind. I don't know if leaving him alone was a good idea. What if a hollower finds him lying there, defenseless?

Smoke swirls in the air when I finally burst into the clearing; a fist of ash wraps around my airway. I pull the collar of my shirt over my mouth and blink away the stinging sensation. The clearing is war torn. The gardens are blackened, littered with charred wood lying in broken piles. A limp body lies in the center, their skin so burned I can't even tell if I knew them. I hesitate. Even after everything that happened, a small part inside of me dies at seeing my childhood burn. The fun I had with Flo, the games I played with Darius—it all billows up in a cloud of smoke.

Aside from the fire, the only light from the village comes from the kitchen shack. Guarded by the small stream, it appears mostly unscathed. I take a deep breath, wrap my hand around the hilt of my dagger, and leave the safety of the trees. Embers sizzle around me and ash covers the ground, but the only other person around is a dead body lying several feet away. Bile rises in my throat when I see their face—blistered and red. I creep to the kitchen shack, the light escaping through the cracks in the wood luring me closer.

"Are they gone?" At the sound of Charles's voice, I press myself farther against the wood.

"Yes," Cynthia responds. "They're heading for the mountains. Alex set everything up for us, now all we need is the wisper."

CREATURES *of the* NIGHT   263

Slowly inching forward, I peek through the window. Charles and Cynthia stand together at the counter over a collection of syringes; Elias lies on the table in the center, his limbs wrapped in silver and attached to the table legs. His eyes are shut, his chest rising and falling at inconsistent speeds. A needle in his arm transfers blood into a container on the ground.

"When will he be ready to move?" Cynthia wonders.

"We just have to get a little bit more." Charles carefully inspects the needle. Elias flinches beneath his touch. "He's only half creature so the chains don't work as well on him as they do for the others. When he's weak enough, we can move him."

"And what about the other creature?"

Charles shrugs. "I don't care what happens to her. Take her blood or finish her. We have a hybrid now, he's all we need."

"I'll leave her outside for now," Cynthia says. "We can take her with us when we go to the mountains."

A chill crawls down my spine when Charles nods. "If anything happens on the way . . ."

"I know what to do." Cynthia steps over to the bench and picks up a syringe filled with a pastel-pink liquid. She taps her fingernail against it, a sly smile creeping onto her face. "Should I send someone after Milena?"

"What?"

"I thought they killed her but something must've happened because she got away."

Silence stretches between them. "No," he says eventually. "We don't need her anymore. We're not wasting time and resources going after her when she's no longer a threat."

"She killed Darius—"

"I said *no*," Charles snaps. Cynthia turns so I can't see her face.

I should move; Cassia's outside, which means she's close. But my eyes are glued to Charles's face, committing his expression to memory, the line between his brows, the twist of his lips, and the way he glares at the floor—proof that maybe my affection for him wasn't one-sided. A stick snaps under my foot. Charles's head turns toward me but I drop to the ground, my body flat against the soil, pulse racing.

Voices continue in the cabin. I drag myself across the ground until I reach the corner. The back door of the kitchen is slightly ajar, but resting against it, wrapped in chains, is Cassia. Against the area surrounding her, her hair looks like a halo. "Cassia!" She doesn't look up, she doesn't even flinch, so I pick up the pebble buried in dirt and throw it at her. She starts and looks at me.

I scramble across the ground toward her. The chains are cold in my hands as I unwind them from her limbs. "What happened?" I whisper. One of the chains clanks to the ground, revealing burned flesh beneath.

"There were too many of them. When I got here, they already had the chains on Elias. I was too late."

The second the rest of the chains fall to the ground, Cassia clutches her bleeding arms to her chest, the red staining her white collar. "Where's Eric?"

"He told me to leave him in the forest."

"He *what*?"

"He said he'd contact someone to get help. He wanted me to help you and Elias."

She looks at the forest. "I managed to contact Bastian and Aliyah a few hours ago—they're on their way with reinforcements." I open my mouth to respond but Cassia grabs my shoulders, pushing my body to the ground and rolling us sideways until we tumble into a bush a few feet away. She presses her body into mine and slaps her hand over my mouth.

Through the leaves, light floods onto the ground as the kitchen door opens and reveals Cynthia. She freezes the second her eyes scan the area, noticing the chains on the ground. "Charles!"

He steps out a few seconds after her. "Where's the creature?"

"She was right here."

"And now she's not. Dammit, Cynthia!"

Cassia's breath is hot against my neck, the cuts on her arms seeping blood onto my skin.

"Find her!" Charles demands. "She can't have gotten far."

Cynthia steps back into the shack before returning with a machete, her eyes scanning the area. I hold my breath as she steps past us. Back by the cabin, Charles curses and then marches in the direction of the tunnel. Cassia rolls off me, grabs my shoulders, and shakes me. "I'm going inside."

"What?"

"They're both gone," she says, wincing as she shifts her body sideways and tries to push herself to her feet. "I have to take advantage of it."

"No. You can barely move. Besides, even if you go in there, the chains are silver, you can't get them off. I'll go. Keep watch, okay?"

She looks like she wants to say something but I pry my wrist from her grip and sprint toward the shack. I advance along the wall, crawling across the ground as I pass the window. The door creaks when I open it. I have to be quick—if Cynthia or Charles sees me here, I don't know what they'll do. The small lantern casts sinister shadows against the wall. Elias lies still on the table, the tube still in his arm and draining into the bucket. I

266   GRACE COLLINS

shudder as I step toward him, then place my hand on his shoulder and shake him. His skin burns. "Elias?"

At the sound of my voice, his eyes open. They're unfocused and clouded. "Milena?"

"I'm here." I squeeze his shoulder. "I'm going to get you out of here." A deep groan rumbles from his chest when he struggles against the chains, his skin searing beneath. "Don't move."

"Go. Get out of here, you can't be here."

"Stop moving." I tug at the chains, but Elias doesn't listen to me, the smell of burning flesh filling my nostrils as he struggles on the table. I put both of my hands on his shoulders and push him down. He's so weak he can barely fight back. "I can't help you if you keep straining on these chains!"

"*Please.*" His eyes fall shut. "Get out of here before it's too late."

I put my hand on his sweat-drenched forehead. "Not without you."

Ducking beneath the table, I attempt to unwind the chains. They're woven throughout the structure beneath, metal loudly clanking as I pull them apart. Despite the chill in the air, sweat beads at the back of my neck. The dirt embedded in my dark skin rubs off onto the wooden floor. The chains fall away. I jump up and wrap my hand around his arm. The skin where the chains were pressed seeps with blood.

"Can you move?"

His eyes flutter open, but he struggles to keep focused on me. "Milena?" The tube in his arm is considerable in size—I don't want to just pull it out but he's delirious and only growing weaker. In a split-second decision, I tear the bottom section of my shirt, slide the needle from his arm, and wrap the shirt in a tight knot around the small hole that seeps with blood.

CREATURES *of the* NIGHT

I turn to face him and put my hands on the sides of his face. "Elias? Elias, I need you to wake up."

"Milena?"

"It's me, I'm here. I need you to move."

His eyes flutter open, gold flecks shimmering in the shadowed room. "I found you."

"Elias—"

"I said I can always find you."

I shake my head and lean over him to put my hands under his arms, trying to tug him upward. Seeing Elias this way makes the world shift. Even the strongest of us can be reduced to deliriousness. His limp body is heavy when he slumps forward, head falling against my neck. Once I've got him in a sitting position, I put my hands on his shoulders. "I'm going to put you on the ground, okay?" I say. "We're getting out of here."

For a split second, his eyes focus on me. "Ana."

"Ana's not here. It's me. Milena."

"I don't want to hurt you."

I pull him closer. "You're not hurting me."

"If I hurt you . . ." His body sways. "You told me to never talk about it, but she was just a baby, Ana."

"Elias, we have to go—"

"She was just a baby and I killed her." He nearly falls backward but I catch him, wrapping my arm around his waist. "I can still hear her screams. I can see the body burning when I close my eyes. I can smell the flesh." His voice is low with pain, his words chopped up and muffled. Wherever he is, he's somewhere far away from here, trapped somewhere in his past, ghosts in his eyes and memories haunting his mind. We have to get out of here.

I step backward, put his arm over my shoulder, and wrap my arm around his waist, stumbling back from the table and taking him with me. But I don't get very far. My entire body goes rigid when I face the shadow looming in the doorway. I take a wary step back, Elias slipping from my grip and crumbling back onto the table. My hand slips behind me to clutch my dagger.

"You shouldn't have come back." Charles's eyes are dark, the color of moss in the shadows.

"What have you done to him, Charles?"

He steps closer. Instinctively, I sidestep so that Elias is behind me and concealed from Charles's view. "You're too late, Milena."

"Please, let him go."

He shakes his head, the candlelight casting shadows behind him. The walls of the room suffocate me. There's something about his presence that makes me feel like a child. "You know I won't do that."

"Let him go or I'll—"

"You'll what?" He laughs because he can see right through me. "I don't need anything from you anymore. You should leave."

"I won't."

"Cynthia will be here soon with the others." He steps over to the table, turning so his back faces me. "If you want to live, you need to go."

The dagger in my hand feels like a block of concrete, the cold hilt like ice against my skin. It would be so easy for me to put it into his back, to push the sharp end beneath his ribs and angle it toward his heart as Eric taught me. But I feel a wave of shame. He's watched me cry over a squashed snail. Charles only stands that way because he knows I won't hurt him. "I'm not leaving without Elias."

"What?" He spins to face me. "*Go.* I don't want to have to hurt you."

"You're hurting me if you take him."

With his lips in a twisted scowl, he stares at me in disgust. "You care about him?"

"Is that so bad?"

"He has creature blood."

"They're not the monsters you make them out to be."

"They're animals."

"And you're a murderer," I say. "I think it's time you took a look in the mirror, Charles."

He lifts his chin. "What's that supposed to mean?"

"You know exactly what it means."

He takes slow and calculated steps forward. I hold my breath, the table digging into my lower back when he stops in front of me. He's so close I have to crane my neck up to look at him. There's a dark shadow on his jaw and a mixture of sweat and dirt across his brow. He looks so familiar but, at the same time, like someone I never knew.

A small dagger dangles from his fingers, similar to the one I have clutched behind my back. But even as I gaze deep into his eyes, I don't see the monster that visits me in my nightmares. I don't see the man who shouted at me when I disobeyed him or the one who's spent the last few weeks trying to kill me. I see the man who once pinned my drawings in his office, and my chest aches. It's so hard to see the bad in someone when you so desperately want to see the good.

"Leave. Now."

I shake my head, refusing to break eye contact. "No."

The door swings open. "I can't find her, she got too—" Cynthia stops. "You found her."

Charles doesn't look at the doorway, his eyes remain on me. I don't know what to do. My head screams at me to run but my heart keeps my feet in place. Elias didn't care why they wanted me; he didn't care that he didn't know me. He promised he wouldn't let them have me and now I have to do the same. I grip the dagger tighter behind me, the muscles in my back aching from tension.

"What are you doing?" Cynthia yells at Charles when he doesn't move. "Grab her!"

He steps forward, his hand wrapping around my wrist. He presses his mouth against my ear. "Go. Run and don't turn back." His eyes are desperate. "Please go, Milena. Get out of here."

I falter, for a second actually considering it. But I shake the thought from my mind, twist my arm from his grip, and press my dagger against his throat instead. "I said no. I'm not leaving without Elias."

"Cynthia, do it," Charles says.

"What?"

"The *potio somnum*." Charles doesn't take his eyes off me, his hands raised high in the air while he talks. "Do it. Now."

"Now?" The air between them is thick with tension; Cynthia looks nervous. "But if we—"

"I said do it!" he yells.

The what?

"We can't!"

"She won't leave while his heart is still beating!"

"What are you talking about?" I shout, pressing the dagger tighter against his throat. "What are you doing?"

"I don't give a damn if she doesn't leave," Cynthia snarls. "I want her dead!"

Charles scowls. "I'll do it myself."

Before I can even take a breath, he spins around and breaks away from my grip. I stumble forward in his absence as he picks up the syringe on the table and launches himself at Elias. "Don't touch him!"

"Get out of my way, Milena."

"No—"

He whacks my stomach and sends me flying backward. I hit the wall with a thump, the world spinning around me as I try to regain my breath and push myself to my feet. An agonizing roar resonates through the walls, and Elias's back arches off the table as Charles stabs the syringe into his arm. I fly forward, thrusting my knife into Charles's back. He staggers backward, the now-empty syringe clattering to the floor feet away from where he falls. My scream chokes as he turns to face me, his eyes wide and mouth agape.

"You—" His words choke halfway in his throat. "—you stabbed me."

I watch in horror, my knife in his back and his blood on my hands. Charles gurgles, his hands reaching to his back and scratching at his skin. I stabbed him. I *stabbed* him. He doesn't look away from me and it's paralyzing, the only part of my body capable of movement are my eyes, and when they shift to the figure on the table, my heart stops. Elias isn't struggling anymore. I stumble over and press against his chest. His skin feels cold, his arms limp.

"What did you do?" I look at Cynthia. "What did you *do*?"

"You're too late."

"No." I press my fingers to his neck, trying to find a pulse. "No, no, no, no, no. You need him. You wouldn't kill him, you *wouldn't*."

"I didn't. But I'll kill you."

She soars toward me and wraps her arms around me with a crushing pressure. I cry out. She grabs my arm and thrusts her dagger into my upper shoulder. White blurs my vision. Cynthia twists me so I'm pressed against her chest and her mouth is against my ear. Charles lies on the floor, his body twitching as he chokes on his own blood, and Elias's arms hang limply off the table. Her mouth presses against my ear. "For Darius."

Her blade presses against my throat, ice cold. I sink my teeth into the hand covering my mouth so hard blood fills my mouth, the bitter taste making me gag. Cynthia gasps, her grip loosening on me. I duck beneath her arms and stumble backward, blood trailing from the wound on my shoulder down to my wrist. Looking around for something to defend myself, I come up empty. My dagger is in Charles's back and the table filled with needles is behind Cynthia. I reach out and wrap my hand around the pot hanging on the wall instead, then hold it toward her.

"Don't come any closer."

She scowls at me. Before she can take another step, the front door bursts open. "Milena!" It's Bastian. Panic flashes through Cynthia's eyes. She looks at me before noticing Bastian in the doorway. Before Bastian can get any closer, she steps toward the back door.

"This isn't over, Milena." She kicks the back door open and escapes the room.

"Go after her!" Bastian yells as I sink to the floor. Movement flashes around me like a light, but I can't focus. Cassia limps through the doorway, her arm thrown over Aliyah's shoulder. Her eyes fill with relief when they land on me, but then they shift to Elias, and the look in her eyes makes me choke on air.

"Elias?" She limps over to him and shakes his shoulder, but he doesn't move. "Elias!" She presses her head against his chest. Maybe I was wrong. Maybe he's unconscious. Cassia lets out an agonizing howl and the hope is extinguished. "*No!*" She pounds against his chest with her fist. "Dammit, wake up!" Aliyah steps forward and puts a hand on her shoulder. "Wake up! Wake *up*!"

I lie discarded against the wall, Charles's blood pooling at my feet and staining the bottom of my pants. Everything is fuzzy but Elias is clear. His arms hang limply off the table. His skin doesn't look so golden anymore. A shadow looms over me as Bastian steps closer, kneeling down so he's at my eye level. But I can't look at him; all I see is Cassia, relentlessly hammering against Elias's chest. Up and down. Up and down. Up and down.

"Milena?" Bastian shakes me by my shoulders. "What happened?"

I open my mouth but no words come out. Bastian has already forgotten me, moving over to Cassia to grab her arms. She screams when he tries to drag her away from Elias. I stare at Charles on the floor. He's dead now, but his eyes are open, his expression vacant as he looks toward me, and a hollowness takes over my chest. All his life, he saw the shifters as the monsters when he was the one who was wrong all along, and he died never knowing his mistake.

CHAPTER SEVENTEEN

When somebody died in my village, the hunters would take the body into the forest at sunrise and return before sunset. We would sometimes have memorial services to commemorate multiple of the fallen, but we never gathered around the bodies like some sort of shrine. That idea is so confronting. Maybe that's why I can't bring myself to attend Elias's funeral.

The cool stone of the windowsill presses against my back as I peer out the window. I hug my legs tightly against my chest and press my forehead against the glass, staring at the scene below. I'm several hundred feet away, but I don't feel far enough. Everything is over. Cynthia got away, Charles is dead, and we're back at the castle. But the hollowness in my chest is stronger than the relief; an ocean of regret and grief surrounds me. And nobody ever taught me how to swim.

Crowds gather around the wooden casket below. It's a cluster of dark clothes and hanging heads, a stark contrast to the euphoria and joy of the last village event in that clearing. Music wafts through the thin glass like a haunting melody. My breath fogs the icy edges of the glass. But even in my thin camisole, I don't feel cold. It's been two days since I killed Charles. Two days since Cynthia got away. Two days since Elias's heart stopped beating. Two days since Elias died.

I barely remember the journey back. I don't know how I got back—how any of us did. The last thing I remember is lying on the floor of the kitchen shack with Charles's blood on my hands and Cassia's screams rattling inside my head. I woke up to an unfamiliar woman with an unfamiliar voice and, for a moment, it was all a bad dream. I didn't kill the man who raised me. Cynthia didn't get away. Elias wasn't dead. But the nightmare didn't end when I woke up.

There's a knock on the door, two firm raps that make me twist my head sideways. Eric leans against the door frame, red eyes finding mine. "Hey."

"Hey." He shuffles closer, moving to stand behind me. "How's your chest?" I ask.

"It's healing."

"That's good." Cassia's at the funeral, her head in her hands as she kneels in front of the casket. My eyes sting and I force myself to look away, noting the red rims around Eric's eyes. "You're not going to the funeral?"

"I already said my good-byes. And you?"

"What about me?"

"You haven't left your room since we got back," he says. "You don't want to say anything?"

"I don't have anything to say." The lie tastes like acid in my mouth, burning all the way down to my stomach. I was there in his last moments. I was there when Charles injected that liquid into his bloodstream and when his hands hung limply from the table. And yet, I didn't get to say good-bye. I lay on the floor and watched as Cassia pounded against his chest, rocked him in her arms, begged for him to open his eyes. "How's Cassia?"

"How do you think?"

There's still a part of me that wants to hate her, to blame her for this entire mess, but I know that isn't fair. I can't hate her for what she did. Hate is an ugly emotion, and it exhausts me. If I'd forgiven Flo for what she did, maybe she wouldn't have died. Maybe her blood wouldn't be on my hands and maybe my chest wouldn't feel as twisted as it does.

The streets outside have been just as dead as the castle, until now. The casket sat alone in the village, flowers scattered around it and handwritten notes from children tucked safely within the foliage. "Are they going to bury him?"

He nods. "In the mountains, with Ana."

"Will you go with them?"

"I won't leave him to be buried by people who barely knew him. Even if he is dead."

I flinch, pulling my legs tighter to my chest. "You don't have to say it like that."

"Say what? That he's dead?"

I shrug and stare out the window. The man by the casket is lifting the bolts, the crowd gathering closer.

"Well, he is dead, Milena."

"I know, you just, you don't have to be so blunt about it."

"What? So you can pretend that he's not?"

"I'm not pretending."

"Yeah, you are, and you have to get over it. Elias is dead and he's not coming back. You can sit there feeling sorry for yourself or you can get up, put a brave face on, and get ready. Because even though you killed Charles, this isn't over. The hollowers got his blood—this is only just the beginning."

"What is *wrong* with you? Look, you can go talk to a stupid casket and Cassia can mope like a child and I won't judge you, so you have no place to talk to me like that."

"You can scoff at Cassia all you like. But at least she's not pretending it didn't happen."

"I said I'm not pretending."

"Say it then. Elias is dead."

"This is stupid."

"If it's stupid then it should be easy. Say it. Elias is *dead*."

I unwind my arms from my legs and walk to the door, opening it for him. The quick movement sends a rush of dizziness to my head. "Just leave me alone."

"No."

"No? Are you kidding me?"

He steps toward me. "If you don't say good-bye, you're going to regret it."

"You don't know anything, Eric." If he's not going to leave, I will.

"I know you care about him. Maybe love him, even." I pause in the doorway, my pulse racing. "And I think he loved you, too, you know." He touches my shoulder, the warmth a stark contrast to the ice in my veins. "He would've wanted you to know that."

All I ever wanted was to be loved unconditionally. But now, I'm not sure I truly understood it at all. I thought I loved Charles, but I was running a marathon that never ended, striving for an approval that I would never get. How can I know what love feels like when the version in my head is twisted? All I know is that after a lifetime of choking on smoke, Elias made me feel like I could take a breath of air. So maybe I do love him, but that doesn't change anything. Love never did me any good.

"If you don't say good-bye, you'll never forgive yourself."

I squeeze my eyes shut. The door to the staircase bursts open and Cassia flies out. Her swollen eyes are on us, hair scattered with leaves. "Eric! Milena! You've got to come down."

Eric tenses behind me. "I told you I wasn't coming to the funeral."

"They opened the casket, everyone is—"

"I'm going back to my room." I turn away.

"Wait!" She grabs my arm to spin me around.

"Let me go, Cassia."

"The body—"

"I said I don't want to see it. What is wrong with you two? I just want to be alone!"

"Milena!" She grabs my shoulders and shakes me. "Listen to me!"

Her eyes burn into mine. When I look at her, I see the cabin. I see his limp body and hear her shrill screams, and it makes my heart ache. But there's something buried within the silver, something that keeps me from slapping her across the face and turning around.

"Cassia?" Eric steps forward. "What's going on?"

"It isn't him."

My blood goes cold. "What?"

"They opened the casket so that we could leave our notes to bury with him and he . . . it's not him."

Eric disappears down the hallway in a blur, and after a few moments, I follow, my head spinning as I stumble down the staircase and burst outside. The icy air hits the back of my throat but I push forward to the clearing where the funeral is, pulling to a stop inches away from the crowd. Eric's already at the front, standing over the open casket with his back to me. Fear and doubt crawl in and I can't seem to move forward. The crowd murmurs among themselves, parting for me. The walk is painstakingly slow, mere feet feeling like miles, my gaze glued to the coffin.

I reach the pedestal, staring at Eric's back. He turns his head to face me, his once dull eyes glowing like a lamp. He nods. My teeth pierce my lip as I lean over the casket. I expect dark hair, tanned skin, golden eyes. I expect to feel a punch to the gut, a twisting in my chest. But I get green, gray, and white. My stomach tightens with recognition as I take in the blood staining the bare chest—a painful reminder of what I did. Charles.

Something else swirls at my chest. Hope. A ray of light in a world that was beginning to feel so dark. "He's not there." But how?

"The casket has been in the village since we got here," Eric says. "Nobody has been guarding it, nobody has been guarding the village. They could've . . ."

I know what he's thinking—it's what we're all thinking. The hollowers switched the bodies. And even though the thought makes my stomach twist, it means something else too. Why would the hollowers come back for a dead body? They wouldn't.

"That means . . ."

Eric's bottom lip wavers. "He's alive."

I turn to face the crowd, my disbelief reflected in the faces that stare back at me. "What do we do?"

"What Elias would do for us." He nods, a breath of air escaping his chest. "We go and find him."

His eyes fall shut as he faces the sky. I do the same, following his gaze to the flock of birds dipping through the pomegranate sky like drops of black paint.

In such a short time, so much has changed. Twenty years old. I thought by the time I reached this age I'd have been on my first hunt. I thought that I'd fit in with the hunters, be best friends with Flo, finally be accepted by Charles. I couldn't have been more wrong.

Before I met the shifters, the things I wanted in life had been so simple. I lived a life of fear, sheltered from the truths of the world that I had been so afraid of. But I'm not afraid anymore. I'm not afraid of the dark, the creatures of the night, of Charles. Because even as night descends around us, stars peek through the shadows. And they shine brighter in the darkness.

It doesn't matter what happened between Elias and me—what lies were told, what secrets were kept—we were destined to know each other, and we barely got a chance. He's still out there, and I'll stop at nothing to find him.

ACKNOWLEDGMENTS

This book started in my year-nine classroom when I scribbled down an idea on the corner of my English book. Of course, the idea was too long for a one-page creative writing assignment, so I tore the piece of paper and took it home. But I had no idea of what it would later become, and without the help and support from so many generous people, this book wouldn't exist.

First and foremost, to my readers: I can never thank you enough. Your support means more than I can say. To Katie, who has given me nothing but unconditional encouragement, thank you for easing my anxieties and cheering me on every step of the way. You celebrate my achievements like they're your own and always remind me to be proud of myself, no matter what.

I owe so much of my gratitude to the team at Wattpad. Thank you to Nick Uskoski, Amanda Ferreira, and Leah Ruehlicke, who took a chance on my story. You, along with fellow writers in the Paid Stories program, helped me realize that something I saw as a silly hobby had the potential to become so much more. I-Yana Tucker, thank you for your kindness and helpful explanations. And a special thanks to Deanna McFadden. Your patience, advice, and insight have been invaluable to me. You've helped me grow as a writer, and I'm so grateful for all that I've learned from you.

Lastly, I thank my parents. As a child who hated reading, your bribery was the only thing that would get me to pick up a book. Without that, I never would've made it here today.

ABOUT THE AUTHOR

Grace Collins first discovered her love for writing when she posted her ideas online at the age of thirteen. She has a bachelor's degree in French and psychology, and is currently pursuing a master's in education. Her debut novel, *Creatures of the Night*, has amassed over one million reads online and received a Watty Award for Horror and Paranormal. Grace lives in Aotearoa/New Zealand, and enjoys spending time in nature, traveling, and learning new languages.

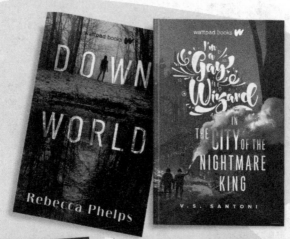

premium

Supercharge your Wattpad experience.

Go Premium and get more from the platform you already love. Enjoy uninterrupted ad-free reading, access to bonus Coins, and exclusive, customizable colors to personalize Wattpad your way.

Try Premium **free** today.